TELL

ME

WHAT

SHE

KNOWS

TELL ME WHAT SHE KNOWS

PAMELA CRANE

Rockin' C Reads
Raleigh, North Carolina

Thank you for supporting authors and literacy by purchasing this book. Want to add more gripping reads to your library? As the author of more than a dozen award-winning and bestselling books, you can find all of Pamela Crane's works on her website at www.pamelacrane.com.

Note to the Reader

If you've been following along with the entire IF ONLY SHE KNEW MYSTERY SERIES so far, you probably caught on that each book in the series takes you to a different decade.

So far we've done the Saturday-Night-Fever Seventies, Elevated-Hair Eighties, Nirvana Nineties, and even a throwback to the Edison Eighteen Hundreds. I get lots of fan mail asking which decade will be brought to life next, and sometimes I don't know until I start writing. And even if I did, I can't divulge those secrets until release day! (Unless you want to bribe me… I'm not above divulging top secrets for copious amounts of dark chocolate, hint hint.)

Without further ado, welcome to the Psychedelic Sixties, baby!

TELL ME WHAT SHE KNOWS

Prologue

June 27, 1969

Tick, tick, tick.

It was the time of night when Alice Belvedere usually slept like the dead, but tonight she could not doze off. *Would not* doze off. She was determined to stay awake, even if it killed her.

Alice didn't consider herself superstitious. Not one to villainize black cats, she in fact had been feeding a stray and named it *Who*, after her favorite band. Alice didn't avoid ladders, but even common sense told her not to walk under one. And she didn't believe in *luck*, good or bad.

Except for tonight. Everyone in Bloodson Bay became superstitious on June 27th.

By the morning of June 28th the town would inevitably return to its logical ways—for the most part. It was a small town with small-town minds, after all.

But June 27th was different. That was the date of the *Bloodson Bay curse*. Every year on that date someone—or something—terrorized the quaint, ordinary town. The news would report on a murder here, a kidnapping there. Some believed a supernatural element was involved, but Alice figured monsters disguised as humans took advantage of the public's fear and let their sadistic sides loose on this day. Either way, she wasn't willing to sleep through it.

Only the dead rested tonight, because, well, they were already dead. They had nothing to fear, nothing to lose. But the living had plenty to fear. Alice, in particular, had *everything* to lose.

The world outside of her bedroom walls ceased to exist as she waited the night out, listening to the *tick, tick, tick* of the Kit-Cat Klock in the hall. The clock's eyes and tail roved back and forth in perfect rhythm, as if counting down to some terrible conclusion, all with an eerie smile on its face.

Drowsy and drunk on exhaustion, Alice felt a terrible void. All day she had sensed something coming, something she was helpless to stop. And she knew it would happen tonight—on *the* night. The *cursed* night.

She had almost closed her eyes when the shrill ring of the telephone in the hall startled her fully awake. What followed was a cold rush of panic that inevitably surged with any middle-of-the-night phone call. *What good news ever came after dark?*

She slipped out of bed and ran to the phone, terrified of something she couldn't name. By the second ring, her fingers closed around the avocado green Bakelite receiver, and she prayed the trill wouldn't wake the baby. *Never wake a sleeping baby* she had read in last month's issue of *McCall's*.

"Hello?" she whispered, her throat tense.

The line was silent. A prank call, maybe. Those happened a lot on this particular date.

"Who is this?" she demanded, her voice louder, now agitated.

If this call ended up waking the baby, no Bloodson Bay curse could compete with her maternal wrath against the caller.

She thought she heard a breath. Then a voice, low and

steady: "Boo! I found you."

It was *him*. Once upon a time, his voice had stirred butterflies in her belly. Now it terrified her. She knew what he was capable of, even to those he claimed to love. The worst part was that she was no better.

"Please… don't do this," she begged.

She waited. He hadn't hung up.

"It's too late," he said after a breathless beat. "I haven't forgotten about you. Or my baby you stole."

Her panic rose. Her heart pounded. Each beat echoed in her ears like the distant thunder of the summer storms that often ravaged her coastal town this time of year. Nearly dropping the phone, her body went numb. Then anger revived her senses. She hadn't come this far, hidden herself from the world, only to be bullied back into submission.

"I'm not afraid of you!" Her words tumbled out in a rush.

"You should be."

"I'll turn you in," she threatened. "I'll tell the police what's behind the locked door in your cellar! I know all about it—"

The truth was, Alice still felt guilty for never telling anyone about the locked door, even all these months later. But telling someone would require her to come forward, and she couldn't possibly do that when she had an arrest warrant for child abduction.

"You know nothing!" he yelled. "Besides, you'll be killed before you make it to the police station."

Then the line went dead.

She slammed the receiver down, the *crack* of plastic underscoring her anger. *It's too late,* he had said. What did that mean? Was this a warning? Or… a distraction?

That thought lingered longer than any other. What did he want from her? The only way to escape him was to hide, *again*, but she was tired of running. Tired of hiding. It hadn't worked so well the first time, had it? He had found her, after all.

Thick, oppressive darkness leaned against the windows of 1 Crow's End Lane, where Alice lived in a mid-century split-level house that belonged to her best friend's parents who were traveling for the summer. Alice couldn't stay here anymore, but where else could she go?

Her parents were dead, and her best friend had a summer internship through her college. The school's *1969 Women's Handbook* strictly governed everything from women's curfews to proper classroom attire to bed-making each morning. Certainly they wouldn't allow a woman and her stolen baby to hide out there.

The baby—she needed to check on the baby.

In the nursery she tiptoed to the crib where a perfect infant slept soundly, nestled under a hand-crocheted blanket next to a Snoopy astronaut toy that the baby was far too young to play with. All safe and sound.

Alice would need to pack everything important for their survival over the next month while she figured things out. So she slipped on her canvas Keds, grabbed her travel case, and packed every gypsy dress and pair of bellbottoms she owned— which wasn't much—along with her meager cash savings.

Nearly an hour later and her packing done, the baby let out a brief cry. She glanced at the clock—it was feeding time. She headed back down the hallway toward the quiet nursery. It wouldn't take long to gather everything the baby needed, then one quick meal before hitting the road.

Her Sears cotton nightgown swished around her bare legs like soft gasps. The nursery door creaked open on achy hinges. Moonlight glowed through gauzy curtains, casting zebra stripes across the crib. Baby powder scented the room, with undertones of the freshly-cut lavender she had placed in a mason jar by the open window. A white moonlit glow barely penetrated the darkness, making familiar shapes morph into something strange and threatening.

"Hey, sweetie. It's almost time to go."

Alice's whispers floated through the bedroom as she yanked open dresser drawers. She moved quickly, almost recklessly, as the seconds slipped away faster than she could catch them. While she rushed across the room grabbing everything she thought she'd need, her shoes—which she had barely afforded, even on sale at two pair for $5—tangled in the hem of her nightgown.

Her body flew forward, and the floor came up faster than she could raise her arms to stop it. She landed with a hard *thump*, face-planting on the shag carpet. Although she wasn't hurt, Alice wept into the fibers.

How could she possibly go on the run with an *abducted* baby when she barely had money to survive? Starting over again, finding new work, avoiding the police—it all sounded impossible, especially after what had happened at her last job…

As she pushed herself up onto her feet, she glanced down at her nightgown, only now noticing she had buttoned it crookedly. In that moment, Alice knew she was up a creek. There was no way she could handle life as a young, single mother in 1969, but she had to at least try.

Grabbing a handful of clothes, she shoved them into her

Samsonite travel case. Tiny onesies tumbled in a chaotic rainbow of polyester and knits. They had to leave before—

A creaking floorboard in the hallway stopped her frenzied packing. Had she let the cat in by accident? She wavered by the door and listened. The scrape of a hard object dragged across glass. Alice peered around the doorframe and found the hallway empty, except for the small telephone table against the wall.

A sudden *tap, tap, tap* behind her startled a gasp out of her. She swung around, her arms raised in defense... and then breathed. It was just the maple tree branch rapping on the windowpane. She shook her head, refusing to let her imagination run wild.

"I will not let him intimidate me. We will be fine." But she branded her baby with a promise she wasn't sure she could keep.

When a dial tone echoed from the hall, its accusatory buzzing didn't make sense. It hadn't been droning on this whole time, had it? She placed the phone on the receiver and checked the time. He could be here any minute.

Tick, tick, tick. The clock relentlessly hammered in her ears like a metronome of doom.

After she packed the bare necessities, she remembered the owl. She couldn't forget the plush, brown owl her best friend had crocheted for the baby. It was the only possession that mattered to her. Where had she left it? Probably in the crib.

Halfway across the nursery she stopped. Something felt *off*. The shroud of absolute quiet. No rustling of tiny legs against cotton sheets. No midnight babbling. Just the hollow sound of her own ragged breathing and the distant chirp of crickets through the window. She raced toward the crib, her knees throbbing from her fall, still clutching the hard-shell case stuffed full of baby clothes, with tiny socks escaping in a trail behind her.

In the dim light, the blankets lay flat and empty except for the lumpy outline of something underneath, a shape all wrong for her child. She warily approached the infant-sized bed, fighting her fear, each footstep across the carpet soft like a shadow. The hum of the summer night outside barely made its way through the brick walls of the house, but suddenly the tension in the room was unbearable.

Her hand was already reaching to scoop up the baby, fingers anticipating the warm weight. The sheets lay rumpled in a strange lump under the dim glow, a misshapen silhouette that made her stomach clench. *Wrong. All wrong.* The air felt empty, devoid of the sweet powder smell.

She reached for the blanket, fingers trembling so badly she could barely grip the fabric, then snatched it back. Beneath the thin cover, Snoopy stared up at her with its black eyes, a cruel replacement for her child. Someone had positioned it carefully right where her baby should have been sleeping.

Her palm slapped against her mouth, muffling the scream that threatened to wake the dead. But it couldn't contain the primal sound that tore from Alice's throat and bounced off the duckling-print wallpaper she'd hung just months ago.

The travel case slipped from her nerveless fingers, spilling fully open on the floor. She picked up Snoopy, its fabric still warm from where a tiny body should have been, the heat a condemnation against her skin. Her knees buckled and she clutched the crib rail to stay upright. The wood creaked under her white-knuckled grip.

"Please, God, no!" The plea came out in heartbroken

syllables.

The *tick, tick, tick* of the clock mocked her. Her baby was gone, and the punishment for her crimes was only just beginning.

Part 1
Tara Christie

Chapter 1

So this was what death row felt like.

The wait. The worry. Each morning wondering if today would be *the day*.

Okay, maybe pregnancy wasn't *death row* bad. But at eight and a half months into what my doctor called a *high-risk geriatric pregnancy*, that was the best analogy I could think of to describe my anxiety over my upcoming labor. I was scared shitless. Literally. I had been constipated for weeks.

It had been seventeen years since I last gave birth. My daughter Nora had a skull the size of a cantaloupe, so I retained perfect recall of all twenty hours of that pain. Body-splitting, vagina-tearing, contraction-ripping pain.

And don't get me started on everything leading up to the birth. My feet ached. The pelvic pressure throbbed. And my stomach wriggled with a fist—or foot, who knows?—poking through my abdomen like that creepy scene from *Alien*. It probably hadn't been the best idea to watch that movie so close to my due date.

I was two weeks away from meeting my Christmas baby face to face, a perfect little miracle in time for the holidays. Well, it would have been perfect if I could get rid of the man who was trying to sue the pants off me.

Just to clarify, I didn't want to *get rid* of Mikhail Pearson like a mobster might want to *get rid* of a loose end. I just wanted Mikhail to disappear… to somewhere like the Arctic Circle. Permanently.

But that was another problem for another day. Today, I was celebrating. I had been waiting for this day since I was a teenager: the demolition of Bloodson Manor.

Bloodson Manor was an abandoned, 150-year-old house on the edge of my horse farm. It loomed like a sore against the blue North Carolina sky, its windows blank and accusing, the weathered boards mocking.

The locals called it the *Slaughter Shed*. It had lived up to its deadly nickname on a fateful June night in 1997 when my friend Emory McAlister was held captive and then murdered in the structure's root cellar. Since then, the house was a constant reminder of death. I was beyond relieved to finally witness its destruction.

Once it was gone, I hoped no more images of Emory's corpse would slide into my dreams. Our sleepy coastal town had lived in terror ever since her death, all of us wondering what our neighbors might be capable of, or worried about whose child might go missing next.

Today, the burden of this house would lift as its walls fell. A lifetime of nightmares would finally end, assuming everything went according to plan—which, given my luck lately, was not guaranteed.

Standing a safe distance away from its threshold—as if anywhere was *safe* these days—I watched an excavator rumble up to the house. Its arm stretched out a clawed bucket that tore into a rotting wall. The crash of debris sent sparrows scattering from the emaciated trees surrounding the property.

I jabbed a corkscrew into the cork of a sparkling cider bottle and twisted, popping out the pulp. I poured three glasses and handed them out. Then I raised my champagne flute filled with my woefully alcohol-free beverage. My mother-in-law, Ginger Mallowan, and best friend, Sloane Apara, stood beside me, our glasses lifted high as the morning sun sparkled in the bubbles of our drinks.

"Cheers to new beginnings!" I shouted into the frigid December wind.

"And to the end of our epic crime-solving era," Ginger added with a pout.

She pulled out a flask from her winter coat pocket and dumped the contents into her champagne flute. Her gaze was fixed on me as she emptied her glass in one swallow.

Ginger blamed me and my growing belly for her recent boredom. Ever since I went on maternity bedrest, life had gotten a lot quieter around here. No murders to solve, no criminals to chase, and for Ginger, no more fun.

"We all know you miss playing detective, Ginger." Sloane, who was Deaf, signed her comment in American Sign Language.

"And we almost got killed because of it," I reminded them both. "Which is why I am officially retiring from catching bad guys."

I rubbed my pregnant belly. This baby was the main reason why our crime-solving girl gang needed to end. I was going to be a new mom again. I didn't need to add *amateur sleuth* to my job description. There would be no more long nights of deciphering clues and chasing killers—not when I had long nights of deciphering baby noises and chasing a toddler to look forward to.

"Tara, you've got to admit that cleaning up the corruption in our town was exciting," Ginger reasoned. "It kept us busy."

"I've got a barn full of manure that needs to be shoveled if you want to clean something." My words came out in white puffs of air.

Ginger huffed.

"I don't know about you, but I'm happy to say goodbye to Tara's Angels." Sloane was referring to the nickname Ginger had dubbed us after we had solved our first murder together: *Tara's Angels.*

To this day I still didn't know how I became the leader of the pack when Ginger clearly enjoyed it more. The sign name Sloane had given us looked like two T's touched to the top of our shoulders that flicked outward, symbolizing angel wings.

"I'm too busy training my new assistant that I don't need any extra drama," Sloane added.

Sloane's business, called Feel the Noize Party Planning, had helped her achieve celebrity status in Bloodson Bay and all over the internet. In fact, actual celebrities hired her because Sloane knew how to create a gala-quality party for a sportsman's lodge price.

"I don't *need* the drama either," Ginger reluctantly agreed.

"But we all know you love it!" I gulped the last of my sparkling cider, now craving something fruity. Or cheesy. Or maybe both. "Speaking of love, I would *love* some Debbie's Diner cheese fries right about now. Who's hungry?"

Sloane laughed, and only then did I realize I'd signed *horny* instead of *hungry.* Luckily, she was a master at lip reading when my sign language skills failed me.

"I could go for her famous banana cream pancakes," Ginger chimed in. "Nothing like watching other people labor to work up an appetite."

A cloud of dust billowed around us as the excavator cleared out another partition, this one tearing open a gaping hole that dropped into the foundation of the house. The root cellar.

I shivered and grabbed Ginger's hand for emotional support. A flickering vision of Emory's captivity there sickened me—and it wasn't pregnancy nausea churning my stomach.

"On second thought, I might need to pass on the cheese fries," I grumbled.

Sloane's gestures interrupted the dangling memory. "Tara, are you sure you're allowed to tear the house down before your trial? Isn't this destruction of evidence?"

I had almost forgotten about Mikhail Pearson's lawsuit, which was the reason I wanted him and his disaster-prone son to disappear. Technically what happened to the son was an accident, so there was no *evidence* to preserve… as far as anyone knew. Was there evidence of other past crimes in the Slaughter Shed? Most definitely. Which was why I didn't hesitate when my lawyer suggested I tear it down. I didn't need anyone poking around Bloodson Manor when I knew it's nefarious history.

I shrugged. "My attorney advised me to demolish it. It shows good faith that I'm taking my liability seriously so no other kids get hurt on my property in the meantime."

What I really wanted to do was shove this frivolous lawsuit up Mikhail Pearson's butt. His drugged-up son, Brock, had been trespassing in the manor when he fell from the second-story balcony onto a rusted, wrought-iron fence. He was lucky enough to walk away with only a punctured lung and broken leg.

I admit, I should have razed this house years ago, but it had been more than two decades since I last stepped foot back here. I had no idea there was a deadly fence, which Mikhail's attorney mentioned more than once during our initial hearing.

I had been pretending the whole eyesore never existed for so long that I had almost convinced myself that it had vanished. *Poof!* But the only thing vanishing these days was my bank account as I wrote check after check to fill the retainer that my attorney was using up.

Anyway, as a result of Brock's trespassing, I was getting sued for damages to the tune of one million dollars. I might end up bankrupt and losing my farm because Brock was a stoned, trespassing, second-story-jumping idiot.

"This makes me glad I never had kids. They're too much trouble," Sloane signed.

I doubted Sloane would feel that way forever. My daughter Nora was my world, and I couldn't wait until she became a big sister. My pelvic floor couldn't wait either.

"If you ever have a child, you'll see they bring a lot more joy than pain."

I failed to mention that at this moment, my back was killing me from standing so long.

"And being a *mamó* means you get all of their love with none of the attitude." Ginger practically bounced when she talked about her granddaughter Nora, who could do no wrong in Ginger's eyes.

"Well, I don't plan on getting married again or having kids,"

Sloane signed back decisively.

I pulled my coat hood up over my head, driving out the chill that seeped between the folds of fabric. The cold retaliated by whipping across my bare face. The baby chose that moment to deliver a swift punch—or kick, it was still anyone's guess—to my ribs, making me grimace and readjust my footing on the slippery mud of what would have been the house's front yard. I tried to glance down at my feet, but my stomach bulged in the way.

"We cleared through to the basement!" one of the workers yelled to the foreman. "You gotta see this!"

Just then, a draft lifted Sloane's designer scarf, which probably cost more than my monthly mortgage, and unwound it from around her neck. The colorful silk billowed in the breeze and floated across the yard and down into the gaping hole the excavator had just gutted.

"Damn," she signed as her scarf got eaten by the muck. "I've heard this house is… c-u-r-s-e-d," her lips moved in unison as she finger-spelled *cursed,* as if signing the actual word would attach its hex on her, "and now that proves it: it stole my juju charm given to me by my grandmother."

Although Sloane could quote the Bible cover to cover, she still held on to the Nigerian superstitions she'd grown up with. One time, I stepped over Sloane's legs when we were sitting in my living room, and she made me walk backwards over them for fear I'd bring her bad luck. And you'd never catch Sloane eating in the dark, which was believed to attract hungry evil spirits. I still couldn't understand the logic of a *hangry* apparition joining her for dinner, but who was I to judge? I was terrified of an empty root cellar.

"I wouldn't say Bloodson Manor is *cursed*," I replied. "Just creepy."

The morning sun cast long shadows across the chewed up basement. As I squinted into the Colonial-era root cellar that had once been used for storage, with its dirt floor and crumbling brick walls, I noticed something that made me wonder if perhaps I was wrong. Maybe it *was* cursed, because what I saw didn't make sense.

"That's weird…" My gaze locked at the far end of the cellar where there appeared to be a—

No, it had to be my eyes playing tricks on me. I turned to Ginger, who propped her asymmetrical sunglasses up on her freshly permed and dyed red hair that had already grown a pinkie-nail's length of gray roots.

"What's weird?" Ginger asked.

"Your fashion sense." I forced a laugh, nudging away the sense of dread.

"Hey, these sunglasses are authentic. Probably worth a fortune." Her neon pink triangular solar shades were a hideous memento from a 1980's Pizza Hut promotional deal for *Back to the Future II*. "I can't believe I kept them all this time."

I could believe it. Ginger was a packrat with more than six decades of crap filling her house.

The demolition crew's machinery grumbled over our conversation, the diesel engines growling louder as the boom reached for another chunk of building. A cascade of wood and brick scattered the sunlight that now streaked across the basement, along with a dank smell that awakened my pregnancy-senses. Half of the house was completely gone now, and the other half stood perfectly intact like a three-story dollhouse a child had taken a temper tantrum out on.

Sloane tapped my shoulder and signed, "Tell the workers to stop! There's something down there!"

So my mind *wasn't* playing tricks on me after all.

I waved crazily to the foreman, who shouted to the crew, "Kill the engine!"

My stomach dropped—this time not from the baby's acrobatics. The excavator abruptly halted, its engine dying. Nothing good ever came from unexpected discoveries in Bloodson Bay.

An argument erupted from the site. The foreman jogged toward us, kicking up dead leaves in his wake, his face pale. He glanced at our champagne flutes, panting.

"Mrs. Christie, you might want to hold off on the celebration. We need to call the cops…"

I waddled after him as he headed to the excavator. "What did you see?"

"I… I don't know. Looks like a crime scene."

"I'll go down and check it out!" Ginger cut in a little too excitedly.

"Absolutely not!" the foreman insisted. "It's an excavation site and could collapse on you."

"Try and stop me," Ginger said.

"Just let me make sure it's safe," he grumbled, then turned to me. "And if your friend gets hurt, I'm not liable."

After passing each of us a hardhat, he explained, "The support beams on the other side of the house are still intact, and there's nothing overhead that can fall on you, but please be careful."

I climbed down into the belly of the basement with Ginger

and Sloane close behind. Each step on the icy earth pitched me like I was in a circus act, especially with my center of gravity completely thrown off by my pumpkin-sized belly.

I knew exactly where to go.

Ginger gasped. "Is that what I think it is?" Her voice hit a pitch that probably summoned every dog in earshot. "That's scarier than me wearing spandex."

Through the rubble and dust, I saw what had alarmed Sloane. What stopped the foreman. And what made Ginger gasp.

A wooden door set into the foundation, its surface covered in cobwebs and grime and—

No, it couldn't be.

I hated that I remembered that door so well that I knew immediately what looked different about it. *No, this was impossible.*

Another flashback from that terrible night returned. The chains and the body and the… Ripping my gaze from the door, I nearly crumpled in place.

The foreman cleared his throat. "Ma'am, do you want me to break through it?"

It wouldn't take much effort. The ancient brick was already crumbling around the edges of the doorframe. I hadn't laid eyes on that door since 1997, but I visualized it in horrifying detail. There was something strangely different about it.

Something unexplainable.

Chapter 2

A message was written in blood across the wooden planks of the door.

"No, we can't go in there," I finally answered, stepping back.

"We have to," Sloane insisted. "You can't ignore this."

Sloane moved closer to examine it, her cream designer boots somehow managing to avoid every speck of dirt. Reaching out, she pulled the handle and swung the door open. As my pupils adjusted, it took a moment to understand exactly what the message meant.

"What were you saying about no more crime-solving, Tara?" Ginger glanced at me. "I guess this means you're coming out of retirement."

I leaned down, unable to make sense of what I was looking at. Whatever it was shifted cautiously, methodically, and then took a tentative step toward me. It had just reached the sliver of light when it rushed me.

I screamed like I was mid-labor. But this was oh, so much worse.

"Rat!" I shrieked as a rodent the size of a cat jumped off a human skull, dashing toward me, then over my foot and up my leg. Its tiny claws pricked through my pants and into my skin before it leaped off me and into the middle of the cellar, then scampered off, disappearing into a dark corner.

"It's just vermin," the contractor said. "I've seen way worse things than that in some crawl spaces."

"Worse than a rat doing acrobatics out of someone's skull?" The rat had distracted me from something far more terrifying, which still loomed in front of me:

The message on the door, and the skeleton behind it.

Beneath a film of gossamer spider webs, the door at the end of the root cellar was covered in dried blood. Not just a spatter. Someone had scrawled words across the planks:

I'M COMING FOR YOU NEXT

The bloody message hadn't been there in 1997. I had no doubt about this fact because it was a detail I couldn't forget, even if I tried. That door—every square inch of its rusty hinges and thick slats—had been branded into my brain, and nothing was on there before.

This meant that the blood was new—or at least newer than 1997. But that was impossible! After Emory's body was discovered, the basement had been sealed off so that no one else could access it ever again. No one could have disturbed it…

Until now.

Obviously, someone had managed to break through the cellar windows that had been sealed shut. Or they'd pulled up the boards that had been nailed over the access panel in the pantry floor above. Someone had been down here. And with that much blood smeared into a puzzling message on the door's surface…

Someone had been murdered. And I was staring at that

someone right now.

"I thought that was a Halloween decoration." The foreman's face turned same gray shade as the corpse we were all gawking at. Then he ran to the furthest corner of the gutted basement and wretched whatever he had eaten for breakfast.

"Aw, honey, it's just a bunch of bones," Ginger answered, unfazed as she patted him on the back. "It ain't gonna bite."

Maybe Ginger *had* missed her calling as a crime scene investigator. She approached the skeleton and scratched her chin.

"I'm guessing it's too late to put my CPR lessons to good use on this fella," Ginger signed to Sloane with a grin.

Sloane had been training Ginger in CPR, but so far Ginger had only managed to break two Resusci Anne CPR dolls. After her last lesson, she was more likely to kill someone than save them. Lucky for this skeleton, it was already dead.

In the hole behind the door, where the glow of daylight reached into its corners, sat a body up against the foundation wall. The skeletal remains lay sprawled out, corroded chains wrapped around what remained of the wrists holding it upright, the metal having left permanent green stains on the weathered bone.

Cropped white hair clung to the skull in patches. Stained jeans and a tattered shirt hung loose on what was left of the corpse. The flesh had long ago decomposed, leaving a faceless skull and knobby appendages hidden under the fabric.

It was exactly what had happened to Emory in 1997, except this time, there was nothing left of the victim but remains. No face to identify. No fingerprints to take. And worst of all, no clues to catch the killer and give him what he deserved.

"What's that?" Sloane signed, gesturing to a paper held in place by a rock next to what remained of its leg.

I take it back. Maybe there *was* a clue.

I knelt beside Sloane—as best as anyone this pregnant could kneel without the belly getting in the way—and reached for a large photographed copy of the *Bloodson Bay Bulletin* spread beside the victim like a macabre welcome mat. When I picked it up using the sleeve of my coat to preserve any previous fingerprints, I checked out the newspaper's date:

June 27, 1969

The first headline announced:

Nixon Gives Hope to 25,000 Troops
Coming Home From Vietnam

I skimmed the articles silently. Reports on Joe Frazier taking the heavyweight boxing title, that week's list of chart-topping songs with number one being "Honky Tonk Women," and a critic's review of *Funny Girl*—none of it seemed relevant. But one article in particular stood out:

Kidnapping Suspect Goes Missing

Early this morning, a woman whom police had been searching for on suspicion of kidnapping went missing from her home at 1 Crow's End Lane.

An anonymous tip was received by the Bloodson Bay Police Department about a woman with a stolen infant residing at the house, until she suddenly disappeared. When investigators arrived at the scene, they noted a packed travel case left behind, and evidence that confirmed the infant was the same one that had been previously reported abducted.

The woman, Alice—

The article ended there. I flipped the paper over, but it was blank. The rest of the article must have been on a different page… a page the killer didn't leave behind.

"Does anyone see another photocopy anywhere?" I asked, walking the perimeter of the basement.

Ginger gave a halfhearted glance around, then shrugged. "Nope."

This wasn't accidental. I held a clue that could help us identify the dead body. But with all of the demolition, it'd be impossible to find if the other half of this news article had blown under a pile of debris.

"The article mentions an 'Alice.' Do you think this is her?" Ginger asked.

Sloane stared at the corpse. "If only skeletons could talk, she could tell us what she knows…"

If indeed Alice was a kidnapper as the article claimed, I doubted she'd spill her sins. Only her first name remained on the page, but without a last name, this meant nothing. Was this skeleton *Alice*? There had to have been a million Alices back in

1969, during the height of *The Brady Bunch* era. Or maybe Alice had killed the biological mother while kidnapping the baby, then hid the body here.

But no. That didn't make sense. This body had to have been put in this cellar *after* 1997, after it had been sealed shut following Emory's murder. If that was the case, this victim could have been here for the past twenty years and I wouldn't have known it. What would the police think? Would they believe me?

The worry made me woozy. The earth was cold and rough against my palms as I tried to push myself back to my feet. The knees of my maternity jeans soaked up the icy mud, but that was the least of my concerns.

"This house has more skeletons than my childhood backyard—and I buried *a lot* of pet hamsters as a kid," Ginger said.

"It isn't a joke, Ging. This is bad." My voice quivered, matching my tumbling tummy as I accepted the grim reality of the situation. "This body being put here isn't random."

First Mikhail's lawsuit, and now a body turning up… and a baby due any day. I had a breaking point and this put me way past it.

Ginger crouched beside me. The fur hem of her coat collected dirt and dead bugs while the sequined trim caught the light. She helped lift me to my feet, then hugged me to keep me upright.

"Honey, I'm sure this murder has nothing to do with you," she said, as if there wasn't a message saying *I'm coming for you next* in front of our faces. "Let's leave it to the police to figure out. I'm pretty sure I have Detective Hughes on speed-dial."

"Then why did the killer go through all the effort to put the body *here*? On *my* property? Whoever killed this person must have known about Emory being murdered in this exact same spot in 1997," I thought aloud. "It's too similar to be a coincidence."

"Isn't that killer dead now?" Sloane asked.

"Yeah, Marvin Valance has been dead as a doornail since last spring." Ginger peered at the bones with the kind of morbid fascination she usually reserved for yard sales.

"But clearly the memory of his crime lives on."

The details of the 1997 murder trial crashed over me like the waves hitting the cliff's edge a stone's throw from where we stood. Every terrible fact of that night had been bolted to my memory, like the shackles to that wall. Marvin's twisted smile as he confessed to torturing Emory. His eyes empty, devoid of humanity, like wells of pure evil. Although this room had been sealed after police took her body away, I could never lock away the horror that haunted this place.

"Do you think this killer is a copycat?" Sloane asked.

"Maybe." But I wasn't convinced. Who would bother to copy a crime that happened so long ago?

Ginger shook her head, her curls crimped like a Slinky a child had stepped on. "Anyone who knew about that case would be too old to be killing people."

"Uh, I was there, Ging. Are you calling me old?" I protested, still feeling defensive about the *advanced maternal age* status written on my OB-GYN medical chart.

"You're a geriatric pregnancy, Tara," Sloane signed with a smirk.

"Which is exactly why I need to leave this up to the

Bloodson Bay Police to handle. My pelvic floor feels like a volcano about to erupt."

"Nice visual," Ginger said, holding her phone out at arm's length, trying to read the screen. "I can't see a dang thing. Who wants to do the honors of calling the police?"

"I'm on it."

I had already pulled out my phone and found Detective Martina Carillo-Hughes' cell phone number in my contact list. As I connected the call, I dreaded this conversation—or interrogation, more likely. Her voice sounded resigned when she answered on the first ring, like she'd been halfheartedly expecting me.

"Tara Christie," Detective Hughes stated bluntly. "Who's dead this time?"

"What makes you think someone's dead?"

"I've dealt with you enough times to know that when you call, there's always a body."

"You should be thanking me. I give you job security."

"No, Mrs. Christie, what you give me is a headache. This better be worth my time."

"Oh, I can guarantee it'll be a case you'll never forget."

As it turned out, I was right.

Detective Hughes would never forget answering that phone call. And I would never forget the day I tried to bulldoze down this house. Because none of us had any idea how twisted this case would become, and how it would change everything.

None of us saw it coming. And none of us would ever forget…

Chapter 3

Alice stared at the empty crib, stung with disbelief. No, not disbelief, because she believed this was happening. She had known for a long time this day would come. What filled her whole body was far worse: guilt.

How had she not heard him sneak into the house? Why hadn't she left sooner? So many questions, and they all pointed the blame at her. She had failed the child. Again.

The hollow *tick, tick, tick* of the clock reminded her that there was no time for despair. There was only time for action as the seconds slipped away like water through cupped hands. So Alice fought to stay focused, even as the obstacles overwhelmed her.

She would have to face her worst fear: Clint Valance.

Clint Valance was no ordinary man. He was the richest, most powerful man in Bloodson Bay. And she had stupidly stolen his child and thought she could get away with it. But Clint was more than his vast wealth—he was cruel and manipulative.

She couldn't go to the police about the baby, or about what he kept behind his locked basement door that still kept Alice up at night. Clint had ensured her silence. And she couldn't show up where he lived, because he would be waiting—most likely with the police *and* a warrant for her arrest. She needed a plan he could never predict.

Think, Alice!

Clint must have snuck in while she was packing and couldn't be too far away yet. She crept into the hallway, every shifting shape a potential threat. He was probably still in the house. Probably watching her at this very moment, holding the baby ransom, like a consolation prize she would never win.

She strained to detect a trace of footsteps or a presence. A creaking floorboard, or a scrape against wood—anything. But the air was eerily silent. The only break in the hush were her ragged breaths and *tick, tick, tick* of the clock.

Could he be waiting outside for her?

She rushed back to the nursery window, yanking the sheer curtains aside, the rings screeching against the aluminum rod. The mercury vapor of a lonely streetlamp painted everything a sickly green, transforming her street into an alien landscape where even the familiar shapes of her metal rubbish bin and mailbox seemed menacing. Her gaze darted from shadow to shadow, searching for movement.

The road was deserted except for her Volkswagen Beetle. Beyond the halo of the streetlight was another parked car, a pale monstrosity mostly hidden around the street's bend. She was about to turn away from the window when the headlights blinked on, and her stomach lurched.

The engine purred to life, and a familiar 1969 white Pontiac Firebird Trans Am drifted forward. She instantly recognized Clint's pride and joy that he waxed to a perfect shine. Her vision blurred as tears pooled, and she stumbled backward, her rear hitting the crib's wooden frame. She gasped for air as the weight of panic had robbed her of it completely.

"Mommy's coming!" Alice cried, her voice breaking.

But she'd never catch up to him now.

She couldn't breathe. She couldn't run. Her mind spiraled like a Tilt-a-Whirl as she reached for the crib to hold her up, the rumpled blanket the only clue that her child had ever been there at all.

Alice wanted to scream, to tear downstairs and across the yard toward the car that was leaving with the baby. She wanted to fling open his car door and plunge a knife into his belly. Or smash a hammer across his skull and watch it crack open, spattering blood across the windshield. Or stab a crochet needle through his eyeball and into the headrest behind him.

But he would probably expect that. That was what got her into this mess in the first place. Alice was too predictable. She needed a new tactic, one he wouldn't anticipate.

With unsteady steps she stumbled out of the nursery, her mind racing through all the possibilities, all of the options to stop Clint. Knives, hammers, crochet needles… the images poured from her darkest imagination, what she might do to him if given the chance. Except that Clint would never give her an opportunity. Alice would have to take her life back by force, just like she had taken the baby.

Then it hit her—the perfect plan. One that wasn't traceable back to her. One that wouldn't land her on death row. One that probably had zero percent chance of succeeding… but she had to at least try.

The air around her thickened with tension and hope, as if the very house was burning, suffocating this last-ditch effort to save her own life. It all hung on her exposing the truth behind the locked cellar door.

There was no time left to reconsider. With a determined sigh, she grabbed the travel case and lugged it across the hallway and down into the sunken living room. Her heart beat so fast, her feet could barely keep up with it.

As she stood at the window, headlights swept over her and across the wall. The beams cut through the night like searchlights, illuminating the dew-covered lawn in ghostly patches. The branches of the old maple tree cast writhing shadows that reached for her with knobby fingers.

Her legs carried her to the den on autopilot, her shoes shush-shushing against the carpet. She rushed to the desk littered with psychology books, and the drawer squeaked as she yanked it open. When she found what she was looking for, she grabbed an envelope, slipped the item inside, and scrawled across the front: *Please Find Him*. It was a final message she prayed wouldn't be necessary if her plan worked.

She propped the envelope up against her favorite framed photo that she wanted to bring with her but couldn't. It was taken four years ago in front of a movie theatre when Alice and her friend stood for over an hour in line to watch *A Sound of Music*. Alice, with the same bob she still had, stood next to a girl with a Twiggy cut that made her look older than she was. Alice wondered if she'd ever see her again after tonight.

Returning to the hallway, she stood beneath the clock ticking away precious seconds. She lifted the phone directory from beneath the rotary telephone table, disturbing a thin layer of dust that clung to her fingertips. The pages crackled as she flipped through them, skimming each name, address, and seven-digit phone number.

She tore out the page she needed, folded it into a tiny square, then tucked it into the waistband of her underwear. This address was a lifeline she couldn't afford to lose, her map to salvation. The rotary dial clicked with each number she spun. A ring echoed in her ear. Then another.

"Come on, pick up." Her voice cracked like thin ice.

A shadow passed over her. She glanced up toward the window. Was that a person moving past the window, or just the maple tree's branches shifting in the breeze?

Three rings. Four rings.

The sound of gravel crunching under tires filtered through the walls, each rock's displacement a countdown. Holding the receiver to her ear, she walked toward the living room window until the telephone cord pulled tight. A car idled in the driveway. A different car—a black Cadillac Eldorado. Clint wouldn't be caught dead in something so conventional. Someone else was here.

Five rings. Six—

A click on the line, followed by a sleep-rough voice. "Hello?"

"Oh thank God." Her words tumbled out in a rush, tripping over each other. "It's Alice… Belvedere."

It took a moment for her name to register on the other end of the line before she heard a response. "Alice? Are you okay? Did something happen?"

"No… I mean yes. Clint's found me and took the baby." She scurried back to the hallway dragging the telephone cord behind her. Her eyes remained fixed on the car outside the window, but the gloom hid the driver's seat from her. "I need your help getting the baby back."

A long groan came next, followed by a cautious reply. "You

know I can't help you with that, Alice. I'm not willing to aid and abet a crime, not even for you."

She had figured this response was coming, but she was prepared. This was her only hope, so it *had* to work. "Please. I have a plan… but you're the only person who can help me carry it out."

"Just go to the police, Alice, and tell them everything. I'll even go with you."

"No! I can't go to the police." Alice nervously twirled the telephone cord around her finger until it drained her flesh white. "They think I kidnapped the baby."

"Well, technically you did. And I don't know how else to help you."

"Then you might as well aid and abet *his* crime—of murdering me. He's going to kill me. We both know this. Either he dies, or I do. You pick." She stared out the window. Something moved in the shadows beyond, an inky patch against the black. "Someone else is here—"

Click. The phone line went dead.

Alice hadn't sensed Clint coming up behind her. She didn't feel him reach past her shoulder and press down the receiver's button. But she saw him now as she turned around, meeting him eye to eye. He grabbed the phone from her grip and set it back in its cradle with devastating gentleness, a mockery of consideration.

"You shouldn't have done that." Clint's voice was smooth as aged whiskey and twice as dangerous, each word dripping with quiet menace.

Any remnant of the man she had fallen for had been destroyed by this imitation. Gone was "Clintaroo," the nickname she had given the version of him who charmed her with wildflowers and whisked her away on a clandestine lunch date of Isaly's chipped-chopped ham sandwiches followed by a matinee to see *Butch Cassidy and the Sundance Kid*. Of course, she should never have allowed herself to fall for him in the first place. His wife certainly didn't appreciate it. Alice had known better, and she was paying for it now.

"I'm sorry," she whimpered.

"It's too late for sorrys, Alice."

"Clintaroo—" she began, hoping the endearment would appeal to a heart she wasn't sure ever existed. "Please don't hurt me."

"*Hurt* you?" Clint snickered. "What you did deserves far worse than that."

"Are you saying you're going to… *kill* me?" She couldn't keep the panic out of her voice.

"You mean like you tried to kill *me*? Eye for an eye, Alice." He sneered, distorting the scar she had left on his cheek the day she went on the run.

"But I didn't mean to—" On the verge of tears, she sniffled and choked back the viscous sob that wanted out.

She could smell the remnants of English Leather shaving cream mixed with his Acqua di Parma Colonia cologne—the same scent Cary Grant wore. She remembered this scent from a year ago when everything had changed between them. The familiarity made her stomach clench with memories she wanted to forget.

"And then you had the gall to kidnap my baby, Alice! What other choice do I have? One of us is going to die tonight, and it's not going to be me. I'm going to finish what *you* started."

The *tick, tick, tick* of the minute hand went on as usual, a countdown to what Alice was certain were the last few minutes of her life.

Chapter 4

My feet throbbed, and the baby's elbow to my bladder was dangerously close to creating an embarrassing leak. I had almost given up waiting for Detective Martina Carillo-Hughes to arrive, but before I had the chance to say, *"Put-a-fork-in-me-I'm-done,"* her police cruiser bumped across the weed-choked field.

The wind whistled through Bloodson Manor's open-air innards, carrying the musty stench of rot and thawing earth. I pulled my coat tight around my bump, shivering against the unnerving atmosphere. Even the baby stilled, as if sharing my unease.

"Here comes the cavalry," I muttered to Ginger.

Detective Hughes and a deputy put on hardhats before they strode past me, straight into the belly of the cellar and toward the skeleton without so much as a hesitation.

"So, Tara, what do we have here?" Detective Hughes asked me as she slapped on a pair of latex gloves.

"There was a message written in blood on the door." I pointed at it.

"I'm coming for you next," she read aloud. "Sounds ominous."

"You're telling me," I agreed.

"And that's not blood." Detective Hughes leaned in to

examine it. "It's… nail polish. That's different."

"Oh good. Now I can sleep soundly tonight," I muttered.

Where the house had remained untouched by the demolition crew, broken windowpanes created jagged patterns across the floorboards on each level. Wallpaper peeled from the walls in long strips like sunburned skin.

My gaze dropped back down to the basement, where Detective Hughes stooped to examine the skeleton, the knees of her black jeans skimming the dirt floor. Her flashlight beam pierced the bones while specks of dust floated around me in the weak daylight, making everything feel gruesomely dreamlike.

Next to me, Deputy Joe Speers—according to the gold name plate attached to his BBPD uniform—grinned at Sloane, who seemed oblivious to his attention.

"Do they know how old the body is?" Sloane signed to me, and I relayed the question to Detective Hughes.

The detective stood and turned toward me, while Deputy Speers wandered suspiciously close to Sloane, signing something to her I couldn't understand from this distance.

"I can take an educated guess, but the medical examiner will be able to confirm it. So here's what I know for sure." Detective Hughes shed the gloves and tucked them into her pocket, then retrieved a pen and pad of paper from inside the breast pocket of her coat. Her boots crunched on dead bugs as she paced. "This isn't a recent death, as you can tell."

"No duh," Ginger commented unnecessarily.

The detective glared at her, then returned to her prostate position at the foot of the skeleton. "We're past the initial stages where you see blood pooling and muscle stiffening. We're beyond decomposition too."

I watched her tap her pen on the remains with the confidence of someone who'd done this countless times. The pen clicked against the aged bone as she pointed out various body parts.

"Notice how there's nothing left inside the cavity? What you're seeing is the skeletal phase—just bones, some remaining leathery skin, and a little bit of connective tissue."

"Like beef jerky?" Ginger chimed in, drawing disapproving looks from everyone—especially me. "What? I'm just trying to get the facts straight."

I fought the urge to gag at the comparison. There went yet another food I'd never be able to stomach again. The detective's mouth quirked up, showing rare amusement.

She tapped the hip bones that jutted out from the buttoned waist of the jeans, then gestured above them. "Hopefully these bones will tell us what happened to her."

"You can tell it's a female?"

"Yep. Notice the wider, flatter pelvis? Built for having babies." She paused and glanced at my stomach, before adding, "As you're well aware, Mrs. Christie."

"What about the clothes?" I peered up at Ginger, wondering about the connection to Alice from the news article. "Did women wear jeans in 1969?"

Ginger rolled her eyes. "We didn't hand-spin our clothes from fresh-picked cotton, if that's what you're asking. And yes, I wore jeans in the late sixties... though back then I was a tomboy and wouldn't know a lipstick if it smacked me in the face."

Judging by the smear of red lipstick on Ginger's front teeth, she definitely had changed since then.

"No, this body isn't decades old," Detective Hughes cut in. "Based on my knowledge of forensic entomology, I'd say the death was about two months ago, possibly… October. Maybe a little earlier."

"Forensic ento-what?" Ginger asked.

"Forensic entomology—the study of insects as it relates to decomposition," the detective answered.

"Plus those jeans are new," Sloane added, fingerspelling the brand name when I gawked at her, then adding, "What? I know clothes, and those are from a boutique in town."

"So we know she liked fashion." I rose and my joints gave an audible *pop*. Spider silk caught in my hair and I swiped at it, making it catch my eyelashes. "Any idea what killed her?"

"That, I'm afraid, remains hidden," Detective Hughes answered. "Speaking of *hidden remains*, you're not hiding anything you know about this body, are you, Mrs. Christie?"

The detective chuckled. Was she actually making a joke for once? She was usually as no-nonsense as the hair pulled tightly in her bun that gave me a headache just looking at it. My heart quickened, wondering what she might suspect about my involvement.

My hands instinctively circled my belly, a nervous habit I'd developed over the last eight months. I wondered if I should tell her about Mikhail Pearson's lawsuit. My attorney had advised me to keep a lid on it to avoid a publicity circus that might harm my case. I figured that especially applied to right now.

The timing of a lawsuit followed by a dead body was terrible, but there couldn't possibly be any link between that and this months-old corpse.

No, definitely no connection.

Sloane waved for my attention and held up the newspaper photocopy we had found, but her signs were too fast for me to catch. Sometimes keeping up with Sloane and Ginger's conversations was exhausting.

"We found this next to the body. Could this victim be the woman mentioned here?" Ginger translated for Sloane to Detective Hughes.

I took a quick picture of the page before handing it over to the detective as evidence.

"Not unless she lived fifty more years after that article and only died recently."

I struggled to piece together how it all fit. What did the article have to do with this body? But I didn't have time to think about it when my phone vibrated, breaking the tomb-like silence. The caller ID showed *Slick & Quick Law Firm*—a call from my attorney that I had been waiting on edge for.

I answered with a hasty, "Please tell me you have good news, because I could really use some right about now."

"I'm afraid not." My lawyer's voice dropped to an unsettling tone that made my insides play a game of Twister. "We've hit a snag in your case. Can you meet me later today?"

"Can't you tell me over the phone?" All I could think of was the billable hours adding up.

"Unfortunately not. We're going to need to have this conversation in person."

I hung up wondering how much worse my day was about to get. If only this victim could tell us what she knew, maybe I'd survive the day. This skeleton wasn't talking… yet.

But if there was one thing I could count on Ginger and Sloane for—other than their shared loved of fashion—it was their talent for unearthing even the most deeply buried secrets.

Chapter 5

I had a huge list of problems, and the body in the basement of Bloodson Manor didn't even make the top two.

Problem number one: I didn't have a million dollars, in the event that I lost Mikhail Pearson's personal injury lawsuit against me. But my horse rescue acreage could be worth that much to the right buyer. And a lot of people over the years had shown an interest in my property. Losing my farm was a reality I had to face.

Problem number two: The trial was set on the same day as my due date. So while all I wanted was to rest and prepare for a newborn, I instead spent sleepless nights preparing for a trial.

Now my lawyer was about to dish out problem number three:

"Did I hear your name come up on the police scanner this morning, Tara?" She said it in a way that made me wonder if this was a question or a statement.

Who still listened to police scanners anyway—other than police? Apparently my attorney was a Millennial woman with a Baby Boomer's fondness for old-school technology. She still used a flip phone for personal calls. I thought those things had gone extinct along with pagers and floppy discs.

"What exactly did you hear?" I asked, but I had a good guess.

"They're investigating a murder that happened on your property. You realize how bad that looks, don't you?"

"I had nothing to do with it. I promise we have nothing to worry about."

Unless I was being framed. Or an unknown enemy was after me. Or the ghost of Emory's killer had taken another victim. Then I definitely had something to worry about.

I shifted uncomfortably in the red vinyl booth at Debbie's Diner, making the plastic seat cover squeak. My stomach pressed into the Formica edge of the booth's tabletop, causing it to wobble and nearly tip my tea onto my lap. The chrome window frame reflected the afternoon sun, blinding me as I averted my gaze to the layer of grime on the glass that desperately needed a good scrubbing.

"While I understand you didn't put the body there, I'm curious why I had to find out about it from a police scanner instead of from you. You do realize I'm your *lawyer*, right? My job is to protect your legal interests."

In my defense, I didn't want her to know. "But it's not relevant to the personal injury case."

She sighed dramatically. "Tara, until the trial is over, *everything* has to do with your case. Unearthing dead bodies on your farm included."

Bella Deere, attorney at law from Slick & Quick Law Firm, sat across from me with a frown that deepened by the second. The pickings for a reputable, ethical lawyer were slim in Bloodson Bay, and despite the law firm's peculiar name, Bella had been nothing but honest and time-consumingly thorough. The billable hours were proof of that.

When my mom recommended Bella to me after her legal

finesse put a stop to a particularly hateful neighbor who sued Mom over her "yard décor," even the unorthodox business name couldn't deter me. If Bella could get my mom's HOA to drop the charges for her life-sized, animatronic Christmas decorations that were still "Rockin' Around the Christmas Tree" in July, then clearly the woman could win *any* case.

"I'm sorry," I said, and I meant it. "I'll know better for next time."

"Next time?" Bella coughed on a mouthful of sweet tea. "There'd better be no next time, Tara. This… discovery makes me wonder what else you're not telling me."

She wanted to know my secrets? Where do I begin? The dark history of Bloodson Manor. Finding a dead girl in the cellar. Facing her killer, Marvin, and putting him behind bars. The recurring nightmares. Take your pick.

"I've told you everything relevant, Bella. I swear."

"Well, I hope so, because right now you're making my job impossible."

Bella's manicured nails drummed against her glass. Her laptop sat open next to legal papers spread between our untouched plates of what was supposed to be chocolate torte but resembled something I'd find in a diaper.

"And just so we're clear, I didn't kill anyone." My throat went dry but not dry enough to stop me from saying something I would probably regret. "And this is actually your fault, by the way. We found that body when we were tearing down Bloodson Manor—which *you* told me to do."

She stared at me silently, then glanced at the door as if contemplating whether to leave. Cue the regret.

"Well, I certainly wasn't expecting a dead body to be

exhumed when I advised that. This could be pretty damaging."

"How damaging exactly?"

"You tell me, Tara," Bella shot back. "How do you think a judge will rule when he hears a body was found on the same property that Mikhail Pearson is arguing as negligently dangerous?"

"Uh, when you put it that way… not good?" I ventured an educated guess.

"This is exactly what we *don't* need." Her voice dropped to a whisper as she glanced suspiciously around the busy diner. "Mikhail's lawyer is going to have a field day with this. An unsecured derelict property near where his son just got injured, and now a corpse?"

"Okay, okay. Just give it to me straight—what are the odds I can still win the lawsuit?" My farm, my home, and my life were all at stake right now.

"Honestly?" Bella's chin dropped as she avoided my eyes. "Next to impossible. When dealing with a personal injury case of this nature, the judge is going to look at a few key things."

She held her hand out, ticking off her red-polished fingers one by one. "First, if there was a dangerous condition on the property that you failed to exercise a duty of care to fix. And second, the age of the trespasser. When you're dealing with a minor—like Brock Pearson is—you can throw logic out the window."

In our first meeting, Bella had exhaustively explained how the law didn't apply to minors. As a property owner, I had a responsibility to eliminate the risk of a trespassing child from getting hurt. She called it the "attractive nuisance" doctrine, which protected child trespassers from things that might attract them, specifically dangers that a child might not realize were a risk to their safety. Things like swimming pools, trampolines… and apparently abandoned mansions.

Of course kids were attracted to danger. It was the whole reason parents existed—to keep their baby from poking a fork in a light socket, or a toddler from touching an open flame, or a teenager from jumping off someone else's balcony and spearing himself in the chest. The law was built around protecting them in their fondness for deathtraps.

A tension headache started creeping into my skull, cleaving through my temples. My stomach churned with lunch that wasn't settling right. A migraine was set in motion and I couldn't even take most pain medicines due to the pregnancy. Could things get any worse?

Why yes, yes they could.

"What could really sink us," Bella continued, "is that Mikhail's wife Darla left him a couple months after the injury, so he's a single dad who will garner the empathy of the court. And he's got a vendetta against the world. There's no reasoning with him."

We had tried everything, but he refused to settle. Bella rubbed her eyes, smudging smoky eyeliner around her sockets. So I was screwed. Case closed.

"Please don't give up on this case," I pleaded. "Just last spring you put the notorious Judge Ewan Valance behind bars. You're the youngest lawyer in the state to win such a huge case. I'm confident you can win my modest case."

I reminded Bella of her biggest career victory to date, though mentioning the monster who had made it his job to corrupt our small town made my skin crawl.

Former-judge-now-felon Ewan Valance had made my life a living hell over the years, mostly in an effort to get his greedy hands on my horse rescue. In typical entitled rich-guy manner, he stopped at nothing to feed his greed. When he had taken it a step too far and killed his own brother Marvin in the process, it all caught up to him. Now Ewan rotted behind bars, and word on the street was that he was too broke to afford the appeal. Former Assistant District Attorney Bella Deere, who was responsible for that triumph, became a town hero.

"Taking down Ewan Valance was different. I was working for the district attorney's office and had more to prove." She straightened her designer blazer.

"And you *did* prove yourself. You took down a giant!"

Her grin was watered-down and weak. "That case made me switch careers, Tara. I'm not the same type of attorney now. Personal-injury law is quite different. And unpredictable. But I promise you, I'll give you my all and hope for the best."

As Bella left to use the restroom, I slumped back in the booth feeling defeated. She didn't have that same winning attitude she had shown during Ewan Valance's trial. Or when she had convinced me three months ago that she was the perfect lawyer to take my case.

Tentatively picking at my chocolate poo-poo torte, I glanced across the diner and noticed a white-blonde head that looked strangely familiar. It took a full minute for my pregnancy brain to catch up and place a name with the face. It was Sloane's new assistant, Sterling Jones, sitting at the counter, absently swiping the screen of her phone.

"Sterling?" I called out, standing up and joining her at the counter. Townies tended to be over-friendly and under-receptive. "Hi! I'm Sloane's friend Tara. We met at Sloane's Halloween event that you helped with."

Her hunched back stiffened straight, then her lips shrunk into a frown. "Oh yeah, Tara. I remember you. The Halloween party was my first gig with Sloane."

"Do you enjoy the work?" I asked, and Sterling looked like she would have preferred a police interrogation over talking to me.

"It's fine." And that was it. A toddler had better conversational skills.

"What do you think of Bloodson Bay? Sloane mentioned you just moved here a few months ago."

"It's… small. Boring. A lot of cow tipping and terrible internet."

I agreed with the terrible internet, but I had yet to meet a person who had successfully tipped over a cow.

"Yeah, it's definitely quaint," I said, fighting the uncomfortable silence.

Something about Sterling rubbed me like sandpaper. When I had mentioned it to Sloane at the Halloween party, she had come to her defense with a vague "Sterling's had a tough life," but I wasn't buying it. There was something more to this girl that Sloane was protecting.

I glanced back at the booth where Bella had returned, tapping her watch. She was on the clock, and every minute cost me. "Well, I better run. I just wanted to say hi."

"Hi. And bye."

Thus ended the most awkward interaction I'd ever had. But then it got even worse. When her gaze skimmed behind me at Bella, her neck grew flushed with red splotches. She knocked over a salt shaker and bolted for the door, leaving a scattering of salt across the stainless-steel counter.

"Strange girl," I muttered as the bell on the door tinkled when it slammed shut. "Do you know her?"

Bella's eyes followed Sterling darting across the parking lot. "No, but she seems to recognize me. I wonder if she's related to someone I prosecuted in court."

The waitress arrived carrying an extra tea along with my check.

"I ordered you a drink to go, Tara," Bella explained. "You look terrible. Drink, get some rest, and stay out of trouble, for goodness' sake. You have a baby on the way and a court case to win. I can't have you collapsing from exhaustion."

At least someone was taking care of me, since lately it felt like I was taking care of everything on my own. Not that my husband wasn't doing his part, but Chris was working two jobs to make ends meet, and I couldn't pile more on his plate.

"Oh, I almost forgot that I brought you a gift." Bella revealed a sparkly gift bag and set it in front of me on the table. "Consider it a belated baby shower gift."

Moving the pastel green gift wrap paper aside, I pulled out a popular diaper bag all the *young moms* were using. "I love it! Thanks, Bella."

"It's a Tiny Tots Tote," she explained. "I filled it with healthy snacks and drinks for you, and diapers and onesies for the baby. I figured you can take it when you're driving around so you stay hydrated."

"It's absolutely perfect. Even Chris won't mind being seen carrying this in public."

I pulled out my debit card, grateful to redirect the subject away from dead bodies and dead-end lawsuits. The waitress returned a few minutes later holding my card out, shaking her head as her huge, dangly Christmas earrings jingled all the way.

"Your card's been declined, hon."

My cheeks warmed with embarrassment. Between the mounting horse vet bills and the renovations at the Loving Arms Children's Home that my farm proceeds were paying for, my checking account was as empty as my brain throughout this whole pregnancy.

I examined the name on my card: *Christopher Christie*. How did my husband's card get in my wallet? That meant he probably had my card, and God only knew what he was buying with it. Probably a beer holster or a potty putter. Yeah, look those up. They're real things.

I grabbed my phone and logged into our bank account. Chris usually handled the finances, and I instantly regretted not being more involved. There it was—a $9 checking balance, right after a $500 charge I didn't recognize. Scrolling through past statements, my stomach dropped faster than Chris's pants on date night. The same charge, month after month, going back years, like a silent thief we'd never noticed. The repeated memo was simply listed as: *A Silver Lining*.

Slipping my phone back into my purse, I started counting dollar bills, praying I had enough to cover the lunch I hadn't even wanted because Bella insisted we meet *in person* for my scolding. She must have noticed my agitation as I came up $3 short.

"I've got lunch covered," Bella offered, sliding her card across the table toward the waitress. "Lord knows you've paid enough attorney fees."

I didn't need the reminder, but at least I got a free lunch from the thousands I was paying her. After the check was paid, Bella handed me my Styrofoam cup of tea and gathered her papers. Her expression was grim.

"We need to get creative if we're going to save your farm and get out of this mess in one piece."

The way she said *creative* made me wonder if I should be worried.

"Right now your focus needs to be on getting that dead body situation solved before the trial."

"And if I don't?" I dared to ask.

"Then kiss your farm goodbye."

Chapter 6

June 27, 1969

"One of us is going to die tonight, and it's not going to be me," Clint warned Alice. And Clint didn't make empty threats.

A voice from Alice's past came back to her now with a sinister vengeance: *"I never make empty threats,"* Alice's mama used to say, usually while whipping her with a belt for an infraction that little Alice couldn't understand at such a tender age. A bleak, ironic chuckle escaped between furious breaths as she imagined Mama's stamp of approval on Clint. After all, Mama had married and died at the hands of a man just like Clint—minus the boatloads of money.

"Not if I kill you first!" Alice yelled, remembering the square of paper secured in the elastic of her underwear that poked her hip bone. She would need that paper later... if she survived.

Her loud, awkward response startled Clint just long enough to give her a second to react. Alice dropped down to the floor, falling out of his grip and jostling the phone table into his side. Within another moment, she had leapt to her feet and dashed down the hallway, at arm's reach from Clint, heading toward the front door. Even though she was smaller and faster, his bulk made him stronger, and that was all it took for him to jump on her and drag her to the floor.

He filled the space around her as he crushed her, then he whipped out a knife, its blade glinting in the moonlight. With one quick swipe, the blade dug into her flesh, piercing her side as it ripped the delicate fabric of her nightgown. Blood blossomed like a crimson flower against the pale cotton.

"Get!" She twisted underneath his massive weight. "Off!" Her elbow jutted out, connecting with the scar on his cheek. "Me!"

He cursed as she scrambled out of his grip, clawing her way forward while jabbing her heel into his nose again and again. That knocked him back enough that she could dart away again. She reached the front door, only glancing back long enough to make sure Clint was still down.

He was, but not for long.

Yanking the front door open, she was almost home free. She'd run straight for his car, grab the baby, and take off for the woods until she could slip back in to get her car keys. But Clint was already on his knees now, and his nose gushed blood that seeped into his shirt collar. He looked angry. Deadly.

She turned back to the doorway and rushed through, taking one step before slamming into a wall. A human wall.

"Fred, grab her!" Clint ordered as he steadied to his feet.

A man wearing an expensive charcoal-gray suit that looked out of place for this early morning hour wrapped his arms around her. He dropped a paper bag at her feet while he secured his hold on her, and she was too terrified to guess what was inside. His face was carved granite, eyes cold as winter frost, and his biceps could squeeze her like a pesky bug if he wanted to.

"Please, Clint!" she begged as he strode up to her, lips

curled in a bloody snarl that distorted the scar across his face even more. "You can't kill me. The police will put you in jail for life."

This time Fred laughed, his spittle hitting Alice's cheek. "Honey, I *am* the police. But I also have a few activities… on the side. Who do you think paid for this nice suit, my new car, or the diamond necklace I just bought my wife? Certainly not my public servant salary."

The weight of this revelation sunk in Alice's stomach. No one was coming to save her or the baby. She had to appeal to Clint if she had any chance of surviving this.

"Clint, you must still love me on some level. What we had was real, wasn't it?" she sobbed. "We created a child together!"

"And you stole that child from me," he growled.

"Only to protect the baby! I know what you've kept locked in your basement. I couldn't let you do that again!"

Alice should have known that Clint didn't have a heart; he only had stone. Fred tightened his grip on her as she went limp. Clint bent down and pulled something out of the bag, then held it up in front of her: a rope.

"The day you did this," he gestured to the ragged scar scoring his cheek, "was the day I stopped loving you, Alice."

It wasn't fair. It wasn't her fault. He had pushed her to do it. She remembered the events perfectly.

It started the day she applied for the position as a part-time housekeeper in the Valance mansion, with its soaring ceilings and marble floors that had made her sensible shoes echo like thunderclaps when she first stepped inside. Working there was a dream come true for a girl fresh out of high school with no other ambitions. But as her dreams always did, it soon twisted into an unrecognizable nightmare.

Clint was the first time she had felt loved, truly seen. But it was all a lie.

Alice and Clint had a forbidden chemistry the moment they met. Her heart raced when he smiled at her, and her body melted at his touch. Just a brush against her skin, or a gentle hand on her shoulder. Until one night when they were alone in his parlor, the firelight dancing across his aristocratic features, and he told her she was pretty. No one had ever told her that, not even her parents.

Eventually smiles turned to kisses, which abruptly shifted their relationship from professional to personal as Clint shattered every boundary Alice had carefully constructed. It wasn't long before kisses escalated into one night of passion. Within three months, his wife suspected something.

Alice could still picture the cold calculation in his wife's eyes whenever she had first noticed the swelling abdomen, like she was mentally measuring it for size. *"You really need to cut back on the sweets, Alice,"* was what she had said near the end of Alice's first trimester. Eventually, the woman realized it wasn't portion control that was the problem. The maid was carrying her husband's baby.

The threat of public shame was more than Clint could bear. And he was not above killing Alice to make the problem go away… but the attempted murder didn't take. Alice fought back, stabbing Clint in the face before she ended up on the run with his baby inside her.

He had been searching for her, for his child, ever since. Months later, Alice held their secret in her arms, an infant with her married lover's eyes. Her world tilted irreversibly on its axis as she prayed every night that Clint would never find her.

Now grabbing both of her arms, Fred spun Alice around while Clint wrapped rope around her wrists. At least they weren't bound behind her back. Then he yanked the cords so tight it cut off her circulation. Her chest constricted, each breath a war against her lungs as Fred squeezed the life out of her.

"I never meant to hurt you, Clint," Alice lied, for she most certainly had been trying to gouge out an eye, or impale his skull if she got lucky. "I was only trying to get away to protect my baby."

His laugh held no warmth. "You think stealing my child and hiding out here is protecting it? That baby is mine too, and face it, Alice—you're not fit to raise a child alone."

His refined features warped into something unrecognizable, something that made her wonder if she'd ever really known him at all.

"So killing me is the only option left?" Her voice cracked on the last word.

"Well, Alice, you can't steal my baby when you're buried six feet under."

"How are you going to explain your sudden new family addition?"

"Oh, that's already taken care of. I have enough money to alter the truth. Like how I paid your doctor to put my wife's name on your medical records. As far as the records show, she birthed that baby, not you." His sneer showed he believed he had already won.

"You won't get away with it."

"Oh, Alice, I already did."

They exchanged one last look, with tears streaking her face

and blood dripping from his nose. They were quite the pair.

Then Clint gave the order and turned away: "Kill her, Fred."

"Wait!" Alice shrieked, shaking her head and beating her bound fists against Fred's chest. "No! Let me go!"

But it was too late. Clint sauntered past her toward his idling Firebird where she heard the faint wailing of her baby trapped inside.

"Nope, you're not going with them," Fred said. "You're coming with me."

"He won't hurt my baby, will he?" The words caught in her throat, raw and desperate, while she searched for an escape route that didn't exist.

"The kid will be taken care of." His tone was eerily matter-of-fact.

Fred dragged her down the porch, forcing her to trip on loose gravel as he roughly shoved her ahead toward the black Cadillac where the trunk gaped open like a metal coffin.

"Get in," he demanded.

"There's no way I'll fit in there!" she cried.

He lifted a gun and pressed it to her temple. "Try."

She barely had time to draw breath before he propelled her inside, her sliced abdomen connecting hard with the spare tire. The lid slammed with terrible finality as her world went black, leaving her engulfed in claustrophobic darkness that smelled of motor oil and rubber.

The engine roared to life with a guttural snarl that vibrated through the metal. All Alice could wonder, as briny tears leaked from the corners of her eyes and soaked into her hair, was if she'd ever see her child again. The thought of never again holding the baby she had birthed, never seeing those puckered lips so much like her own, made her chest constrict with an ache far worse than the wound in her flesh saturating the trunk with her blood.

She tried to shift positions, but every movement sent fresh agony through her body. The car lurched forward, and soon the crunch of gravel gave way to smooth pavement, each bump and turn disorienting her further as she fought to stay conscious, to memorize the route, to hold on to some thread of hope that she would outlive this nightmare and see her precious baby once more.

And if she did survive the night, the vengeance she had planned would be the stuff of Clint's worst nightmares.

Chapter 7

After lunch with my attorney, I spent the rest of the day in bed with a stomachache, the typical aftermath of eating Debbie's Diner greasy fare. I didn't return to Bloodson Manor until the next day—and by then, the body was gone. But an outline of its shape remained in the patch of dirt, surrounded by bright yellow caution tape.

Unfortunately, any chance of me winning Mikhail's lawsuit—and keeping my farm—hung on solving this murder. So here I was, ducking under the tape and poking around when I should have been on bedrest.

"Shouldn't you be resting, Tara?" Sloane signed to me as I managed to get myself tangled in caution tape.

"And miss out on all this fun?" I signed back, finally ripping myself free.

"Exactly!" Ginger cut in, clearly oblivious to my sarcastic expression that didn't convey in sign language. "Why sit around watching *Columbo* when you can *be* Columbo?"

Although I wasn't feeling one hundred percent, I chalked it up to the fact that I would probably not feel one hundred percent ever again. First there would be the sleepless nights of early motherhood and endless nursing. After that the exhausting stage of negotiating with a toddler terrorist who learned the word "no."

There would be a brief break when the child was in elementary school and could wipe its own bum and feed itself. But then middle school hit along with the hormones, and everything went downhill from there. In the blink of an eye your child became an adult, off at college and only coming home when it needed money or clean laundry.

Oh, how I missed Nora.

A wave of dizziness hit me. I steadied myself against a weathered beam while Sloane swept her flashlight across the debris-strewn floor, illuminating a century of forgotten junk and animal droppings. Possum, by my deduction. When it came to animal poop, I was an expert. It came with the territory of running the Rockin' C Ranch Horse Rescue. I figured my poop knowledge would parlay nicely into motherhood.

We had only been exploring a few minutes before Ginger's phone belted out an instrumental refrain from Sir Mix-a-Lot's "Baby Got Back." Her face scrunched as she answered the phone, then she wandered into the field out of earshot.

I could only see her furrowed brow from where I stood, but those deep-set wrinkles conveyed bad news. When she returned, she was oddly quiet as she shoved the phone in her pocket without so much as a snarky remark.

"Everything okay, Ging?" I asked.

Ginger didn't answer me at first, then mumbled a distracted "yeah" as her pocket pinged. A text had come in, and she cupped her hand around her phone as she read it, as if trying to keep me from seeing it.

"Sorry, gals, but I have to go," she blurted out.

"You're the one all gung-ho on investigating this," I reminded her. "And now you're flaking out?"

"It's an emergency," was all Ginger said. Then she was gone.

I exchanged a look with Sloane, who gave an equally confused shrug. Ginger rarely left without some kind of pomp and fanfare.

"So what are we looking for?" Sloane signed, getting back to business.

"Clues to figuring out why someone chained a body down here." I guessed the signs for *clues* and *chained*. I never expected I'd need to be proficient in investigative terms when I first started learning ASL. "Though, maybe this is just a waste of time."

"Or maybe not…" Sloane gravitated back to the door and snapped a picture of the threat: *I'm coming for you next*. "Since this is nail polish, do you think we're dealing with a woman killer?"

While it wasn't as common, it had crossed my mind. "If so, what woman hates me enough to kill someone, and leave a threat for me here, of all places."

"She'd need to be connected to Marvin Valance to pick this exact location."

That left only members of the Valance family, and there were a lot of them. And if our perp was a *married* woman, she would have changed her last name to her spouse's. It was a needle in a haystack dilemma, but at least we had our first lead: Our killer was a woman.

Sloane cast a look at the setting sun. "It's getting close to suppertime."

I had no desire to eat after still feeling the effects of yesterday's lunch, but a nap sure sounded good.

"And I don't want to be here when it gets dark," Sloane added.

I couldn't agree more. "I'll drop you off at home," I offered as we hopped into my truck.

"Thanks. It's too bad Ginger couldn't stay. She would have had a field day with this," Sloane signed when we paused at a red light.

Ginger was usually an open book and runner up for most talkative person in Bloodson Bay, second only to the town mayor, Rose Crabtree. So her unexplained, abrupt exit had me worried. The way her normally rosy cheeks had gone ghostly white when she'd read her text message... something was wrong, and it wasn't like her to keep a secret from me, her own daughter-in-law.

"We better keep an eye on Ginger," I signed to Sloane, glancing briefly over at her while I drove.

She nodded in agreement, her dark waves bouncing. In the winter's early dusk, her phone lit up and blinked, the glow bursting in fast beats through the slit of her coat pocket. When she checked her message, a red exclamation point filled the screen.

"Oh no. It's a security alert from my office. Would you mind dropping me off there instead?" Sloane used her voice, as the night had deepened the gloom, making her hand gestures barely visible.

I nodded my fist with a brief *yes*.

During the drive, she kept trying to reach her assistant, inspecting her phone with increasing frustration. I wasn't surprised that Sterling hadn't replied; the girl was bizarre, and I trusted her about as much as I trusted the can of condensed milk

I found in my pantry this morning that expired in 2015.

Along Sloane's office building, under a stretch of streetlight, I parallel parked my truck. I didn't like the shadows in this part of town at this time of night.

Sloane shoved her phone back in her pocket. "Dead zone."

I checked my service and saw my bars were hanging on by a thread, until the connection dropped completely, leaving both our phones useless. In Bloodson Bay, that usually meant either a storm took down the signal or Mercury was in retrograde.

"I forgot to tell you I saw Sterling yesterday at Debbie's Diner," I said. "She practically ran from me like I had rabies. Is she usually that social?"

Sloane chuckled. "Yeah, that sounds like Sterling. A little jumpy. She's had a tough life. After what she did—" Sloane shook her head. "Never mind."

What *did* Sterling do? I didn't want to pry, but I sure could have used some hot gossip about someone else to distract me from my own scandal-worthy life right now.

We hopped out of the truck—or in my case fell like a bowling ball—and headed toward the entrance of Feel the Noize Party Planning. The windows were an ominous black and the door was closed and intact. It didn't appear as if anyone had broken in—but then again, one never knew what to expect in this part of town that the locals called the Trick Tract.

Don't even try to say it three times fast.

A week ago, some kids blocked every business entrance off with caution tape and made chalk outlines of bodies in front of every door. And last month, someone had stolen all the garden gnomes from Rose Crabtree's yard, only to arrange them in a perfect circle around the town square fountain. I secretly applauded the prank because I hated Rose Crabtree, and for good reason.

"I'm heading in," Sloane signed. "Do you mind waiting for me? I'll only be a minute."

"I'm not letting you go in alone! I'm coming with you." I waddled behind her a good five paces because Sloane was unfairly long-legged.

The doorknob easily twisted under Sloane's grip—it was unlocked—making me clutch my belly protectively. Being pregnant had turned me into a nervous wreck, but I wasn't about to let my best friend investigate a security alert alone, even if every horror movie I'd ever watched screamed this was a terrible idea.

Sloane's brow furrowed. "That's not good. Someone was— or still is—here."

"Maybe it's just Sterling…" I hoped.

"Then why are all of the lights off?" Sloane pointed out.

The door creaked loudly as we entered the gloomy gray hallway that opened up into an even darker pitch-black waiting area. Sloane fumbled for a light switch on the wall while I tried to enable the flashlight of my phone. A crash echoed from somewhere further inside, followed by the distinct sound of glass shattering.

I yelped, gripping Sloane's arm hard enough to probably leave marks—but she had no clue why because she hadn't heard it. My heart rammed against my ribs as pregnancy hormones sent my imagination into overdrive, conjuring images of masked killers and vengeful apparitions.

Sloane snapped up the light switch, shoving the office into blinding light, making both of us squint against the sudden brightness. The fluorescent bulbs buzzed to life with an angry hum that matched my already-frayed nerves.

A window hung open in the kitchenette across from the main office space, the white curtains fluttering in the night breeze. Something had hefted itself outside, leaving behind knocked-over coffee mugs and scattered sugar packets. My fear first suspected a rat, due to the memory of yesterday's rat encounter still fresh. But I quickly shot that down, because whatever had been in here made a human-sized mess.

"Did you see what jumped out the window?" Sloane looked as horrified and confused as I felt.

"No, did you?"

She shook her head. "I think we scared whoever or whatever was in here out through the window."

"Does anyone else have a key? Like a cleaning service?"

Sloane raised an eyebrow at me. "You think a housekeeper would have escaped through the window to avoid getting caught cleaning at night?"

Okay, good point. "No, but maybe she left the door unlocked and had opened the window and forgot to close it before she left."

"In December?"

So it wasn't the most logical conclusion, but it was a lot easier to digest than a masked killer, vengeful apparition, or rat, which were my only guesses so far.

"Only Sterling and I have keys, and I don't hire a cleaning service. It must have been Sterling. That's the only reasonable explanation."

A skittish personality, a secret past Sloane couldn't talk about, leaving the entrance unlocked… I wondered if there was something more to Sterling than Sloane knew. I couldn't shake the sensation that something about that girl's reaction at the diner didn't add up.

"Everything looks okay," Sloane signed warily after we did a sweep of the office.

"I don't trust your assistant," I said, picking a business file up off the floor and setting it on the desk. "Maybe you should look for a new one."

"Do you know how hard it is to find someone reliable in this town? And willing to learn sign language to communicate with me? I can't give her up." Sloane's features softened. "Besides, I'm her last chance at fixing her life."

Fixing her life from what, though? Obviously, she had done something bad enough to ruin it in the first place.

"Tara, you of all people should appreciate helping someone in need and giving people a second chance."

Sloane was right. My life was built around people—and horses—who needed another chance. The Loving Arms Children's Home, the Rockin' C Ranch Horse Rescue. Those places were refuges for children and animals at the mercy of others for their very survival. But something about Sterling felt sinister, more calculated than vulnerable.

Still, I kept that thought to myself, knowing how stubborn Sloane could be once she'd made up her mind about someone. I hoped she was safe from this someone, an edgy woman with a secret past.

Chapter 8

"October."

Detective Martina Carillo-Hughes's voice crackled through my speakerphone as I pulled up my driveway.

My headlights passed over my garage door, casting a succinct beam of light on someone standing on my porch before the figure was plunged back into darkness. I sat in the truck, unable to make out who it was while I listened to the detective through my truck's speakers.

"The forensics team believes the body was placed in the basement sometime in October, as I suspected," she continued explaining, her voice competing with the blast of heat through the vent.

The timing lined perfectly with Mikhail Pearson's lawsuit against me. What a coincidence. A deputy had delivered the Summons and Complaint to me in September, Mikhail suing me for negligence. One month later, a dead body was planted on my property. That didn't look good for my case. God forbid the body have a connection to Mikhail, or I could be looking at murder charges.

"Any idea yet who she is?" I asked weakly.

This conversation was making me queasy. Though, these days, everything made me nauseous.

"The medical examiner is working on it. I checked the

missing persons database, but there were no local women who disappeared in October." Detective Hughes paused. "At least, none that were reported missing."

"So… what now?"

The din of conversation filled the background as Detective Hughes sighed into the phone line. "Well, I figure we might need to expand our search, so it's going to take some time."

I highly doubted the victim lived outside of Bloodson Bay. No one knew about the Slaughter Shed except for the locals, which meant the killer lived in our town. And more than likely, the victim did, too.

I had read somewhere that most killers hunted within five to twenty-five miles from their residence. I guess even psychopaths preferred the creature comforts of home. I didn't mention this to Detective Hughes, though. I figured she wouldn't appreciate my armchair detective input.

"And," Hughes continued, "I'm outsourcing a forensic odontologist to examine the dental evidence, since Bloodson Bay doesn't have the resources for that."

Outsourcing dental records? That sounded time-consuming, and time was not on my side. My attorney had been clear about that—an open investigation about a body on my property could easily be used against me to prove my negligence, to the tune of a million dollars. Responsible people tended to notice when their property was being used as a murderer's dumping ground. I needed this case closed as soon as possible.

"How long do you think that will take?"

"It shouldn't be too long before they have an ID," the detective answered.

In police speak, *not too long* could mean anything from days to years. Probably not two weeks, which was when my baby was due. Perhaps I needed to help move things along after all. Ginger would be thrilled to hear this.

"What do they think killed her?" Based on the condition of the body, could they even tell? There was hardly anything left of her.

"We're still determining the cause of death. There is no evidence to show that she was murdered in the basement of Bloodson Manor, if that's what you're wondering."

I hadn't been wondering that at all, actually. But now I was. If she had been killed right under my nose, I could never forgive myself for that.

"Is there anything I should do in the meantime?" I offered futilely.

"Just stay local in case we have questions."

I didn't bother to remind her that I was about to pop out a baby any day and had no plans on jet-setting anytime soon.

I hung up just as the shadow waiting on my porch lunged toward my truck, and I almost hit re-dial for the police. I didn't like the looks of whoever was ambling toward me, creepily hunched over, their silhouette noticeably bobbing up and down with a severe limp.

Could I, at eight months pregnant, defend myself against a hobbling attacker? Probably not. My water would break before I even got a punch in. Playing it safe, I locked my doors and triggered the truck's alarm, hoping to scare off whoever it was. Or at least draw the attention of my husband inside the house.

The headlights started flashing as the alarm shrieked, and the figure rushed toward the truck, arms waving wildly. When the person smacked up against my window, I realized who it was and shut off the alarm.

"Ginger!" I screamed as I opened the truck door, letting all the heat out. "What the h-e-double-hockey-sticks is wrong with you?"

I had been practicing not swearing since I'd have a baby in the house who would soon be listening to and repeating everything I said. I figured I'd need as long as possible to break my cussing habit.

"What's wrong with *me*? What's wrong with *you*? You nearly gave me a heart attack!" Ginger's wild curls framed her head like a huge halo, and her kimono fluttered in the breeze like an exotic bird taking flight.

"You almost caused me to go into labor," I retorted.

"I'll take that as a thank-you." Ginger waited while I shut off the engine before she said the four most dreaded words in the English language—or in Ginger's case, smushed into three words: "We gotta talk."

"Nooo," I groaned. "What now?"

"Word on the street is that Mayor Crabtree wants you out."

Rose Crabtree, our town mayor, had a dream: to revitalize Bloodson Bay. By *revitalize* she meant turn our charming little town into a premier tourist destination. Developers had been trying to accomplish this for years due to our beachfront real estate, but Bloodson Bay lacked that certain appeal that vacationers wanted. Like more than one restaurant option and decent entertainment.

"She wants me out? What does that mean?"

"Crabtree wants your land, Tara."

"Get in line. What does she want it for?"

"Her idea of modernizing the town is turning your farm into

an entertainment complex with go-karts, trampolines, and arcades," Ginger explained. "She wants to speak with you. Try to strike a deal to sell."

I hauled myself out of the truck with a groan, not sure what I dreaded more: the drop from the seat to the concrete, or discussing this further. I was so tired of being the hot topic of Bloodson Bay.

Every movement sent a spike of pain through my sciatic nerve. Apparently, I wasn't the only one with leg pain. Ginger staggered beside me into the house, favoring her left leg. Once inside, I caught a glimpse of a nasty bruise, purple as an overripe plum, peeking out from below the hem of a shrunken cropped top that would fit my newborn baby better.

"How did you get hurt?" I asked.

"A door jamb jumped out at me."

I was about to call her out on this lame attempt for an excuse when she blurted, "So, with everything going on, I'm sending you away."

"Say what?" I asked.

"You need to leave town. Take a break from all this—the dead body, Rose Crabtree, everything. I'm sending you and Chris on a babymoon."

"I can't leave town." My hand automatically moved to my very pregnant belly because no explanation was necessary. "Besides, it's almost Christmas, and I have doctor visits lined up until my due date." The thought of rescheduling all those appointments spiked my anxiety even more—if that was possible.

"Just for a couple days. For your own safety and sanity. Please."

Did Ginger know something I didn't about the body? Why would I be unsafe in my own home? But a babymoon did sound nice, since everything would change once the baby arrived. This was my last chance to get in some quality hubby time with Chris. And sleep. Oh, how I wanted sleep. And bladder control would be nice, too, though I didn't want to get ahead of myself.

"I don't even know where we'd go," I realized. "The police told me to stay local."

"Oh, I know the perfect place! I've already made the arrangements for you."

Uh-oh. I didn't trust that at all. Ginger considered a romantic getaway spending a weekend at the So-So Southern Motel in the heart of the town's crime district.

"Don't worry," Ginger quickly added. "It's not a motel. It's near the beach."

I decided to trust her this once because I was too tired to argue. When I headed into the kitchen to make tea, Ginger grabbed her purse and followed me with a wince.

"Are you okay?" I asked. "You look like you're in pain."

She scoffed, her green eyes flashing with defiance. "I've never felt better in my life!"

She stumbled slightly with a grimace, contradicting herself, then dropped her purse. It flew open, scattering a bajillion things across the kitchen floor.

"Hell's bells!" Ginger yelled.

We both dropped down to our knees, grabbing handfuls of crap and shoving it back in her purse. Wadded up tissues, a Lip Smacker lip balm from the 1990s, a Fiona Apple CD… Her purse was a time capsule.

I reached for an envelope and noticed that the top left corner had a return address from the Bloodson Bay Correctional Facility. The familiar address made my heart skip a beat as I recalled visiting my husband there not too long ago, when he had been held on murder charges. What the heck was Ginger doing with a letter from the county jail?

My fingers itched to open it up and read whatever secrets it contained, but Ginger caught me staring and yanked it from my grip. She held the envelope against her chest like it contained state secrets.

"Got a new pen pal?" I teased, but Ginger wasn't biting.

"I need to head home. It's getting late."

After Ginger left, I wondered what other secrets she was keeping from me. Between the jail letter and her mysterious limp, Ginger was turning into quite a puzzle today. But I didn't want another puzzle to solve.

Maybe a babymoon was exactly what I needed.

Chapter 9

A babymoon turned out to be the last thing I needed.

None of my clothes fit. My shoes could barely contain my swollen feet. And I experienced a sudden case of carsickness that made every mile torture.

I fixed my gaze out the passenger window as Chris navigated the winding coastal roads, while the seatbelt cut into me like a dull razor. A morning fog hung low, revealing rare glimpses of the gray Atlantic Ocean between the mounds of sand dunes and sprigs of sea grass.

"I'm really starting to regret this trip," I said as Chris pulled up to a house with a series of life-sized lawn ornaments lining the driveway. And filling the yard. And pouring up onto the porch.

My mother's house looked like Christmas *and* Easter had exploded all over it. Between the ceramic bunnies dotting the garden and the crosses adorning every window, it was a shrine to her two greatest loves: Jesus and rabbits.

Then there was the Christmas décor. A human-sized Santa wearing a polka-dot bowtie, a nutcracker holding a teacup, a nativity of dogs… and that wasn't even the half of it. I was walking into a holiday house of horrors. Chris carried our luggage past neon pink flamingos guiding a sled and what appeared to be a Santa-dressed bunny.

"It's just for a couple days," Chris reminded me as he pushed up his glasses. "We needed to get out of Bloodson Bay and away from the drama."

"So we come *here*?" If we wanted to get away from drama, we should not have come to my mother's house.

"Well, I'll take drama involving animatronics and HOA complaints over corpses and lawsuits any day."

Chris heaved my suitcase up onto the porch with an exaggerated groan. Out of habit I had packed enough outfits for every possible scenario, including a dress for a hypothetical black-tie dinner, even though I doubted I'd be able to squeeze a thigh into it, let alone my entire body.

Within half an hour of settling in and conversing with my mother about whether I was eating enough, whether I was eating too much, or if she could touch my shifting belly just one more time—she was up to fourteen times, but who was counting?—I decided it was time to explore downtown Wilmington. My ankles were already swollen from the two-hour drive, and if I had to endure one more lecture about the benefits of drinking pineapple juice mixed with castor oil to induce labor, I was going to scream.

In the 2000s, I admittedly was hooked on teen drama television. What girl wasn't? *Dawson's Creek. Gilmore Girls. Gossip Girl.* Even *Golden Girls* when my mom controlled the remote. All the *girls*, but most importantly, *One Tree Hill.* And so I dragged Chris to every *One Tree Hill* film location we passed. And if we didn't pass it naturally, I would find a detour that forced us to.

In typical super-husband fashion, Chris indulged my constant stops and excited pointing, though I could tell by his patient smile that he didn't quite share my enthusiasm for every park bench and storefront that had ever appeared on the TV show setting.

"This is where Lucas and Peyton had their first kiss!" I grabbed Chris's arm, bouncing until I nearly induced myself.

"You know I have no idea who Peyton and Lucas are, right?" Chris laughed at my fan-girling.

"Don't tell me you've never seen *Dawson's Creek* either. Some scenes were filmed right there," I added as we walked up the Banks Channel.

Back then Chris was probably too busy watching NASCAR or *South Park*, but he pretended to enjoy my lengthy series recap regardless. By late afternoon, we had wandered up to a crowded Christmas event that had taken over the beach. Wilmington's historic waterfront caught fire under a burnt orange sunset, making every filming location look even more magical than it did on screen. I now knew why filmmakers and photographers called it the *golden hour*.

"Only one more, I promise. Over there is—" I froze mid-sentence, spotting a familiar white-blonde head bobbing through the crowd ahead of us. The distinctive platinum shade was unmistakable, even from this distance.

What on earth was Sloane's assistant doing here?

But when the figure turned, it was just a teenage girl who happened to share Sterling's distinctive hair color, right down to that expensive-looking platinum sheen that usually only came from regular visits to a high-end salon. Maybe pregnancy brain was making me paranoid.

It wouldn't be the first time my hormones had me seeing conspiracies in coincidences. Last week, I'd been convinced the mailman was secretly replacing our bills with identical duplicates—it was the only logical explanation for why our bank account never seemed to grow. Oh, that and having a ranch full of horses whose upkeep kept us poor, I suppose.

"Hey, Tara, are you okay?" Chris tenderly squeezed my hand, his palm reassuringly steady against mine.

He always sensed when my mind spun off into wild tangents. Or maybe I was just that easy to read. Either way, Chris kept me grounded.

"I thought I saw someone I knew." My voice wavered with uncertainty.

There was something oddly familiar about the girl that bothered me, like a word stuck on the tip of my tongue. I watched her disappear into the crowd, trying to place where I might have seen her before. Being approximately the size of a small whale these days, all my energy went to the baby, so my memory wasn't exactly firing on all cylinders. The third trimester was doing a number on my usually sharp mind, turning it into something resembling warm pudding.

"Who?" Chris asked, adjusting his glasses and searching the spot where my gaze was locked.

I pulled him ahead, pointing her out from a distance.

"Over there. See the white-haired girl?" My finger traced her path through the sea of people, her head like a beacon.

When she turned to face us, I swear her eyes met Chris's from across the beach, and his mouth gaped open. "No, it can't be her…"

His grip on my hand tightened.

"It can't be who?" I turned to study his expression, noting his calm demeanor crack around the edges.

He shook his head. "No one. It's not possible. She's way too young, and it's not the same hair. But the face looks so much like hers… a girl from my past."

The way he said it spiked my curiosity. A past girlfriend? Co-worker? But then she turned away before I could get another look. Chris led me out of the crowd, briskly guiding me toward the ocean.

"Let's get away from here," he insisted with a strange urgency.

We reached the beach as tiny snowflakes began drifting down, melting as soon as they touched the sand. But soon the flakes started sticking, layering the beach in pure white. It rarely snowed here, and the sight was dreamlike, nature's own delicate confetti coating the shore. I burrowed deeper into my coat against the winter chill, and Chris wrapped his scarf around my neck before he kissed me. It was a perfect day, a perfect babymoon. Even the mysterious girl-sighting couldn't dampen it.

"I can't believe it's snowing. A Christmas miracle!" I exclaimed, then sighed. I glanced at Chris, his expression distant as he stared down the beach where the girl had been. "Honey, where are you?"

"Huh?" He looked over at me. "Oh, I'm here, babe."

"No, you're somewhere else. Somewhere… sad."

"I don't want to ruin the mood."

"Chris."

It was all I needed to say. We didn't keep secrets. Not anymore, at least.

He toed the snowy sand, shoulders hunched. "That girl… she dredged up something I had tried to forget." That was all my husband offered for a long minute, but then he continued, "Something happened here, on this same beach, shortly after my parents died."

That was before Nora was born. What could possibly bother him from such a long time ago?

"That girl reminded me of someone who went through something horrible... because of me." Then he said nothing more.

It was the first time he had ever mentioned this part of his past, and it was a pretty big bomb to drop without more explanation. My husband dedicated his life to helping people, not hurting them. Was there a reason for that—had he done something terrible that he was trying to make amends for?

"Chris, what are you talking about?" I pressed. "What happened?"

He sat down on the sand, and after a little physical struggle, I joined him. I sat between his legs as he held me from behind, and his mouth was so close to my ear I could feel the warm breath behind his words.

"It was my birthday, and to celebrate, the guys threw me a beach party. I drank too much. We were hanging out around a bonfire, acting wild. You know how guys can get. Anyway, some girls joined us on the beach."

"Excuse me?" I turned to look back at him because if my math was correct, we were most likely married at the time. "Are you about to tell me you cheated on me?"

He quickly added, "No, it wasn't like that. I swear, I wasn't talking to any of the girls. In fact, I was pretty out of it. But then I saw something happen... and I just... watched and did nothing."

Whatever it was, it had to be bad. Bad enough that twenty years later, the blame still haunted him.

"What did you see, Chris?"

He swallowed hard. "I watched one of my friends take a girl behind the dunes into the caves. Toward Lover's End."

Lover's End was not nearly as romantic as it sounded. It was basically a cave formed from a huge collapsed pipeline that discharged municipal wastewater into the ocean. Not only was it disgusting, but it was dangerous, too. Several kids had drowned from getting stuck in the channel during high tide with no way out. It showed just how apt the Lover's End name was, because any guy that took a girl there to make out would guarantee the end of that relationship.

"People went there to make out all the time, Chris." I didn't understand what he was so upset about.

"There's more to the story," he said. "As he was pulling her toward the caves, she called out my name and mouthed something to me. It might have been *help*, or something like that, but she definitely knew me. I didn't know for sure what she was trying to tell me, but I just… froze. I didn't do anything. I never stopped it. I was too drunk to react. The next day, the news reported a girl missing, last seen at Lover's End, and… I knew it was her, and it was my fault."

I remembered that case vaguely. I couldn't tell you the girl's name, but Lover's End was a cautionary tale after that. I had no idea my husband had witnessed it. Every parent used that girl's disappearance as a warning to their daughters.

"I thought the news said she ran away." My voice grew quiet as the gravity of what Chris was telling me sank in.

The gentle crash of waves against the shore suddenly felt

ominous.

"Even so, I could have stopped it and I didn't. I still get nightmares about it." Chris's voice cracked. "Maybe everything bad happening to us now… maybe I deserve it."

I shifted around to face him, hugging him tight. "Honey, that's not true. It's not your fault."

"I should have told you sooner, Tara. I'm sorry." He broke my heart as he sobbed into my hair. "I've tried to make amends by donating to a rape crisis center every month, but nothing can undo my failure to act. A girl was traumatized because of me."

So that explained the monthly $500 charge I had found. "I meant to yell at you about that but I totally forgot in all of the chaos."

"I'll stop if you want me to. But I felt like it was the least I could do after what I did… well, didn't do." Chris's shoulders sagged against me. "I let something terrible happen to that girl and I'll never know the truth."

The raw pain of his confession was a side of my husband I'd never seen before. For years he carried a burden I hadn't known existed. I felt torn between despair for him and rejection for me because he didn't trust me enough to share this.

"Why didn't you tell me?"

"I was ashamed, Tara."

"You were young and made a mistake, Chris. But you can't go back and change it. You have to move on."

I reached over and held his hand, feeling the slight tremor of his fingers interlocked with mine. Seeing him this devastated tightened my chest with worry. His anguish made me want to wrap him up, somehow shield him from the weight of his own remorse. Then he voiced the question that had clearly been tormenting him, his words barely above a whisper:

"How can I move on when I feel like it's not over yet?"

With that question, I felt it, too—that crushing, suffocating burden of responsibility that had been visiting our household like an unwelcome guest. I couldn't move on, either. Not from Brock Pearson's near-deadly accident. Or Mikhail Pearson's lawsuit. Or the mystery woman's body found in Bloodson Manor. Or the fear that I wouldn't be a good enough mom to my baby. But all of that was at home. Right now we were sitting on a beach, dusted with once-in-a-lifetime snow, together.

"The only way forward is through faith, Chris. Bad things happen, and we can either let them break us or forge us in fire. The pain we endure empowers us to be stronger, more empathetic, more resilient. Don't let it destroy you."

My hand tightened around Chris's, as if holding on could anchor us to this perfect moment, away from the spiral of what-ifs that threatened to drag us both under.

Chapter 10

That perfect moment lasted just about twelve hours.

By late morning, I awoke to find Chris's side of the bed empty and my mom's sing-song voice dragging me unwillingly from a particularly crazy dream involving a nudist beach and swimming with sharks. Me in the nude surrounded by pointy teeth didn't scare me half as much as my reality, though.

"Wakey, wakey, eggs and bakey!" My mom, Eloise Reynolds, was a bundle of energy from dawn until dusk… and sometimes the late-night hours in between, especially ever since she hit menopause. "Time to rise and shine, sleepyhead."

And she loved using annoying cliches.

"Where's Chris?" I asked.

I preferred to deal with my husband first thing in the morning instead of my mother. He knew better than to greet me with "wakey, wakey" and "rise and shine."

"He had to head home early this morning, dear. His sister Peace called with some horse crisis that couldn't wait."

Of course our babymoon got cut short. What else was new? Now I was stuck on my romantic getaway with my mother. *A little Eloise went a long way*. Oops, I guess I used annoying cliches too. *Like mother, like daughter*.

By the looks of the snow coming down outside the widow next to my bed, I wouldn't be getting home anytime soon. In the south, just a threat of "weather" put the town in a state of emergency as everything shut down.

"I've got brunch on the table for you. And you'll never guess what it is," Mom said. Her voice was a bit too chipper for my ears so soon after waking up, even though it was close to noon.

"Uh, eggs and bacon?" I took an educated guess, which my mom's impressed expression affirmed was correct.

Mom always made eggs and bacon when I came to visit, and the eggs were always undercooked and runny, while the bacon was overcooked to a burned crisp.

"Egg and bacon *sandwiches*," she corrected, "since it's almost noon, dear. And I brought you tea."

On the dresser across the spare bedroom sat a mug of steaming tea. Beside it, my phone beeped.

"Oh, that reminds me," Mom said, "your phone has been chirping nonstop for the past hour. I took a tiny glimpse at your messages while you were sleeping to make sure they weren't important. You should probably reply. It looked urgent."

"Seriously, Mom? I'm a grown woman. You don't check another woman's text messages."

"You're not just *some woman*, Tara. You'll always be my troublemaking daughter, and I'll always be your nosy mother."

I rolled my eyes like the teenager she seemed to still think I was and then held out my open palm. "Can you pass me my phone?"

She handed it to me, and my blood pressure rose with a lightheaded flush when I saw the number. Over a dozen text messages. And most weren't even from Ginger. There were numbers I didn't recognize. I groaned and shifted to my side, already dreading whatever fresh chaos was about to be unleashed on my morning.

Mom hovered over me, stealing glimpses of my screen:

Who did you kill this time, Tara Christie?

Stop bringing our property values down and leave town!

This is your final warning. Leave or we're going to #cancelrockin'cranch!

Have you checked our town Facebook group posts recently? It's not good.

That final text was from Ginger, who added half a dozen emojis at the end, ranging from shocked cat face to upside-down face to drooly face. Though I couldn't figure out what that last one had to do with anything.

"Oh dear, what's going on now?" Mom's cheerful tone was at complete odds with her words. She had a knack for delivering bad news like she was announcing I'd won the lottery.

I pulled the quilt over my head, surrounded by the overwhelming presence of her ceramic rabbit collection watching me from every shelf.

"I don't know and I don't care." My words came out muffled, but my whine carried through the blanket.

"You can't hide from your problems, Tara." Mom yanked the covers back with the enthusiasm of a game show host revealing a grand prize. "And remember, for every problem there's always a solution."

"And when there's no solution?" I asked.

"Then you drink tea!"

I sat up as she handed me a cup of peppermint tea, my swollen joints making the simple act of movement feel like an Olympic event.

"I have a suspicion this problem is a pretty big one."

I was certain it had something to do with the corpse found at the manor, since word spread fast in Bloodson Bay. But what could be so bad that people wanted to run me out of town? Or worse—*cancel* me?

"Let's find out together."

I sipped the over-sweetened tea and winced. "Don't you have decaf coffee instead?"

Mom scoffed, as if I'd just asked her for motor oil. "Decaf? I don't buy decaf. I'd rather drink sewage than decaf. At least sewage has character."

"Then regular coffee it is," I demanded. Why did I sense I'd need all the caffeine I could get in order to handle today?

"Absolutely not. Caffeine is not good for the baby."

Mom wagged her finger at me like I was sixteen again and trying to sneak out to a party. Which I never did, by the way. I wasn't the type of cool kid that got invited to parties. Maybe I would have gone to book club parties, but no one had those back then.

"Mom, the baby has a couple weeks left in here." I patted my baby bump. "I don't think caffeine at this stage will cause any harm."

I tried to sound reasonable, though reasoning with my mother was like trying to convince her she had too many lawn ornaments. It would only end in an argument. Or a lawsuit. That's how she had found my lawyer, after all.

"Sorry, not on my watch." She perched on the edge of the bed, pointing to my phone. "Now let's rip off the Band-Aid and deal with the problem."

I inhaled the disappointing aroma of peppermint, wondering how many more days of this herbal torture I'd have to endure. Once I settled back against my pillows, I prepared myself for whatever drama had captured the town council's attention this time. The post was easy to find, pinned to the top of the Facebook group page:

The Bloodson Bay Town Council has decided to schedule an impromptu meeting to vote on whether or not to demand the removal of one of its townspeople due to property liability and negligence. After the fateful incident where Mikhail Pearson's son Brock was injured on Tara Christie's farm, another significant event has been brought to our attention. A body was found on her property earlier this week, which leads us to make the difficult decision to vote Mrs. Christie out of town. She has brought nothing but danger to our quaint town and must be stopped. Voting starts tonight at 6:00 p.m. Local police will enforce the results of the vote.

The poster was anonymous, but I suspected who the proverbial "we" was. Half the town had it out for me ever since

Ewan Valance had targeted my farm and actively recruited the town council to push me out. Someone even had the gall to come to my home after dark and leave a message on my doorstep saying: *I know what happened in Bloodson Manor, and you will pay.*

Mayor Rose Crabtree had enthusiastically led the charge against me. Whoever "we" was, they had no legal right to demand I leave. But they could certainly make my life hell if they wanted to.

"Why on earth would anyone want you gone?" Mom's hand pressed to her chest, as if the idea of anyone hating her daughter was unfathomable.

"I'm guessing this is because a body was found in the basement of that abandoned house in the back of the property."

Mom tut-tutted me. "Oh yeah, Bloodson Manor. I had warned you about the liability of owning an abandoned house. If I recall, I had even offered to try to sell it for you. I could have gotten a good price, considering its historical value."

"Stop." I didn't need her real estate spiel, not now.

My mother had done a stint as a realtor, specializing in selling abandoned properties to house flippers. When I was a child, she would drag me to every condemned or foreclosed house across town, assessing what kind of profit she could make on the sale.

"Anyway, it looks like the town council is trying to convince the voters that I killed someone."

"You—a killer?" My mom laughed, and under any other circumstance, that description was laughable. Chris and I saved lives, we didn't take them. We rescued horses, we ran a foster care facility. But someone really had it out for me. "Why would someone accuse you of such a thing?"

"I don't know," I answered glumly.

But I could think of several reasons. It could be payback from Ewan Valance for being a thorn in his side. Or someone wanting to get their hands on my property, which was worth millions. Or maybe I cut someone off in line at the grocery store and they've been plotting my demise ever since. It was Bloodson Bay, where anything could happen and did happen.

I started reading through the comments. One in particular stood out. It was also posted anonymously:

It's about time we get rid of the Christies and the Loving Arms Children's Home along with them! It only attracts riff-raff and must be eliminated to restore our town's honorable legacy.

No one in my age demographic said *riff-raff,* so that narrowed down the commenter to everyone over fifty? Sixty? I had no idea who used that word, really. But with all of the likes the comment was getting, it seemed that was how a majority of the town felt.

I checked the time. Home was a couple hours away, but I would have plenty of time to make it to the meeting… if I could drive, that is. Chris had taken our truck, and it was snowing. I had no experience driving on snow-covered roads, and snow plows were unheard of in this region.

"I need to get back in time for this meeting," I announced. To save my farm, my children's home… and my sanity.

"You can't drive in this, Tara. It's too risky with you being pregnant. If you got in an accident…"

"Can you drive me?" I begged, trying not to sound as desperate as I felt.

"I can't drive in snow. Plus, my night vision is awful." She rapped on her glasses for emphasis. "These aren't just a fashion statement, you know."

I wondered if Sloane would be able to pick me up. I knew it was a huge ask, but my life depended on it. So I sent a quick text to her, and she replied right away, saying she'd be here in two and a half hours. Help was on the way!

Four hours later, Sloane still hadn't arrived. The meeting was at six, and it was almost four o'clock. That gave me two hours to make it, which would be cutting it way too close. Sloane should have been here by now. I'd never known her to be late—tardiness was usually *my* specialty.

I texted Sloane again, my fingers drumming nervously on the kitchen counter as I waited for a response. Nothing. So I attempted to video chat with her, hoping maybe she was stuck in traffic and would answer. Again, she didn't pick up.

My mind wandered to every possible worst-case scenario: She had gotten in an accident on the icy roads. Her car had broken down and she was stranded somewhere in the freezing cold. Or worse, Ginger had decided to come with her and offered to drive, in which case it'd take until midnight.

"Maybe Sloane got lost?" Mom suggested, though we both knew that was unlikely.

With her top-of-the-line GPS and borderline obsessive punctuality, Sloane getting lost was about as probable as me giving birth to a unicorn—which given how much this baby poked seemed only slightly less likely at this point.

"Wait—someone's here," Mom announced.

Headlights zipped across the window, catching the falling flurries in their beams like a spotlight on dancing stars. I squinted through the frosted glass. It was Sloane's car, but it wasn't Sloane driving. It took me a minute to recognize who it was. Through the veil of swirling snow and ice-crusted glass, there was no mistaking the driver.

We would have two hours trapped together. Two hours to learn everything I could.

Chapter 11

Snowflakes whipped across the windshield as Sterling white-knuckled the steering wheel. I flinched at every gust of wind that buffeted the vehicle, the hairs on my arms standing on end with nervous energy.

It had been the longest two-hour car ride of my life with little to no conversation. Between sips of bottled water and handfuls of trail mix from my Tiny Tots Tote, I had tried making small talk. But Sterling's one-word responses and nervous glances in the rearview mirror wore me down to silence.

I would have rather been anywhere else than on this dark road in this icy mess with a perfect stranger—but here we were, crawling along at a snail's pace while I speculated over what I'd face at the town hall meeting where she was dropping me off. The way Sterling kept anxiously checking the rearview mirror wasn't helping my nerves one bit.

A wave of vertigo pulsed through me, urging me to throw up, but I held it in. Was this early labor? It had been so long I had forgotten the signs. I shifted uncomfortably in my seat, my queasiness making it impossible to find a comfortable position.

It was odd how Sterling jumped at the sound of a passing truck's horn and side-eyed me every few minutes. For someone who worked at a party planning company, she seemed neurotically reclusive.

Sloane had mentioned that Sterling was shy when she'd hired her, but this seemed more than simple social anxiety. Like the way her fingers drummed impatiently against the steering wheel, and she practically leapt out of her skin at every flash of headlights that brushed across our car.

It had me seriously questioning her ability to handle the chaos of the lavish events Feel the Noize Party Planning was known for. The distrustful glares were what really got me wondering about her past. I worked with traumatized youth at the children's home, and Sterling exhibited similar traits. Then again, maybe I was just being extra critical because my back was killing me.

Eventually I resorted to staring out the passenger-side window. My phone chimed with a text message from Sloane somewhere after the terrain transformed from sunset beach to dusky woods to black fields:

So sorry I couldn't pick you up, but Sterling offered to do it. I got caught up in the library's archives. But good news—I have another clue!

A warning would have been nice. My horses give better conversation than Sterling.

You won't be mad at me once you see what I dug up!

An image popped up on the screen, and I would have kissed

Sloane if she was here:

All's forgiven! Wait until Ginger sees this.

I already sent it to her and Detective Hughes. Stay safe on the roads!

The picture Sloane had sent was the remaining half of the newspaper article we were missing. Finally I'd be able to start filling in some blanks. I read the article in its entirety:

KIDNAPPING SUSPECT GOES MISSING

Early this morning, a woman whom police had been searching for on suspicion of kidnapping went missing from her home at 1 Crow's End Lane.

An anonymous tip was received by the Bloodson Bay Police Department about a woman with a stolen infant residing at the house, until she suddenly disappeared. When investigators arrived at the scene, they noted a packed travel case left behind, and evidence that confirmed the infant was the same one that had been previously reported abducted.

The woman, Alice Belvedere, had worked as a maid in the home of Clint Valance. Due to unprofessional behavior, Alice had been fired, but later that night returned to abduct their newborn baby. The Valances had not seen her since and reported it to local authorities.

When Alice's whereabouts had been discovered with the help of a private detective, Alice disappeared from her Crow's End Lane home, leaving the baby behind. While the family celebrates the return of their child, Alice is still on the run and is considered armed and dangerous.

If you have information regarding the whereabouts of Alice Belvedere, please contact the Bloodson Bay Police Department.

The thought of someone kidnapping a newborn was scary enough, but what chilled me most wasn't the child theft. It was the address. *1 Crow's End Lane.* Not only did it sound familiar, but I had a strange attachment to it. I had been there once, although I couldn't remember when or why.

"Was that Sloane texting you?" Sterling's voice broke into

my thoughts.

"Oh, yeah. She was explaining why she couldn't pick me up. But I appreciate you coming to get me in this snow."

"No problem." Sterling's response came out clipped.

"How did you end up working for Sloane, by the way?" I already knew the story Sloane had given me. I wondered if Sterling's version would match.

"I answered an ad in the *Bloodson Bay Bulletin* for an assistant."

So far so good.

"Did you already know sign language?" I asked.

"No, but when I looked up Sloane's company and saw she was Deaf, I learned enough ASL to get through the interview. Since then I've been practicing so that I'm almost fluent now."

"Wow, didn't you start working for Sloane in September?"

"Yeah, I guess I'm a fast learner."

Only three and a half months to master another language? That was impressive. Maybe I wasn't giving her enough credit.

By the time we reached Bloodson Bay's exit, it was close to six o'clock and the winter sky was inky black. Red lights began to flash in the distance behind us, their strobe reflecting off the fresh snow. Even in the dark, I watched Sterling's pale face go chalk-white.

Without warning, she gunned it through a red light, nearly getting us T-boned by a pickup truck. The other driver swerved as he laid on his horn, his rusty F-150 fishtailing on the slick road. Our car slid sideways, the tires losing grip on the snow-dusted pavement.

I grabbed the door handle, my skin pinching between the metal as Sterling veered onto the berm, slamming to a stop right before we smashed into the guardrail. Gravel and slush sprayed up onto the window as the ambulance that had been behind us sped past and on up the road.

When Sterling hit the gas again, my heart threatened to jump straight out of my chest as my muscles clenched with whiplash. I silently prayed my water wouldn't break right here in the passenger seat.

"Stop the car! Are you trying to get us killed?" I screamed.

Sterling's foot jutted down on the brake, and her impromptu Mario Kart impression left me terrified. I had no desire to risk another mile with her. This was definitely not the mild-mannered assistant I'd pegged her to be. This girl was seriously deranged.

"What the hell is wrong with you? That was an ambulance!"

"I'm so sorry. I thought they were police lights, then I hit ice and-and… I lost control… and—"

Sterling didn't finish her thought. Instead, she began sobbing. Now I regretted yelling at her because as soon as she began crying, I began crying, and before I could stop, we were both stuck in one big, inconsolable cry-fest.

"It's okay," I finally reassured her, and myself while I was at it.

I couldn't even begin to speculate why her kneejerk reaction to police lights would be to flee.

"You just need to drive more carefully, okay? And when you see an emergency vehicle, you're supposed to slow down and pull over, not start some high-speed chase."

My dizziness intensified and my brain buzzed with a dull ache. My rapid heartrate physically hurt. Something was wrong. This was not labor as I remembered it.

Eventually Sterling wiped her tears and pulled back onto the road. A lot didn't add up about this girl.

She'd shown up in town in September, right before the woman in Bloodson Manor was allegedly murdered. And then there was her erratic driving, like she expected the devil himself to be tailing us. There was way more to this woman, with her mysterious past and superior sign language skills, than met the eye.

Why was she so terrified of the police? And why did she take off when she saw my attorney at Debbie's Diner? So many pieces to her puzzle. I was afraid of what I would find if I put them together.

A sudden impact lurched us forward, thrusting my neck into a crooked angle. Someone slammed into our rear bumper with enough force to make my teeth rattle. I turned around to look through the rear window, my heart in my throat.

Oh no. Road rage at its craziest.

It was the driver of the F-150, his grill now smooching our bumper as we sped on. Sterling gassed it harder, managing to put a couple feet of distance between our bumpers, but the driver persisted. Another slam jolted us, and I grabbed the dashboard to brace myself.

"I'm calling the police!" I had already dialed the 9 on my phone with trembling fingers.

"No—no police!" Sterling snapped with panic.

She stepped on the gas like she was trying to push it through the floor, took the next right with a squeal of tires, and left the truck behind in a spray of dirty slush. The move was so sudden that my phone went flying from my hand and skittered somewhere under the seat. I began to fish around for it, bending in half as best I could with all that baby in the way.

Minutes later, she screeched to a stop outside of town hall. I clambered out of the car unsteadily, trying to get my footing on the slippery sidewalk, then turned around to thank her for the adrenaline rush and early labor. But the minute the passenger-side door closed, she peeled away, leaving me standing in the swirling snow.

I'd let Sloane deal with the dent fender and trying to find the truck responsible for it. I already had too much to worry about.

Thank God right then Ginger appeared beside me, her red hair smushed under a green beanie and dusted with white flakes that made her look like a festive Christmas elf. Her emerald eyes widened when she saw me.

"You look like something the cat dragged in, honey… though he'd have to be a pretty big cat," Ginger said with a chuckle.

"This is what you look like after a high-speed car chase. Something's seriously wrong with that girl," I muttered, wrapping my arms around myself as a gust of icy wind whipped me.

After the way she'd bolted like a spooked horse, my speculations were working overtime. Where did Sterling learn to drive like that? Normal people couldn't stunt-drive around corners as if the hounds of hell were on their tail.

"Honey, we gotta get in that meeting. It's fixin' to get ugly in there." Ginger nodded toward the town hall doors.

The moment of truth had arrived. I needed to know what Rose Crabtree was planning. I would not give her all the say in whatever drama was about to unfold behind those heavy wooden doors. Being pregnant might slow me down, but it wouldn't stop me from standing up for myself, swollen ankles and all.

Ginger and I walked inside together, my belly leading the way as we crossed the threshold. The crowd fell silent, all eyes turning our way like synchronized puppets on strings. The faces were a blur of familiar townspeople I'd known for years, their features swimming together in my heightened state of anxiety. Everyone grew motionless. All except for one.

Across the room, a man turned toward me, his gaze following the crowd's like a predator spotting prey. His expression darkened when he saw me, transforming from neutral to murderous in the span of a heartbeat, and he burst toward me in a forceful gait that made several people stumble out of his path.

His face contorted with rage as he charged, nostrils flaring, spittle flying from his lips as he yelled, "You!"

I had been prepared to face almost anything… except for *him*.

Chapter 12

On the drive to town hall, I had prepared myself for the inevitable questions about the woman's body found in Bloodson Manor. To my shock, this was not about that after all. In fact, I never could have anticipated Mikhail Pearson charging me like a teenage girl in her favorite store with her mom's credit card.

"You're the reason my son is in the hospital!" Mikhail's embarrassingly loud accusation echoed off the low ceiling, causing the room to collectively gasp. "And you're the reason my wife is *dead*!"

His face turned an alarming shade of purple as he jabbed a finger at my collarbone, his whole body vibrating with barely-contained rage. His wife was *dead?* I had no idea what that had to do with me, but I didn't get a chance to ask because he was on a rampage.

"Did you kill her? What did you do to Darla?"

My jaw dropped. "Mr. Pearson, I don't know what you're talking about. I've never even met Darla."

I hadn't dealt with Darla during the lawsuit, only Mikhail. He clearly didn't believe me because he was no less than an inch from my face, berating me.

"I will make sure you rot in jail for this!"

I instinctively took a step back, knocking into a table behind me. I pivoted to find several large vases of flowers and framed photos of a woman adorning a warm, gentle smile and sparkling blue eyes. One look at the pictures and I realized what it was.

Oh no. A memorial to Darla.

Dead Darla. The wife that Mikhail thought I killed.

The images seemed to capture Darla in various moments of joy—laughing with Mikhail in a Debbie's Diner booth, holding a baby presumed to be Brock in a hospital bed, and posing in a wedding gown in front of the sportsman's lodge. But the last I'd heard, she'd left him and filed for divorce. Nothing about being a murder victim.

A shiver ran down my spine as I wondered what was really going on here.

"Please listen to me, Mr. Pearson. I had nothing to do with Darla. I don't know anything about it."

"Liar! My darling Darla is gone, and it's all because of you." He stumbled over her name and gestured to the memorial.

Darling Darla wasn't the impression Mikhail had given over the summer during notorious screaming matches in their front yard that, on more than one occasion, summoned the police. Darla had been known to frequent every bar in town, every night of the week. And when she wasn't drinking, she was buying drugs and apparently sharing them with her own son.

Mikhail must have conveniently forgotten they'd separated on not-so-pleasant terms, with him throwing her clothes onto their crispy brown lawn while their neighbors watched from behind twitching curtains.

I only knew these sordid details about the Pearsons because my attorney had brought his public embarrassment up as a possible reason Mikhail was so adamant about suing me. Bella speculated his lawsuit might be more about revenge than justice, considering how the whole town had witnessed his marriage imploding.

Broken hearts tended to want to break others along with them, and Mikhail's heart seemed determined to shatter everything in its path, including my bank account and my life.

"Why are you blaming *me*?" I demanded.

His accusation was baseless, but the townsfolk's murmurs confirmed that they had already passed judgment against me, too.

All I knew was that the last anyone had seen Darla, she'd been storming out of the Last Call Bar after a slap fight with another woman and some choice words that had made even the drunk looky-loo patrons blush. The town gossips insisted she'd run off with a trucker she'd been doing tequila shots with, though no one could agree on whether he drove a red semi or a blue one.

First Mikhail filed a ridiculous lawsuit over Brock's injuries while the boy was trespassing, and now he was accusing me of *murder*? None of this was my fault and yet I was getting hit with the most creative lawsuits his evil genius lawyer could imagine.

It had been Brock's fault for throwing a drug party. The "Curse Day Parties"—as they had been coined—had apparently been going on for a couple years on June 27th at the abandoned Bloodson Manor, right under my nose. But most kids were smart enough not to brag about their drug crimes. Until Brock took *getting high* to a new level. Jumping off the second-story balcony level, that is.

Clearly, Brock wasn't the brightest crayon in the box. I desperately wanted to point this out to his father, but I managed to hold my tongue. His ex-wife was dead, after all. I could force a little empathy.

When he stopped yelling and spitting, I got a quick word in: "Why do you think I had anything to do with Darla's death?"

My voice came out shakier than I'd intended, partly from anger and partly from humiliation of all the witnesses watching this unfold.

Mikhail's hands clenched into tight fists at his sides like he was holding back a right hook to my face. If I wasn't pregnant, he might have followed through. I'd seen that look before during the initial lawsuit mediations. The man had all the self-control of a lit firecracker, and there was no guessing what would trigger his explosion.

"You murdered my wife as retaliation for the lawsuit."

Several murmurs vented around me, and dozens of eyes bore into me. The whispers caught fire, spreading through the spectators with gasoline vengeance. Just what I needed—more gossip about me, the lady who let kids throw drug parties in her abandoned mansion. Wait until they found out a woman's remains had been discovered there too.

"I'm really confused. I thought Darla took off with some guy. What makes you think she's dead?"

Mikhail leaned in, and I flinched and blocked my face with my hands in case that punch was still coming.

"Because the police just ID'd her body chained in the basement of Bloodson Manor."

Chapter 13

Darla Pearson was the identity of the body we had found? Now that *did* sound a little incriminating.

Slivers of facts slid together into a clear whole. Detective Hughes had determined that the victim was killed and disposed of sometime in October. Darla had left Mikhail only a couple months earlier. I believed both the killer and victim were local, and sure enough, that fit.

If I were a bettin' woman, I'd put down my life savings—which wasn't much—on Mikhail killing Darla for leaving him, then planting her body on my property to frame me so he could win his million-dollar lawsuit against me. He had all the motive for murder, whereas I had none. I only needed to prove it without letting him know I was on to his scheme.

"I'm sorry for your loss, Mikhail. I didn't know—"

"Don't act as if you didn't have something to do with it!" Tears streamed down Mikhail's face and his body shook with each ragged breath.

The tough-guy facade crumbled before my eyes, revealing raw grief underneath. I reached out a hand and touched his shoulder in a halfhearted attempt at consolation, but he shrugged me off like my human contact scalded him. He wanted none of it from me, the person he claimed killed his wife. Though I had to admit, I would have never thought Mikhail was this good of an actor. It was Emmy-Award-winning level.

"That one-million-dollar lawsuit you're going to lose?" he continued. "That's only the beginning. I'm going to make sure you go to jail for life." His threat was hard and cold.

I hoped the police would agree that none of what Mikhail accused me of made sense. I sure as heck wouldn't kill Darla and dump her body in an abandoned house on my own property, then stupidly start a demolition project that would expose myself. No intelligent mastermind would do that.

Clearly Mikhail had to realize nothing pointed to me—I had no motive and no means. But he was too dead set on turning me into the villain… and framing me for his own crime.

Ginger rested a hand on my shoulder. "Sugar, don't it strike you as odd that for two and a half months that woman was dead and we're only just now hearing about it? Not even a missing person's report?"

Good point. Detective Hughes had searched the missing person's database and Darla's name didn't come up. Why hadn't Mikhail reported his wife missing? Before I could respond to Ginger's surprisingly sound logic, a sharp pain ripped through my abdomen. I didn't feel well. Was it the trail mix I had eaten? No, this was more than a tummy ache. Another searing pain stabbed through my entire body and I doubled over as warm liquid gushed down my legs, pooling on the meeting room's cheap linoleum floor.

"I have to go!" I grabbed on to Ginger for dear life. "Call Chris!"

I dry-heaved and clutched my belly, which began to throb with an intensity that made my knees buckle. I had forgotten how painful labor contractions were, as if someone was wringing out my insides like a wet dishrag.

"Now!"

My voice came out as a strangled yelp. Of all the times for this baby to make its appearance, it had to choose the middle of a heated, public confrontation with Mikhail Pearson.

Mikhail's expression warped into an ugly sneer. "Oh, trying to run away from your guilt?"

"No, you idiot." Ginger came to my defense. "Can't you tell she's about to give birth, you asshat?"

Another contraction snatched and wrenched my abdomen in its tight fist. I tried to make my way to the door, but Mikhail persisted in blocking me.

"If you don't move aside, I'll deliver this baby all over your precious tribute to Darla!"

That seemed to do the trick as I shoved past him. Ginger held me up, guiding me through the doors and out into the parking lot.

"Come on, honey. Let's get you to the hospital before you drop that baby in the middle of this meeting."

Her grip was surprisingly strong for someone who spent most of her time baking questionable casseroles and thrift shopping. But in this moment, there was no better friend I wanted by my side as another wave of pain dropped me to my knees.

I hunched over on the sidewalk, but this time not from labor. My stomach chose that moment to empty all over the pavement, but what I saw as I heaved again and again was not undigested trail mix.

It was blood.

Part 2
Ginger Mallowan

Chapter 14

My daughter-in-law—and also my best friend—was in the hospital and no one would tell me what in tarnation was going on.

It was terrifying. I had no idea if Tara had given birth to my grandbaby, or why she was yacking up blood. And every time I asked the front desk, and any nurse that passed by, and every doctor I could catch up with, I kept getting told, "We'll keep you updated." Well, it had been hours and no one had updated me on a dang thing.

I was pacing the waiting room with a bouquet of cheerful yellow daisies I had bought at the gift shop when a doctor finally approached me, dressed in blue scrubs that matched his eyes.

He pulled down his face mask. "Are you Ginger Mallowan?"

"It's about time! Is Tara okay?" I cut to the chase.

It felt like forever before he answered. I couldn't wait a moment longer to know what was happening to *the* most important person in my life.

"Yes, she's able to see you now."

I followed the doctor, nearly stepping on his heels, all the way to Tara's labor and delivery room. I burst in past him, dropping the flowers on a little table as I rushed to her bedside. The big ol' smile plastered on her face could've lit up the whole dang county. At her side stood my son Chris, and in her arms lay a bundled, hospital-grade blankie.

"How's my girl?" I said, then kissed her flushed cheek.

"Tired. And happy to introduce you to your grandson!"

Tara looked utterly beautiful, as radiant as a June morning. I stroked her hair, which was pulled back into a messy ponytail, while damp strands clung to her forehead.

I gazed down at the newborn boy. "He's perfect! Did you pick a name yet?"

Tara and Chris had been debating for months over names. When they finally narrowed down the boy choices, Chris wanted something cowboy classic, like Duke. But Tara wanted something meaningful, like Phoenix. No one cared that I preferred Cillian after my Irish great-granddaddy.

In all fairness, I wasn't the one pushing a watermelon out of a hole the size of a pea, so my opinion didn't matter. When Tara and Chris exchanged a look, I read the unspoken words between them.

"No name yet?" I grumbled. "You've only had nine months to pick one…"

"We want to get to know him first," Tara said with such adoration in her voice that I instantly forgave her for all the stress she had caused me last night vomiting blood.

"And how's mama feeling?"

"Much better. I'm already in love."

Her hospital gown was sticky with sweat like she'd been wrestling wildcats… or birthing a baby. I'd birthed three of them—babies, not wildcats—so I knew baby-birthing made wildcat-wrestling look like child's play.

"Want to meet him?" Tara held out the baby for me to coo

over.

I oohed and ahhed. His tiny mouth made the sweetest little O-shape as he yawned, and those itty-bitty fingers were already curling around my pinky like he'd been practicing for weeks in her womb.

"Where's big sis?" I asked, looking around for Nora.

"She ran down to the cafeteria to get something to eat," Chris answered. "She's been texting Eloise every hour with updates. It was a long night for all of us…"

Tara stifled a yawn that would've done a hippo proud, and I noticed the dark circles under her eyes that spoke of hours spent bringing this precious miracle into the world.

"You had me worried, hon. With the blood last night, I thought…" I could barely speak my worst fear. Losing Tara would kill me. I could never survive it. "I thought something horrible had happened to you."

The doctor breezed in with a chart clutched in hand, saving me from becoming an emotional mess, which would inevitably make Tara an emotional mess. Southern ladies were prone to such outbursts.

"Mrs. Christie, congratulations on your beautiful baby boy." He beamed at Tara, but his expression faltered as he scanned her paperwork. He dropped the chart into a plastic bin that hung on the wall, then sat at the foot of Tara's hospital bed. "How are you feeling?"

"Like I just gave birth," Tara replied with a grin.

"Good, good." The doctor paused, glanced up at Chris, then at me. "Look, Mrs. Christie, something unusual came up during your labor last night."

He must have registered the sudden panic in Tara's

expression, because he quickly amended, "Don't worry, the baby's fine. And you're fine. But I do need to discuss something with you—a complication."

"What kind of complication?" Chris interjected.

"Maybe *you* can tell me." It was almost imperceptible, but did the doctor just *glower* at Chris? If I'd ever seen a glower, this was it.

"Why would I know anything?" Chris looked as baffled as I felt.

"I didn't want to bring it up last night, but there was something concerning we found in your wife's bloodwork."

Tara glanced at Chris, then the doctor. "What was in my blood?"

The doctor hesitated, his eyes darting between Chris and Tara, then settled accusingly on Chris. "I need to speak with your husband. Privately."

"Me? Why privately?" Chris asked. "Tara and my mom should be present for whatever you want to say, since it concerns her."

"I need to show you something first." The doctor was insistent as he rose from the bed and stared at Chris. There was no mistaking the glower this time. "Can you please follow me to my office?"

This wasn't a question, and Chris didn't have the option to refuse. It brought back a memory from fourth grade when the principal came to escort me to his office when I got caught borrowing answers from my classmate's test. After getting paddled, that was the first and last time I ever cheated. This felt a lot like Chris was about to get paddled for something he'd done wrong.

The doctor led Chris out of the room, leaving me with an anxious flutter in my stomach.

Chapter 15

I knew without a shadow of a doubt that my son did *not* attempt to poison Tara, no matter what proof the doctor presented. Chris loved his wife with all his heart, and he loved Nora and this baby, too. He would never have tried to hurt any of them. But the doctor wasn't convinced. And the police would have to be involved.

It only took Tara and I five minutes to figure out why the doctor had escorted Chris out of the room, and why he suspected him of poisoning Tara.

"What do you think that was about?" I had asked Tara the moment Chris and the doctor were out of earshot.

Tara's gaze locked onto the chart the doctor had left behind at the foot of the bed. "Ging, can you grab my chart and read it to me?"

I rummaged through my purse—Lord have mercy, it was like Mary Poppins' carpet bag in there—finally producing a magnifying glass with a flourish. Tara raised an eyebrow, and I couldn't blame her. My purse was known to contain everything from emergency snacks to used tissues to a deck of cards in case I wanted an impromptu game of Solitaire. Good thing, too, since I did a lot of Solitaire while waiting for an update on Tara last night.

"Why do you have a magnifying glass in there?" she asked

with a hint of amusement.

"I lost my cheaters and can't read a darn thing without them. But this works even better."

I grabbed the chart and peered at it through the circle of glass. My eyes scanned the page, and my heart skipped a beat as I spotted something strange.

"Tara, sweetie, it says here you've got a high level of... ethylene glycol in your blood."

Tara's face blanched. "What's that?"

I took a deep breath, trying to process the information. "It's a toxin, honey. It's found in antifreeze."

"How do you know that?"

I shrugged, feeling a mite smart. "I watch a lot of crime shows."

"How did I possibly ingest antifreeze?" Her voice trailed off, and I could see the fear creeping in. "Oh my gosh, it could have killed the baby!"

I squeezed her hand, trying to offer what little comfort I could. "I'm sure as soon as the doctor saw this, he checked the baby. Don't worry. He said everything's fine."

But nothing was fine. Someone had tried to poison my pregnant best friend and grandson. Tara's eyes hung on mine, a fierce determination burning in their depths.

"I need to find out who poisoned me," she said, her voice low and deadly.

"That explains why you threw up blood yesterday. Do you remember feeling sick at all before that?"

"Honestly, the past five days have been a blur, ever since we found that body. I've been nauseous, anxious, exhausted— you name it, I've been feeling it. What should I do?"

"I got this. You focus on the baby." I nodded, my mind racing with possibilities. "I'll get to the bottom of it, hon. I promise."

I'm coming for you next, the threat on the door in the Bloodson Manor cellar had said. This was no accident. It was attempted murder.

That afternoon, as I left the hospital, the cold winter air slapped me like my *máthair* once did when she caught me wearing white after Labor Day. Breaking the rules of fashion had been an unforgiveable sin back then.

I gazed up at the sky in wonder, watching delicate snowflakes dance their way down to earth. It was still snowing in Bloodson Bay, a rare and magical occurrence that happened about as often as Rose Crabtree passed up a chance to gossip. A season of miracles, indeed.

I was determined to get Tara a miracle of her own—to find out who poisoned her and who planted Darla's body in the Bloodson Manor basement, which I suspected were one and the same. Someone in this town was playing a mighty dangerous game of Risk, and they were about to learn that this redheaded Southern lady knew a few games of her own—and I was especially good at connect-the-dots.

When I reached my car, I moaned in frustration. The windshield was covered in a thick layer of ice, and I had nothing to clean it with. Down here in Dixie, not a single soul thought to keep an ice scraper in their vehicle.

Staring at the near-empty slush-covered parking lot, something made the hair on the back of my neck stand up straighter than a Baptist preacher's collar. I pulled out my phone and nearly dropped it twice from my sparkly-mittened grip, then

I dialed a number I knew by heart.

"Hello?" a voice answered.

"I need to see you," I said, barely above a whisper. "Urgently."

There was a pause on the other end of the line. "Is it really worth driving in this weather?"

I took a deep breath, my mind racing with everything I needed to get off my chest. "Yes… there's something I must confide in you. And it can't wait."

"Meet me in an hour. This better be worth risking my life."

"I assure you it is. I'm risking my own life telling you."

Chapter 16

I had one hour to kill, and I knew exactly where to spend it. In jail.

Well, not in jail as much as jail-adjacent in the visitor room, where I sat across from the latest love of my life, Gunther Jones, a gray-haired fox of a man who looked even skinnier than when I had seen him yesterday. His drab, prison-issued jumpsuit hung on him like a dressed-up skeleton.

"Aren't they feeding you?" I asked.

Gunther smiled. Actually, he had been smiling the whole time since we sat down, but it grew across his face a little more.

"Yeah, they feed me fine. But I don't want to talk about me. How are you? How's your hip? You're limping."

Yesterday I had banged my hip on the metal door jamb on my way in when the guard began frisking me. I couldn't help that I was ticklish. Besides, the nasty bruise was worth that young man getting handsy with me.

"You want me to show you?" I playfully lifted the hem of my shirt up just enough to show some skin. A little flabby, but to a man in jail, lady flesh was lady flesh, no matter how wrinkly.

"Ooh, a strip tease!" Gunther exclaimed too loudly. Several guards and inmates pivoted to stare, and I suddenly felt risqué and covered myself. "Can I ask the guard to give us a conjugal visit?"

"Hush, you! I'm not here for your pleasure this time. I'm here for advice."

"Of course, Ging. Anything for you."

I sighed, wondering why I was even here. How could Gunther help from behind bars? How could anyone help with what truly bothered me? But Gunther's earnestness prodded me to continue. I decided to just dive right in.

"Someone tried to hurt Tara…"

"And you want me to arrange some kind of tragic accident?"

Gunther winked, but he wasn't kidding. And if I knew who was behind the threats, I might have even taken him up on the offer.

"No, silly! I want to protect Tara, but I don't know how. I feel… hopeless and helpless."

He waited before he answered, thoughtfully. "Hope isn't an emotion reliant on perfect conditions, Ging. In fact, hope a peaceful mutiny against despair. It thrives in the worst of circumstances."

That was pretty dang eloquent for a man who spent his days surrounded by cuss words and threats.

"Well, I'm definitely in the worst of circumstances, and feeling useless and old. Every day is a chore to wake up and face the reality that my days are numbered."

"That's when you need hope most. It's not victory over your problems, but a tenuous invitation to keep going despite them. Even when the world is dangerous and fear bends your knees, hope rises. Hope won't make you outrun your worry but help you pace beside it, and each step will remind you that something meaningful can be rebuilt from ruins."

I realized who I was talking to—a man stuck in jail giving me a pep talk about hope—and I instantly regretted this whole conversation.

"How insensitive of me! I shouldn't be talking about hopelessness to you of all people."

"Ging, of course you can talk to me. But you know what I'm going to say—that your purpose doesn't go away with age. And you have a lot to offer the world."

"You mean my accumulated years of vast wisdom?" I joked, because no one had ever accused me of being wise.

"I was referring to your accumulated years of well-practiced snark." Gunther always knew how to get a laugh out of me. "Have you talked to your therapist about it?"

Gunther was the only one who knew I was talking to a shrink. I didn't know exactly why I kept it a secret, except for the stigma my family had placed on mental therapy. I was coming to realize that sometimes, we all just needed to talk to someone who would listen without judgement.

"Yeah, I've told her how I feel."

"And is it helping?"

"I guess. But what would help more was if I was ten years younger and didn't crumble at the slightest bump. You know you're getting old when your back goes out more than you do."

"So you're not dating anyone other than me?" Gunther probed.

"You know I don't like talking feelings."

"I guess you don't want to hear how much I love you then, huh?" Gunther said, reaching out and cupping my hand.

"My friends would kill me if they knew I was talking to you, let alone telling you I love you.”

“I don’t care what your friends think. And maybe you shouldn’t either.”

What was the point of all this? What future did we have? What future did *I* have? At my age, the fire department was on standby when I lit my birthday candles.

Gunther squeezed my hand, and for a moment I felt alive.

The guard glanced over, darting a warning shot at us. “No contact,” he grumbled.

We released our hands and said our goodbyes, but long after I left, I still felt Gunther’s warmth, as if the mere thought of him gave me hope. Then I wondered if I would ever feel hopeful again.

Chapter 17

Dr. Lea Dreyfuss's office resembled my childhood home, down to the antique floral sofa, two velvet club chairs with crocheted blankets hanging on the back of each, and tea set sitting on a shiny credenza that would have looked perfect in my own living room.

Her knack for tasteful décor might have been what sold me on picking her as my therapist. Or it could have been because she was about my age, had great fashion taste, and always offered homemade cookies so warm and fresh I wondered if she had an Easy-Bake Oven in her office.

Our sessions felt less like head-shrinking and more like I was talking to a close friend who wore a darlin' hot pink pantsuit and served delicious refreshments. At extreme odds with her cozy office was the incessant buzz of nail salon equipment next door, droning through the thin walls. Soft 1980's love ballads played in the background just enough to drown out the noise.

Great clothes, great music taste, and a great baker? Dr. Dreyfuss was a lady after my own heart. I almost passed her up when I discovered she was located in a shopping plaza where anyone in town could catch me walking inside. I could imagine the rumors flying when word spread that I was seeing a therapist.

That's close-minded, small-town folks for you—my own

parents being of the same ilk when they were alive. But I soon got over it when I realized half the plaza was vacant real estate, and no one ventured into this dangerous part of town without a death wish. And anyone with a death wish probably needed therapy, too.

A crooked frame hung behind Dr. Dreyfuss's desk, displaying her psychology degree from 1972, the gold lettering faded but still gleaming with a hint of pride. Potted plants and knickknacks took residence on every surface. I fidgeted with the worn armrest, the familiar scent of old books wrapping around me like a warm hug.

"The stress is killing me, Doc." I squeezed the plush owl that had been sitting on my chair while I lamented over everything that had happened the past few days. My biggest fear was that my new grandson might end up in the crossfire. "What should I do?"

"What exactly are you worried is going to happen?" Dr. Dreyfuss prompted. She always answered every question with a question.

"I don't know, I could lose my best friend. This lawsuit drama is getting worse by the day. First his idiot kid Brock gets impaled, then he sues Tara, and now Mikhail's ex-wife turns up dead in Bloodson Manor… and Tara ended up poisoned. This all can't be coincidence."

"Don't you think you should let the police deal with that?"

Now Dr. Dreyfuss was just being irritating. "I can't sit back and watch my daughter-in-law's life get ruined!"

She crossed her legs and adjusted her bulky glasses that made her gray eyes look even larger. Then she attempted to smooth down her short, gray hair that matched her eyes exactly.

While I think she had intended it to be a sleek pixie cut, her hair stood at attention every which way, reminding me of the bedhead buzz cuts I had given my sons all through elementary school.

"Why are you making Tara's problems your problems?"

I hmphed. "That's what family does, Doc."

"I see. So you want to be needed?"

"I never said that," I denied, even though it was probably the truth.

"Have you ever considered setting boundaries between the two of you?"

"You don't need boundaries when it comes to family," I insisted.

"Look, Ginger, I don't blame you for your concern about your daughter-in-law, but you can't take the world's problems on your shoulders. It almost sounds like you thrive on drama." Finally Dr. Dreyfuss had run out of questions, but this statement felt worse.

What she was implying was ridiculous, and I would have said exactly that if it didn't sound so accurate. Instead I said, "The drama thrives on me."

"I'm assuming the police are investigating?" Another question that was more annoying than helpful.

"Of course, Doc. The strangest part," I said, locking my eyes on hers, "was what was left with Darla's body."

I glanced up to make sure I had her full attention. I did. Even she couldn't resist a little drama.

"A newspaper clipping from 1969 about a missing woman named Alice Belvedere. She vanished without a trace from her home. I can't figure it out, but I think it has some connection to

Darla's murder."

I paused, studying her. I didn't want more questions, I wanted answers. Some advice, some guidance. Anything that could help Tara.

I wasn't expecting Dr. Dreyfuss's mouth to drop open and her eyes to bulge with surprise. "Did you say Alice Belvedere?"

Based on Dr. Dreyfuss's college graduation year, they might have been around the same age and lived in the same town.

"Yeah, did you know her?"

It caught me off-guard when a tear slid down her wrinkled cheek like a raindrop on a dried leaf. She dabbed at it with her sleeve, her hand trembling slightly. She hesitated, sniffling and blowing her nose while I waited for some kind of explanation that might make sense of everything. But she shook her head.

"Oh dear, look at me! I'm supposed to be helping you, not the other way around. I vividly remember that 1969 case... I had almost forgotten about it."

Almost forgotten... as in, she had *not* forgotten. Alice must have been someone important to her. Her hand trembled as she reached for her water glass, the ice clinking against the sides.

"When you called, you said you had something to confide to me, Ginger. What did you want to talk to me about that was worth driving here in a snowstorm?"

How interesting that she hadn't answered my question on whether she knew Alice.

"There's something weighing on me, Doc. A secret I've been keeping. I don't know if I should tell my friends."

"Is there a reason you want to keep whatever it is private?" she asked.

Shame over who it involved. Guilt for feeling the way I did. Loving Gunther Jones was too complicated to explain.

"I'm afraid people are going to judge me and try to convince me to stop," I decided to say cryptically.

"Do *you* think you should stop?"

"I don't know. I don't know if it's good for me or not."

The truth was, I knew latching my heart to a convict was bad for me. But something about Gunther made me feel so vibrant, so alive. And nothing that felt this good came without a price.

Gunther Jones was a mistake I had made and could never recover from. I had fallen for him during a tumultuous time when my ex-husband played with my heart and broke it. After my ex died, the spot in my heart became vacant. Gunther moved right in.

After Gunther was sentenced to prison for his affiliation with the Russian mafia, I had sworn to Tara that I'd stay away from him. And for the most part, I'd kept my promise. I refused to visit him in prison—for the first couple months, at least. Then in one moment of weakness I caved.

It was a slow fall from grace, I'm ashamed to say. First, I couldn't keep my filthy little mind from dreaming about him. Then writing him. Then responding every time he wrote back. I was addicted to his love letters, to his attention, to the risk and the secrets. And now I couldn't go a day without visiting him.

As Dr. Dreyfuss was watching me, her expression softened. "Why are you worried about being judged by your friends, Ginger?"

I shrugged, feeling a twinge of guilt. "I don't want them worrying about me. They've got enough on their plates with

Tara's… situation."

Standing up, Dr. Dreyfuss smoothed her pink pants that shimmered as she walked to the bookshelf, and I made a mental Post-It note to ask where she bought them. She grabbed a book and handed it to me. It was her latest release, *I've Fallen and I Can Get Up!* The cover featured a cartoon version of Dr. Dreyfuss on the floor, waving a cane in the air with a feisty expression that made me chuckle.

"You know why I never retired, Ginger? I found purpose in helping others, just like you found purpose helping your friends." The gray of her eyes caught the light behind her glasses, which had slipped down to the tip of her nose.

"You think I have purpose?" I asked, as if a person with *PhD* after their name affirming it gave more weight to its truth.

"Of course! Purpose isn't always big and bold, Ginger. Sometimes it's small and silent. And just because things feel like they're falling apart, that doesn't mean you can't pick them back up. Whatever secrets you've got, trust that your friends will carry you through if it gets messy. You're allowed to make mistakes, Ginger. And when you do, that's what friendship is about—being the hand to lift those we love."

I flipped open the book, feeling a surge of gratitude. "You're right, Doc. We all need a purpose in life. And I've found mine in helping my friends, no matter what."

Even if that friend was Tara dealing with a lawsuit that had gotten out of hand, or Gunther needing encouragement while in prison. Friends came in all shapes and sizes and purposes.

"Have you ever had a friend who would go to any lengths to help you?" I asked. "Who would be there to catch all your tears when your decisions end up going to hell in a handbasket?

Someone to shatter the rules then piece together the fragments with you?"

Dr. Dreyfuss considered my question. "Once. I've only had one friend like that in my long life, and she was taken from me too soon. But I understand what you mean—we didn't follow the rules, and we had no boundaries. We were like two peas in a pod, causing all sorts of mayhem together. And that mayhem cost her her life."

I shook my head sadly for her loss. "That's a rare friendship, Doc. I'm sorry you lost yours. That's why I'll do anything to help Tara."

I fiddled with the charm bracelet on my wrist that had mine, Sloane, and Tara's birthstones, thinking about how blessed I was to still have them both in my life, despite all our misadventures. They hadn't given up on me yet.

Dr. Dreyfuss shrugged, her thick shoulder pad slipping crookedly off one bony shoulder. "It was a long time ago."

"Time doesn't erase what you had," I said.

"Hm. You're wiser than you look." Then she muttered, almost to herself, "You said an article about Alice Belvedere's disappearance was left at the crime scene, huh?" Her tone changed, becoming more clinical, professional.

I studied her. "So you *do* know something about the 1969 case? Please, if there's anything you can tell me that could help solve this mystery, you'd be saving my friend's life!"

I got up from my seat, stood before her, and knelt. Yes, the arthritis hit my knees to the bone, but this was urgent. I was as desperate as a possum in a pickle barrel. I needed her to understand that.

Dr. Dreyfuss slumped in resignation, her gaze dropping to

the floor beside me. "It was so long ago, Ginger."

"Please! You're my only hope. You said you stuck it out in this job to help people. Well, help me!"

She stood and stepped around me, heading to her filing cabinet. The metal drawer creaked when she opened it. The sound reminded me of the moment we opened the door in the Bloodson Manor cellar. I hated that everything seemed to come back to that.

"I need to show you something." Her voice trembled slightly, like foliage caught in an autumn breeze.

Her weathered hands rifled through manila folders with practiced efficiency. The way she hunched over that drawer told me whatever she was about to share weighed heavier on her conscience than my homemade biscuits. She slid a folder out and passed it to me as I returned to my chair. I had to read the typed name across the top twice before I believed it.

"You think you've got secrets, Ginger? Well, I've got one too, and I've been keeping it for far too long."

Chapter 18

My *máthair* used to say that everything comes full circle.

As Dr. Lea Dreyfuss parked her 1978 AMC Gremlin—the same model and shade of puke green mine used to be!—I understood what *Máthair* meant. Somehow divine purpose had brought me and Dr. Dreyfuss together. No, not because we shared the same love of 1980's fashion or at one point drove the same car. But because the address we arrived at simply could not be happenstance:

1 Crow's End Lane

That's right. Dr. Dreyfuss personally knew of this house, and this was the address from which Alice Belvedere had disappeared. Somehow, both of us had been drawn to solving the mystery behind Alice's death. There you have it: divine purpose.

The house was a one-story, modest brick dwelling on a lonely, dead-end street that looked like it had been forgotten for decades. It was hidden behind a postage-stamp-sized yard with dead weeds taller than me. A bare tree grew next to the porch, and a number "1" clung to the front door, the black paint chipped and faded.

On my seat sat the manilla folder Dr. Dreyfuss had shown me with Alice Belvedere's name typed across the top. Inside was a sparse collection of newspaper articles, police reports, and photos. Clutching my phone, my fingers were adorned with my collection of lucky rings, including my father's gold wedding band and the Claddagh Celtic knot ring Sloane bought me for my birthday. I aimed the camera at the house and snapped a picture, then texted it to Tara:

Guess where I am!

Tara would definitely want to see this.

The property stood short and stout, ivy clinging to the brick. As Dr. Dreyfuss led me up the front steps, something darted past a window, disturbing the tattered lace curtains draped across it. I nearly jumped out of my skin.

The movement was so quick, I almost convinced myself I'd imagined it, but my instinct told me it was real. And honey, my instinct hadn't steered me wrong since 2009, when I thought I could still wear a tube top without a bra.

I squinted through the glass pane, trying to catch another glimpse of whatever—or whoever—had made those delicate curtains shudder, but now they hung as still as a portrait in a museum. They were probably just as old, too.

A streetlight buzzed to life down the block as dusk encroached. I wanted nowhere near this place, but I knew it must have been important if my therapist dragged me here.

If only my *máthair* could see me now, showing up at this abandoned house with my therapist like some kind of geriatric Nancy Drews. The whole situation had my nerves jumping, but there was no turning back, no matter how loud the voice in my head ordered me to run.

"Let's head inside," Dr. Dreyfuss announced as she pushed a key into the lock.

Near the foot of the door were fresh flowers in a vase, like a tombstone memorial. Who would leave flowers here, and why? I felt a sudden urgency to stop her from entering. My hand instinctively reached out to grab her arm, the colorful bangles on my wrist jingling in protest.

"Wait, Doc," I whispered, nervously searching the porch corners, as if the shadows themselves might be listening. "Be careful. I think someone's here."

She rolled her eyes and chuckled, the sound husky from years of nonstop talking to patients like me.

"No one's come down this road since Alice disappeared," she said. "I guarantee no one is inside, Ginger. This house has been sittin' here like a ghost, just waitin' for the kudzu to claim it." She patted my hand with a gentle, papery touch. "You're just spooked, that's all."

But I knew what I saw and felt, a shiver of unease that had nothing to do with the fading light. The lock clicked open. The doorknob turned. Then it occurred to me that I had never told her the address Alice had disappeared from. And how did she get the housekey?

"Doc, how did you know about this address?" I asked.

One thin, gray eyebrow arched behind her cat-eye glasses. The quiet wait for her response wrapped around me, putting a stop to my anxious breathing.

"Because this was my family's home. I grew up here, and my parents let Alice live here before she—" The words landed like an explosive in my lap.

"You *own* this? I ain't trying to be rude, but it looks like a crack house. Ever hear of a lawnmower? Or a handyman?" I gave the property another onceover. "Or a blowtorch?"

"You'll see why I kept it," she said as she pushed the front door open.

I stopped short of crossing the threshold, an involuntary tremor running down my spine. Pushing past a terrible sensation that this was a huge mistake, I stepped into the house. A bitter chill seeped into the house's bones.

A faint scent of hardcover books and stale air wafted over me, carrying whispers of the past. The dim light coming through the windows illuminated an interior in shocking contrast to the exterior. It was charming, with vintage furniture, down to the space-age, mustard-plaid sofa nearly every 1960's home had.

Despite the cold but cozy atmosphere, an undercurrent of unease hummed through the air. A gust of winter air followed us in, prickling the fine hairs on my arms before I slammed the door shut on it, swathing us in darkness. Dr. Dreyfuss led the way, her eyes scanning the space searching for something, but her composure showed the tiniest crack of uncertainty, as if something felt off. Questions raced through my mind and my heart pounded in anticipation—of what, I didn't know. A foreboding.

As I moved a few more steps into the house, the shadows seemed to grow longer, like wispy fingers reaching out to snag unsuspecting ankles. What was I looking for, anyway? A hint of a secret that had been hidden here for over five decades? My quest seemed like searching for a needle in a haystack, except I didn't even know what kind of needle I was searching for. But Dr. Dreyfuss's determination was infectious. I was both terrified of and addicted to the thrill.

A floor lamp sat in the middle of the living room, and a flick of a switch turned it on. The window with the lace drapes extended across one wall, and the furniture looked like it was well preserved from 1969, when Alice had last been here. The floorboards creaked as I walked around, pausing at a telephone table holding an old-fashioned, avocado green rotary phone.

Across the living room was the *pièce de résistance*: a vintage, mid-century tube record player stereo console. As I lifted the wooden lid, a flashback from my youth hit me with memories of standing on my daddy's feet as we rocked around the clock while my mama did a terrible impression of Elvis's rubber legs dance move. On one side was the radio, and on the other was a turntable with several records stacked next to it. I picked up an album—*Sgt. Pepper's Lonely Hearts Club Band* by the Beatles—tempted to see if the stereo still functioned… until something stopped me.

An unnatural pitter-patter. The frantic beats were too random to be mechanical. Someone else was here. I sensed eyes probing, and not in the sexy way Gunther had ogled me when I gave him my strip tease earlier. I turned around to find Dr. Dreyfuss staring at a row of framed pictures on an end table, but my stealthy observer stayed hidden, the presence marked only by a subtle *thump* from another room.

"Did you hear that, Doc?" I asked, but the sounds immediately stopped.

Her expression was unreadable as she walked stiffly toward me, her steel gaze making my skin crawl. "I'm sure it's just the house shifting."

Sure, houses shifting sounded like footsteps.

"Do you want to know about Alice or not?" Her words were punctuated with puffs of warm breath disappearing into the frosty air.

"I came to this creepy house with you, didn't I?" I answered briskly.

"Alice was my closest friend," Dr. Dreyfuss began, taking the album from my hand and positioning it on the record player. She adjusted the needle, turned the knob, and the Beatles' intro filled the room. "My folks basically raised her after her mother disowned her. When she got pregnant, I was off at college so they let her live here with the baby to protect her."

"Protect her from who?" I asked.

"Sit," she ordered me.

My joints were throbbing, so it didn't take much convincing for me to drop my achy bones onto the couch that poofed a cloud of dust up around me. Dr. Dreyfuss settled into a club chair across from me, the soft lamplight glow casting fake warmth around us. She exhaled another white cloud of breath, her eyes locking onto mine.

"The night Alice disappeared, she left a message behind…"

Then she stopped, dangling that mystery in front of me.

"And?" I could barely speak above a whisper, as if it would awaken the ghosts that lingered within these walls. "What was the message?"

She took a moment, her expression growing somber with the memory. The lines on her face deepened like the grooves on the well-worn record. My chest constricted, anticipating her next words.

"I think it was intended to be a clue to help me find her," she said finally.

"What was the clue?" My voice carried a desperate edge I couldn't contain, the question tumbling out of my mouth.

She shifted closer, and I leaned in to catch her words, my hands clutching the armrest so hard my arthritic fingers felt like someone was holding a Bic lighter under them. For a moment, I imagined this space full of life and chatter between two best friends, but now it was shrouded in menacing secrets waiting to surface.

"I never figured out what it meant before she was murdered."

All I knew about Alice Belvedere was that she had run off with her baby in 1969. Fast-forward to now as Darla's body was dumped in Tara's abandoned house along with an article about Alice. What was the connection? Who was the father? What happened to Alice? There was so much missing from the news article, and Lord knows I've watched enough bad television dramas to spot plot holes from a mile away.

"Did they ever find Alice?" I asked.

"No, but I know she was murdered by the baby's father." Her words were heavy with remorse as she fiddled anxiously with the hem of her pantsuit jacket.

"How can you be sure?"

"Because I know her killer." The anger in her voice could've cut glass. Her chin lifted slightly, defiant. "And I know what he was capable of. Which was why I stopped pursuing justice for Alice. I couldn't risk losing anyone else I loved."

The way she said it gave me chills that not even my warmest cardigan could chase away.

"So that's it—you gave up?"

"You have no idea what I went through, Ginger. What I

lost."

"I don't understand why you let her killer walk free!"

She whirled around to face me, her gaze intense. "He killed my parents, Ginger! Is that what you want to hear—that not only did he kill Alice and take her baby, but he murdered my parents."

With terrible timing, that's when Cyndi Lauper interrupted us. Not her in the flesh, obviously, but her song "Girl's Just Want to Have Fun" ringing from my purse, blending discordantly with Paul McCartney's crooning. The ring tone meant Tara. I answered at the lyrics "when the work-ing day is done."

My anxiety instantly jumped to worst-case scenarios. "Are you and the baby okay?" I answered the call.

"Yeah, we're fine," Tara said. "I got your text and picture. That house—it's 1 Crow's End Lane, right?"

"Wow, good guess."

"It's not a guess. I remember being there as a kid. It was forever ago, back when my mom was a realtor scooping up abandoned properties. She took me there hoping to get the owner to sell. And when she found out a young mom had disappeared from that house, I'll never forget what she had said to me."

Tara held out as the baby cooed in the background.

"Well?" I verbally nudged.

"My mom said, 'There's only one family in this town evil enough to kill a woman and take her baby, and rich enough to pay off the police and media to cover up the crime.'"

We all knew who that was: the Valance family.

Chapter 19

June 27, 1969

The Cadillac Eldorado hit a pothole, smacking Alice's skull against the trunk floor. The impact sent a burst of stars dancing behind her closed eyelids. A rubbery smell from the spare tire she was crammed up against filled her nostrils while she wriggled against the rope cutting into her wrists.

A faint scent of gasoline clung to her clothes, making her stomach churn. Where was Clint's goon taking her? And when she got wherever they were going, what then? As Alice struggled to free herself, the cord only cut deeper, its rough twine fibers biting into her skin like tiny teeth. Her mind grasped at partial images of an escape plan, but none would fully form and all of them felt hopeless.

Even without the blood seeping from her wounded abdomen, Fred was bigger and stronger than her. She considered aiming a kick at his face when he opened the trunk of the car, but what if he never did? What if he planned to leave her trapped in here until she suffocated to death?

She had a sinking feeling she was running out of time and options. Then the car stopped. She slowed her breathing and listened. Were they somewhere public? A place where someone could hear her if she cried out?

"Help!" she screamed as she kicked at the trunk. "Help me!"

Her throat burned raw from screaming and her legs ached from the awkward angle, but she wouldn't stop. Not if there was any chance someone could hear her.

But her hopes charred to ash when the car rumbled back to life. As the car drifted forward, the tires crunched over gravel. Each bump and turn disoriented her in the abysmal darkness. Minutes stretched out as the vehicle wound its way along twisty, rutted roads that took her farther from home, and farther from her baby.

Her chest tightened with each passing moment, each dip and curve, until they finally slowed to a stop. Keys jangled, followed by heavy footsteps. She prepared herself to kick, fight, anything to catch Fred off-guard. But when the trunk popped open, she was instantly blinded. Light flooded the trunk directly into her pupils, rendering her flails useless as she squinted against it. Something hard swiftly smashed into her face, and her nose cracked with a snap.

As she was yanked out of the trunk and thrown onto her knees, she realized what Fred had broken her nose with: the grip of his police-issued handgun. He stood above her, one hand aiming a flashlight at her face and the other hand propped on top of it holding a pistol. When she scuttled out of the narrow beam of spotlight, she caught a glimpse of her surroundings.

Pine trees towered around them on a narrow dirt lane cutting through dense woods. No houses or lights in sight. The smell of blood and wet earth overpowered her senses. She felt drained of a strength, but she would never show Fred.

"Is Clint such a coward he can't deal with me himself, so he paid you to do his dirty work?" Alice's voice dripped with venom despite the terror coursing through her.

She'd be dead in a few minutes anyway. There was no point holding anything back.

Fred's face remained impassive. "You should know he doesn't like to get his hands dirty."

"So instead of protecting and serving, you're going to kill me? Is that what you've resorted yourself to, *Officer Fred*?" Alice spat his name out because she wanted him to know he would not get away with doing this anonymously.

"BBPD doesn't own me," he stated.

She studied his expressionless face in the moonlight, searching for any hint of justice or humanity that had once attracted him to policework, but she found none. *Just another one of Clint's mindless henchmen*, she thought bitterly, remembering how her former employer had always expected everyone to obey. Even her. How stupid she had been to open her heart and legs to him!

Alice only had a moment to think, to react. A primal urge to survive pushed her to her feet as her mind raced through her limited options: beg, fight, or flight. None seemed particularly promising against a calculating, armed man who killed for a living. So she did what any bound, desperate woman in her situation could do: she ran.

Her Keds at least offered her decent traction as she bolted into the tree line. Branches lashed at her face and snagged her nightgown as she crashed through the underbrush. Her lungs burned with each ragged breath.

A gunshot chased her deeper into the woods.

"Stop! Get back here!" Fred's footfalls pounded close behind her, but she was smaller and could more easily navigate through the brush, even with her arms bound. For once, she had an advantage.

She ducked behind a massive oak, pressing her back against the rough bark. Her chest heaved as she tried to quiet her breathing by clamping her bound hands against her mouth to muffle the sound. Despite months of dusting Clint's furniture and scrubbing his floors, then having his baby, this was where she ended up—hiding from his thug trying to kill her.

Twigs snapped nearby. Closer. Closer. Each crack of a branch sent fresh jolts of panic through her tense muscles, and she silently cursed herself for not seeing this coming, for not realizing sooner what kind of man Clint Valance truly was beneath his polished veneer.

Suddenly, it was quiet—too quiet. Had he left? The eerie silence pressed in around her like a suffocating blanket, broken only by the pounding of her heart and the soft rustle of leaves overhead. Since becoming a mother, Alice had developed a sixth sense about danger—and right now, every instinct screamed that this false calm was merely the precursor to something worse.

As she peered around the tree, a startled owl took off, wheeling into the darkness. She hadn't seen Fred creep up behind her until it was too late. A gunshot peeled through the night air, shattering the silence like a hammer through glass.

Alice fell.

Chapter 20

"The person who killed Alice was—" Dr. Dreyfuss paused, then her gaze turned to flint as she laced the name with hate, "Clint Valance."

Clint Valance—Dr. Dreyfuss confirmed the same name that Tara had mentioned to me on the phone moments ago. The Valances were pure evil back in 1969 and pure evil still today. Only the Valance family had the power and means to make a woman disappear and then bury the case for more than fifty years.

But Dr. Dreyfuss had left out one crucial detail.

"What was Alice's connection to *that* family?" I couldn't imagine any *nice* girl associating with the town's most notorious crime family.

"She worked for them after high school," Dr. Dreyfuss answered. She got up from her chair and paced up a small set of stairs into a hallway.

I rose and followed her. By now, the Beatles were playing "Lucy in the Sky with Diamonds" as Dr. Dreyfuss ambled into a nursery where a crib took up one wall. She stared at the tiny bed so long, I wondered if that was all I was going to get.

The song was halfway over before she turned to glance back at me. "She was their maid. And then got pregnant with Clint's baby. But it wasn't that simple."

"Nothing ever is," I agreed.

"I suppose there's no point withholding the truth about Alice anymore, is there?"

I propped my elbows on the crib's drop-rail, the kind that had since been banned, and for good reason, too. I almost lost a finger in my son's crib back in the 1980s. My swollen knuckles cracked as I picked up a toy—a Snoopy dressed like an astronaut. I remembered seeing this back when we had toy stores. This house really had been untouched since the 1960s, though I still sensed an unwanted presence that I couldn't shake.

"Go on," I urged.

I wanted to get the juicy details over with so we could finally leave this tomb of a house. With a quiet resolve, she picked up where she had left off.

"I knew Alice since we were kids. We were so alike, and yet so different. I was the independent, academic one, and all she wanted was to be a wife and mother." Nostalgia crept into each word. "Even as little girls, I would trade her all my baby dolls for her books."

And then there's me, neither maternal nor smart, I thought. Instead, I was the bad girl who chased the bad boys. The letter from Bloodson Bay Correctional Facility in my purse reminded me that I hadn't outgrown that toxic trait, and Tara had almost found me out. I needed to be more careful.

"After high school, Alice took a job as a housekeeper for the Valance family," Dr. Dreyfuss continued. "Clint Valance and his wife. But it didn't take long for Alice and Clint to get swept up in an affair. He was a rich, charming womanizer, and she was young and dumb."

It was a tale as old as time. I knew young and dumb well. I

had been an expert at it when, barely out of high school myself, I fell for motorcycle-riding, leather-jacket-wearing Rick. God rest his wicked soul.

"Let me guess," I interjected, predicting the outcome from personal experience. "He left her with a baby and empty promises."

"Sort of," Dr. Dreyfuss answered. "When Clint got Alice pregnant, she had no choice but to run. She had stupidly dreamed of some kind of happily ever after with him, but Clint was only interested in the baby—his flesh and blood, his property. He wanted nothing to do with Alice. But the only way she'd give up her child was if she was dead."

"So you think he killed Alice and abducted the baby?"

She nodded, and a tear slid into a fold of her cheek. "I've known it all these years and have been carrying this secret the whole time."

"So Alice disappeared and was never heard from again?"

"Sadly, yes. Taken from this very house."

The mystery hung in the air begging to be solved. I felt a dormant fury rising up, a sense of outrage on behalf of Alice and her lost child. But as I looked at Dr. Dreyfuss, I saw the weight of her secrets bearing down on her, hunching her back and clouding her eyes.

"Why didn't you tell the police?"

Dr. Dreyfuss's focus glided to the floor, and she physically drooped. "I tried. Believe me, I tried. And that was my first mistake."

"What do you mean?"

"When I saw the news, I knew the media had it wrong. So I told the police Clint Valance probably killed her—Alice would have never just disappeared without contacting me. The very next day, I was fired from my job at the mental asylum. I realized then and there that I had no idea what I was up against—that Clint owned Bloodson Bay. He had everyone on his payroll back then."

"The Valance family still does," I corrected her.

Well, until last spring, when Clint's son, Ewan Valance, was thrown in jail. But even a jail cell was no real threat. Ewan's conviction was currently being appealed. Tara and I had talked about it to the point of exhaustion—what if Ewan got released? Would he come after Tara seeking vengeance?

Or had he already? It wouldn't shock me if Darla's body in Bloodson Manor was Ewan's way of saying, *"I'm coming for you next."* And the timing of Tara being poisoned with antifreeze couldn't be coincidence.

"Anyway, it's haunted me ever since," Dr. Dreyfuss admitted. "There wasn't much more I could do. And even if Alice had somehow survived, back in 1969, as you probably know, an unmarried mother had few rights, especially not against a man like Clint Valance. It all seemed hopeless. I was scared of what Clint would do to me next, considering he easily made my friend disappear."

I couldn't blame her. The Valances made a living making people disappear.

"Did you ever find the baby?" I asked.

"Clint and his wife raised him as their own and no one questioned it. Clint's wife was a bit of a homebody; she never left the house, so no one would have known if she'd been pregnant or not. And back then the family stayed out of the spotlight. There was no internet to research people. Everything about them was hush-hush, and I decided I'd let it go after my parents died."

Dr. Dreyfuss headed to the nursery door and I trailed her warily. She stopped in the doorway so abruptly, I nearly rear-ended her.

"That's the worst part, Ginger, that Clint's son is unaware that he had a birth mother who loved him—and who died trying to protect him."

She led us back into the living room while I mulled over everything she had told me. My brain latched on to one specific detail.

"Hold your horses! Did you say Clint's *son*? You know for sure the baby was a boy?"

Dr. Dreyfuss nodded. "Yes, Alice had named him Julius. He was as sweet as pecan pie, too."

I only knew of two Valance sons—Ewan, and his younger brother Marvin who he killed—but Ewan was the firstborn, the one who carried the family mantel. "Do you think Julius is Ewan Valance?"

"You mean Judge Ewan Valance—the one who was arrested for drug trafficking, theft, kidnapping, and murder?" Dr. Dreyfuss shuddered. "Lord, I hope not. That is not the legacy Alice would have wanted for her son."

"But it fits, doesn't it? He's the oldest, the baby that completed their family."

"I suppose it fits," she considered. "You could probably confirm it by looking up his birth date in the public records, but keep in mind that they altered the birth certificate to say Clint's wife was the biological mother. They could have also changed the birth date to match whatever birth timeline they wanted.

Records back then were easy to fake if you had money."

The room fell silent, the only sound the soft ticking of a cartoon cat clock hanging on the wall. Perhaps that clock was one of the last things Alice had looked at before she disappeared.

I imagined the countless what-ifs that must have intruded on Dr. Dreyfuss over the years. We shared a mutual understanding of being bound by our secrets, our fears, and our determination to uncover the truth. But together, we could bring her closure.

"What happened to Alice's missing person's case?" I asked.

"They dropped it because Alice's body was never found. No body, no crime, I guess. But I always knew…"

The gray of Dr. Dreyfuss's eyes glazed over like she was lost in thought, as if the memories were rising to the surface like bubbles in a stagnant pond.

"To this day, I've wondered about Alice's fate. Maybe I don't want to know after all."

That didn't make sense to me. How could she not want to know what happened to her best friend?

"Are you sure, Doc? If you really want to know the truth, I'll help you find it."

"To what end?" Dr. Dreyfuss asked.

"To the ends of the earth! You can't give up. You need closure—not just for you, but for Alice."

"It's been so long, though. Where do I even start?" It was as if she drifted away for a moment. I thought I saw a trace of something—regret, sorrow—but then it was gone.

"You mentioned something about a clue…" I reminded her, but I was cut short by the distinctive clatter of metal. This time, there was no mistaking the sound, and it was closer than before. "You heard it that time, right, Doc?"

Her eyes widened as she peeked down a hallway that led past the den and circled around to the kitchen. "I stand corrected. That is *not* the house settling."

I stood guard in the living room while Dr. Dreyfuss wandered around the corner to investigate. "It sounded like it was coming from the kitchen. I'll check there, you check the den."

I may be old, but I wasn't senile enough to go wandering into shadowy corners of an abandoned house in search of whatever was making strange noises. But the longer I put it off, the longer until this night would end. So I pulled up my big-girl britches and headed into the dark hallway.

Upon entering the den, one look told me this had been Dr. Dreyfuss's personal library once upon a time, as books lined one wall, covering every subject from bipolar disorder to xenophobia. A large poster depicting the anatomy of the human brain hung on the wall above a desk.

I switched on a hideous, mid-century-modern-style desk lamp. The three frosted shades were attached to curved brass rods that looked like something you'd see in *The Jetsons* Skypad Apartment. I began to explore the room, noting a collection of old papers stacked neatly on the desk.

On top was a typed police report from June 27, 1969, with the typewriter's letter "Y" slightly crooked on every page. It detailed the date, time, and location of Alice's disappearance, along with the details Dr. Dreyfuss had already shared with me.

When I flipped over a yellowed photo of two teenage girls squinting against the sun with the beach behind them, two names were neatly hand written in perfect loopy cursive on the back: Lea Dreyfuss and Alice Belvedere.

One girl had a bob, and the other had a pixie cut and wore cat-eye glasses almost exactly the same as Dr. Dreyfuss wore now. Apparently her taste in eyewear was consistent.

An envelope was buried near the bottom of the pile with the words *Please Find Him* scribbled messily across it. Opening the envelope, I found a black-and-white picture inside, along with a key. I retrieved my magnifying glass from my purse and began scrutinizing the image. A spark of recognition flared within me, and a shiver ran down my spine.

I knew how to find out what happened to Alice.

On my way to tell Dr. Dreyfuss, a shrill scream, followed by something shattering, echoed from the kitchen, startling a trickle of pee from my weak bladder. Then Dr. Dreyfuss shrieked, "Get away from me!"

I dropped my magnifying glass and dashed through the dining room that led to a closed swing door. Dread crept up my spine like a cold draft. Everything was quiet.

A dull *thud* reminiscent of a body hitting the floor froze me mid-step. My pulse faltered while I braced myself, imagining I'd confront either a massive Edmund Kemper-like brute, or some bespectacled Ted Bundy-esque serial killer.

"Doc?" I yelled, swinging the door partway open. "Are you okay?"

Nothing but dreadful silence. I stepped forward, but the door wouldn't budge any further than the width of my hand. I peered through the gap, and the blockage appeared to be… a pair of pink pantlegs? Ramming harder, the gap opened just enough to reveal Dr. Dreyfuss covered in blood, and I felt my consciousness shrinking at the sight.

This time I heaved my shoulder against the door, and it shoved Dr. Dreyfuss aside enough for me to squeeze through. The sight instantly turned my panic into nausea. Blood. And something else I never in a million years would be able to overwrite in my memory.

Chapter 21

My mind whirled like a tornado in a trailer park when I saw Dr. Dreyfuss lying spread eagle on the kitchen's linoleum floor, her head sliced open in a yawning gash. Bright red oozed down her nose and lips. But that wasn't the worst of it. Crawling across her lap was a cockroach the side of a rat. I'm talking Amazon-jungle, horror-movie big.

"Did I kill it?" Dr. Dreyfuss was slowly regaining consciousness as she reached up to her forehead and ran her fingers across the open wound gushing like a geyser.

If I wasn't feeling so faint, I would have thrown up.

The roach hopped off her lap, then *tap, tap, tapped* its way across the floor toward the cabinet. I scuttled after it, aimed a foot over it, and stepped down. I squished its yellow innards out both sides of the bottom of my shoe in a loud crunch that made Dr. Dreyfuss gag. When I was certain it was dead, I plucked the ginormous bug off the floor and dangled it in front of her before I tossed it in the garbage can.

She grimaced. "That thing attacked me!"

Skimming from a splintered plate to a metal pot on the floor to Dr. Dreyfuss's split forehead, I was trying to put two and two together on how a bug could bring down a grown woman and cause all this collateral damage.

"How on earth—?"

"It was running across the counter and hid behind a plate when I came in," she explained. "So I grabbed a pot to trap it under, but I missed and dropped the pot and knocked the plate on the floor. That's when it flew up at my face, so I tried to duck out of its way. I misjudged and cracked my head on the edge of the counter and knocked myself out. Does it look bad?"

The lump forming above her eyebrow was already turning black and blue beneath the gash.

"Nah, 'tis just a flesh wound. But you might have a concussion. We should probably get you checked out."

Dr. Dreyfuss rose to her knees while mine buckled beneath me at the sight of so much blood. Bug guts, skeletal corpses, even vomit I could handle. Blood, not so much. I handed her a towel to press against her forehead and closed my eyes, needing a moment to compose myself.

"Think you can help me bandage it?"

I shook my head. "Doc, no Band-Aid is big enough to stop that. You either need stitches or a super-absorbency menstrual pad… and considering neither of us has had a period since Beanie Babies were popular, I don't think we have one on-hand."

"Oh, malarky. I'll just press a towel to it," Dr. Dreyfuss problem-solved. "And by the way, I've got a storage room with 200 Beanie Babies, so I'm counting on them to make a comeback."

I didn't want to admit that I had quite a collection of my own that I had yet to be able to sell. So much for that investment scheme.

After Dr. Dreyfuss tended to her wound, we headed into the den where I showed her the photograph and key I had found.

"Did you ever figure out what this key unlocks?"

"No idea. Some instructions would have been helpful."

I picked up the picture and held it out to her. "This is the clue you were talking about, right?"

Dr. Dreyfuss plucked the photo from my fingers and gazed at it. "Yes. I remember taking this picture…" she whispered, almost wistfully. "But I don't know how this was supposed to help me find Julius."

"Look at it more carefully," I prompted her.

In it, Alice was sitting upright in a hospital bed holding a newborn infant wrapped in a blanket. At her bedside stood a mustached doctor wearing thick black glasses and smiling broadly.

"What did the police say when you showed them this?"

Clearly this was undeniable proof that Alice had a baby. How could the police argue against photographic evidence?

"They claimed there were no hospital records indicating she gave birth, and no birth record for a Julius Belvedere, either. So they shrugged it off, saying it must not have been Alice in the picture. As if I was lying about it." She sighed heavily. "It's not like it matters anyway. I don't know how this was supposed to help me find Julius. You can't even see him in the blanket."

"That's because this wasn't a clue to finding Julius." I pointed to the man wearing the white lab coat in the photo. "It was a clue to finding *him*. The doctor is who we're searching for!"

Dr. Dreyfuss's mouth dropped open. "How did I not realize that's what Alice meant?"

We had a respectable witness to Alice's labor and delivery—the doctor who delivered Julius! And from the way he wrapped his arm around Alice and the kindness in his smile, he appeared to genuinely like her. There was a good chance we could get the truth from this man… if he was still alive.

While the doctor looked young enough to be in his thirties back then, that would put him in his eighties now. Would he even remember delivering this specific baby fifty years ago? Probably not. But we had to at least try.

"Any chance you remember the doctor's name?"

Dr. Dreyfuss frowned. "Unfortunately, no."

I held my cracked magnifying glass over the image, hovering it over his kind face where his mask had been pulled down over his neck. Roving my way down his body, I stopped at his shoulders. A name was embroidered on his white medical coat.

The letters came into focus, and I felt a surge of excitement: Dr. G. Kildare.

"Got it!" I exclaimed. "We'll look up every G. Kildare we can find who is roughly eighty years old. Hopefully we'll get a hit."

"I think we should just let it go," Dr. Dreyfuss grumbled. "What if he's not local anymore?"

"Then we'll call him. Or text him. Or email him. Or send a smoke signal if we have to! Why are you being difficult when we're so close to finding out what happened?"

"Maybe I don't want to know…"

"Do you want to avenge Alice or not? Do you want Clint Valance to pay or not?" I demanded. "Now's your chance."

"Ginger, I'm too old to play detective. It was one thing to bring you here, but it's another thing to go poking around in other people's lives asking questions." Dr. Dreyfuss groaned wearily.

Her fidgety, weathered hands betrayed her, and I could tell she was wrestling with her conscience. Digging up skeletons didn't come without dirty fingernails and danger.

"Have you got something more important to do?" I raised one carefully penciled eyebrow that I imagined had started sweating into the folds of my forehead. "A hot date with your crossword puzzle, maybe?"

"You need to learn to respect boundaries, Ginger." She gave me that stern look she'd perfected over months of psychoanalyzing me, then shoved past me out of the den. "This doesn't concern you."

The rigid, logical therapist in her had made a comeback, as if we hadn't crossed every doctor-patient boundary hours ago into something more akin to friendship… or accomplices. I chased after her, following her into the living room where she was already grabbing her purse and car keys.

"Actually, it does. Alice is connected to a body left on my daughter-in-law's property. So I'm in this, whether you like it or not. And if you want the closure you deserve, then you need to learn to break some rules, Doc," I shot back. "This time, you know you can't beat me, so you might as well join me."

"How do we know this message was referring to the doctor?" She sounded so defeated it broke my heart.

"I'll prove it," I declared, though I had no idea how I would do anything of the kind.

Glancing around the living room, I tried to put myself in Alice's shoes during her last night here. The news article mentioned she had packed a travel case, but what would she have done next? Most people would have contacted someone for help.

I spotted the telephone table in the hallway where a rotary phone sat next to an ancient phone book. I blew off the inch-thick coating of dust and opened it. Flipping through it, I skimmed the pages, searching for one in particular. While the phone numbers were too short to be relevant to this century, it wasn't a number I was looking for. It was a name.

And the page I needed was missing.

Chapter 22

Every last name from Kenmore to Kirkland had been ripped out of the 1969 *Bloodson Bay Citizen's Telephone Directory*. Only a torn edge of a page remained in its place.

"I told you so!" I yelled at Dr. Dreyfuss, who looked at me as if I had truly gone the way of the cuckoo bird. "This is proof that Alice contacted Dr. Kildare before she left. The page where his number would be is missing from the directory."

I slapped the phone book for emphasis. She couldn't deny that this was pretty convincing.

"Fine, Ginger, you win."

I always do.

And then divine purpose hit again: Finding Gregory Kildare's home address was as easy as three clicks on the online white pages. There was only one G. Kildare approximately eighty years old in the Bloodson Bay town limits. But when I searched his address, I got an unusual result. Nothing I had ever seen before.

While the listing showed a mailing address, when I looked for directions, there was no road access to his residence—only large plots of crops surrounding the house. It looked like we'd be taking the cornfield less traveled.

"Got four-wheel-drive on this thing?" I asked Dr. Dreyfuss half an hour later as her Gremlin crawled along with a worrisome clanking.

"No, but you're paying for the tow truck if we get stuck."

Every mile took us further into rural territory, where gravel became dirt roads leading deeper into no-man's land with no cell service. Ditches lined the single lane, blocking any turnaround. Night draped thick and dark over us, with the occasional sliver of moonlight through stalks of corn. It would have made a perfect horror film setting.

My sensitive bladder threatened to spill with every bump, and I was glad for the bladder control pad I had put on this morning. Here was some girl math for you: Childbirth times three plus old age equaled leaks from unexpected places at unexpected times. One sneeze after too many sweet teas and my pants were doomed.

The car coughed and sputtered, the suspension growled in protest. Dr. Dreyfuss gripped the steering wheel so tight it turned her knuckles as white as the coconut snowball cookies she had served today during therapy.

Lord help me, but her car had been around longer than my late husband—and was probably equally unreliable, too. The headlights cut yellow paths through the black, catching the occasional glint of a startled deer's eyes on the berm, which made me jolt every blessed time.

"I swear this field gets denser with each mile." Dr. Dreyfuss's voice trembled like the brown leaves clinging to the shoots.

"Did you know three kids disappeared from this corn maze?" I asked, unable to resist stirring the pot a little. "And they say their ghosts haunt these fields, looking for people to torment," I added with a dramatic flourish.

The cornrows seemed to lean in, their stalks tangling together in a macabre dance, as if trying to lend some credence to the local legend. The dim dashboard lights cast her face in an eerie glow. I shot her a reassuring smile, but my own mind began to wander… those missing kids, the feeling that we were being watched. And now, the sinking suspicion that this rusty hunk of junk car might just leave us stranded in the middle of nowhere.

"Those are just stories to keep kids from wandering off," she concluded.

But the dense canopy gave me the creeps. The GPS had lost its signal miles ago, which was just about the time my stomach started doing the Texas two-step. When we reached a weathered mailbox with KILDARE spelled out in peeling gold letters, I exhaled relief that I hadn't just led us to our deaths.

A car-width overgrown path led us through a field of dead weeds to a Victorian-style house that had seen better days, and those better days were probably sometime during the Roosevelt administration. Mildew plagued the wooden siding, and several shutters hung crooked, creaking in the faint breeze like my joints. Crunchy leaves carpeted the wraparound porch, and a swing rocked slowly with the breeze, as if occupied by a ghost.

I shot a sideways glance at Dr. Dreyfuss, wondering if she was thinking the same thing I was: Was it too late to turn back?

"Maybe this wasn't such a good idea." Dr. Dreyfuss stopped at the foot of the porch steps.

"It's just an old man in an old house. Nothing to be afraid of."

I squared my shoulders and marched across the warped boards up to the front door, my sensible shoes making each plank groan like it was personally offended by my presence. The brass knocker, shaped like a snarling lion's head, echoed hollow through the house when I gave it three sharp raps.

Only silence. No one seemed home, which wasn't exactly surprising, given the house's state of neglect. Still, it was disappointing. Then I remembered the key I'd found in the envelope with the photo. I slid it into the lock and turned.

Click.

It worked! I couldn't help but feel a surge of pride that I was mastering this chess match of a cold case. I turned the icy handle, and the door slipped open with a long *creeeeak* that would've made any horror movie director proud. I peeked in, squinting into the gloom. It was dark as a bear's belly in here.

"Anyone home?" I called out.

After a long moment, I stepped inside, noticing how Dr. Dreyfuss hung a safe distance back. She wasn't as attuned to the sleuthing life as I was. All those years of shrinkin' heads had probably made her overly cautious. I, on the other hand, had lost any trace of self-preservation when it came to facing danger. The thrill of excitement was ticklin' my toes as I walked into the dusty depths of the derelict house.

"Looks empty," Dr. Dreyfuss deduced.

A door slammed shut somewhere inside. A gust of wind, maybe?

Then a slow, rhythmic *creak, creak, creeeeeak.* Maybe it wasn't the wind. Definitely footsteps. Human ones this time.

The approaching resident of this creepy house was apparently too much for Dr. Dreyfuss, who instantly turned and ran out the front door, leaving me to fend for myself.

"I've got a weapon!"

I held up my handbag, ready to swing it at any attacker. Since it was heavy enough to give me permanent spinal scoliosis, it could easily knock someone out.

A faint form appeared under an arch that led into the house's gut, then the silhouette moved into the dim moonlight pouring through the open front door. A frail woman with white hair glared at me, her outstretched hand holding a gun. I sized her up as she floated toward me like an apparition, gauging my odds. We were about the same age and size, although I had stupidly brought a handbag to a gunfight.

"Why on earth would you threaten me in my own home?" the woman snarled. Her eyes seemed to look right through me. Past me.

"Oh, we're sorry!" Dr. Dreyfuss apologized, coming to my rescue. "We didn't realize anyone still lived here."

"We're looking for information about a Dr. Gregory Kildare." I tried to steady my frazzled nerves, but the unsettling stillness seemed to amplify every quiver.

Her thin lips barely moved as she replied, "No one has called him that in ages, not since he retired."

She slowly lowered her gun-wielding arm to her side. I shot a reassuring glance toward Dr. Dreyfuss, who resurfaced next to me now that the imminent danger had passed.

"So I take it you know him?" Hope floated in my chest like a warm bubble. We might finally be onto something.

"Don't you mean *knew* him?" The woman's jaw tightened, deep lines appearing around her mouth as she frowned. A storm brewed behind her stare, an unspoken pain and anger that lingered beneath the surface. "Who are you, and why are you here?"

We should leave.
"We were hoping to find Dr. Kildare," I answered.
Then she asked me something that changed everything:
"I thought you were supposed to be looking for his killer."

Chapter 23

June 27, 1969

The crack of a gunshot split the air. Splinters of tree bark scattered across Alice's hair. And when the bullet hit her, she fell.

A moment before this, however, the air had stirred with the flap of an owl taking flight, making Alice flinch, which then caused her heel to sink into the mud. The dip yanked her backwards, then down, until her tailbone hit soft, wet earth just as the bullet zipped across the tip of her ear. The tiny missile was close enough that she felt its vibration and heat burn her skin, but far enough that her life was spared.

Her kidnapper's eyes widened with surprise. "Lucky girl."

The owl had saved Alice's life, and she momentarily thought of home, where the crochet owl Lea handmade for Julius still sat in his empty crib. Lea was her only hope. If her best friend found the envelope with the photo and the key, she would understand what to do: Find Dr. Kildare, the only person with the evidence to take down Clint Valance and save Julius.

With no time to process her miracle, Alice scrambled up to her feet. Adrenaline masked her aching muscles and the soaked nightgown that clung to her like a cold second skin. She charged forward, ramming her shoulder into Officer Fred's knees with all the fury of a mother protecting her child.

The tall man's knees buckled in a grotesquely wrong direction. The impact knocked the breath from her lungs and sent shockwaves through her teeth. They both went down hard on the pine straw, Fred's grunt oddly satisfying in Alice's ears.

Branches snapped and shrubbery crunched, and the earthy scent of decay permeated around them like nature's own pungent perfume. With hands stuck together, she clawed for purchase in the wet terrain, determined not to let Fred gain the upper hand.

The gun thumped to the ground, inches beyond Alice's reach. Lunging forward, she savagely reached out and closed her fingers around the grip, the metal against her palm both terrifying and reassuring. She stumbled backward, mud squelching under her shoes, and her heart hammered so hard she was sure it would soon give up and stop beating.

When Fred pushed himself upright, his face twisted with rage as the moonlight snagged on the cruel angles of his features. Her hands shook as she raised the gun. Aimed it at him. One breath. That's all she allowed herself. Then she pulled the trigger.

The gun kicked in her hands with a force she hadn't expected, sending a spasm through her outstretched arm. The sound echoed across the woods, ricocheting off trunks and brush and fading into the heady summer night, leaving behind a deafening silence broken only by a grunt.

Her fingers felt numb. Somewhere in the distance, an animal huffed and took flight, its light-hooved gait beating a frantic retreat further into the darkness.

Fred's expensive suit was now stained with mud and forest debris… and a slow blossom of blood. Red bloomed across his chest like a grotesque flower, spreading quickly through the fabric before he crumpled, his mouth opening with a hollow sound of disbelief.

She didn't wait to see if Fred would survive. There was no time. She had to get as far away from here as possible.

Alice ran to the Cadillac, her legs wobbly and threatening to give out with each exhausted step. She felt for the folded paper still tucked in her underwear, the only thing that could save her now. Thank God it hadn't fallen out.

The car door handle slipped out of her clammy grip, and she had to try twice before she opened it. She breathed so hard she could barely hear anything else, though in the back of her mind she registered that she'd just shot a policeman. She had either killed him or he was somewhere behind her in pursuit.

Sitting in the driver's seat, she stared dumbly at the ignition. For a moment she wondered if this all was real—the gunshot, the officer crumpling to the ground, her son gone forever. But the sharp pain in her side and the acrid smell of gunpowder clinging to her clothes was a bitter reminder that it had all been terrifyingly real.

She leaned over, feeling for the metal seat track underneath. It felt sharp enough to do the trick, so she sawed the rope back and forth until the twine around her wrists frayed.

Next were the keys.

"Where would he put them?" Her voice came out scratchy, foreign to her own ears.

She flipped down the visor—not there. Then she checked the interior—the dashboard, the other seats, even the floor. The keys weren't in the car, which meant they must be in the absolute worst place they could be: Fred's pocket.

Leaving the safety of the vehicle, she forced herself back toward the spot where she had shot Fred. The dense canopy disoriented her as she retraced her paces, winding through the brush aimlessly. She hoped she wouldn't get lost as the clouds tucked the moonlight away, making every step hazardous. When Alice finally reached the clearing, her breath stopped.

This had to be the right place, but there was nothing there except trampled weeds and mud. The vacant space scorned her.

No body. Just empty darkness stretching in every direction.

"No. That's not possible."

The shot hadn't killed him, but she was certain he had bled too much to survive much longer. Flicking her gaze over every inch of forest surrounding her, she didn't detect any movement. No form stood out of place, no human sound cut into nature's cacophony. Nonetheless, her fingers tightened around the gun's grip as she expected him to spring out at any moment.

She could try to hike until she found a road, but she had no idea where she was or how many miles until she'd reach civilization. Grim reality sank in: She would never make it out of these woods alive without the car key. And the only way to get it was to find Fred… before he found her.

"I thought you were supposed to be looking for his killer."

The white-haired woman's question caught both me and Dr. Dreyfuss speechless.

"Someone killed Dr. Kildare?" I clarified. Of all the rotten luck, the one person with possible answers was dead when we were so close to solving this…

"You're the police, aren't you?" the woman asked firmly but warily. "I thought you were here because you finally figured out who murdered my husband."

Before I said anything, I held up my hands so she could see I was unarmed. I had no idea how trigger-happy she was. She sure looked like a straight-shooter in every sense of the word.

"Oh, I'm sorry, we're not the police."

The woman's eyes narrowed on Dr. Dreyfuss. "I figured with her pantsuit she was a detective."

Dr. Dreyfuss shook her head with a wry smile because no detective would wear a hot-pink pantsuit. "No, I'm actually a therapist."

Then the woman nodded at me. "And she is your patient, I take it?"

I felt a flush rise to my cheeks, but the woman's words were more teasing than malicious. "What gave it away?"

The woman's smile widened. "No sane person your age

would wear that in public, dear."

I bristled at her comment, feeling a surge of defensiveness for the bold geometric-patterned sweater I had proudly owned and worn since 1983.

"My personal style has nothing to do with my sanity—or lack thereof!"

"Back to the topic," Dr. Dreyfuss intervened, her voice returning the room to a professional calm. "You said Dr. Kildare was murdered?"

The woman's expression turned somber, her eyes cloudy with cataracts and tears.

"*Greg*—he preferred Greg." She paused, collecting her thoughts. "He was killed a few years back."

"I'm sorry for your loss," I sympathized. "I never did get to put the man responsible behind bars."

She paused as if reconsidering this conversation.

"Can you tell us what happened?" I asked.

She deliberated for a moment, then sighed. "I might as well. The police apparently don't give a damn. Greg was shot on his way to the police station to come clean about his part in a woman's disappearance long ago."

I exchanged a look with Dr. Dreyfuss, feeling a sense of intrigue.

"Was the woman you're referring to Alice Belvedere?" I dared to ask.

She glanced over her shoulder at a cheerful kitchen off to our left, its gingham curtains and matching tablecloth giving off the kind of homey vibe that made me think of Dr. Dreyfuss's fresh-baked cookies and sweet tea on a summer afternoon. The outdated kind of kitchen my *máthair* would have loved and

Sloane would have hated.

"You know what? You've already let yourself in, so you might as well make yourself comfortable and I'll tell you all about it. It's been lonely since Greg died. I could use the company."

"You'd trust two virtual strangers?"

She shrugged. "Well, you certainly don't look like a threat. Plus I have a gun and you don't. Besides, it's about time the truth came out to *someone*. Follow me—it's a long story that can only be told over tea and cookies."

Maybe she trusted us, but could we trust *her*?

She led us into the kitchen, where the scent of freshly brewed tea and cinnamon wafted through the air, then she placed a plate of gingersnap cookies on the table. I chuckled—despite our shared namesake, they were the one cookie I didn't care for.

Handing me a smiley face mug, she poured it full of tea from a ceramic polka-dot carafe. As I wrapped my hands around the warm mug, I caught a whiff of Earl Grey and felt a little more at ease. I took a sip, my suspicion melting into mild mistrust.

"Can you start from the beginning?" Dr. Dreyfuss prompted in her most therapeutic tone.

The woman's expression turned grim. "Back in 1969, my husband delivered a baby for Alice, and the biological father forced Greg to falsify the birth record. When Alice attempted to run away, things got out of control and Greg helped cover up murder by burying the body."

A jolt of shock hit me. Dr. Kildare had helped kill Alice.

"Greg was a loose end," the woman continued. "It wasn't

until he planned to come clean to the police about everything when he ended up shot right outside the police station. The police said it was probably a gang-related drive-by shooting, and conveniently, no cameras got any footage. But I know he was targeted to ensure the truth stayed buried."

I furrowed my brow, perplexed that she could be so cavalier about her husband being part of Alice's murder cover-up.

"You knew what he did in 1969… and you both let years go by before going to the police?"

The woman's eyes bore into my soul. "You don't understand. He took a big risk to come clean and it killed him! My husband was a good man, and he felt guilty about it for the longest time, but he never told a soul. I was the only person who knew."

My mind raced with too many questions to sort through.

Dr. Dreyfuss's voice interrupted my thoughts. "Did Greg happen to have proof of who Julius belonged to, or what happened to Alice?"

The woman leaned forward, and her hand quickly rested on the gun. A moment later her arm twitched. Then the gun was aimed at Dr. Dreyfuss.

"How do you know Julius's name?"

"I knew the mother," Dr. Dreyfuss answered.

"We're here to help," I tried to assure the woman. I didn't want to scare her off by telling her that somehow this was linked to another recent murder, and the body count kept rising. "We just need to know if there is any tangible evidence of what happened to her and the baby."

"You mean something like the original birth certificate?" The woman chuckled, but the gun didn't waver. "Of course

Greg kept it. My husband never was one to do as he's told, and that hadn't changed since I showed up on his doorstep in the middle of the night in June of 1969."

Chapter 25

June 27, 1969

Spanish moss hung like a funeral shroud, and not a single night bird called out. Alice stood over the spot where Fred had fallen, focused on the bloodstain that soaked into the soil.

The sight transported her back to another time, another place—Clint Valance's house, where she'd mopped up countless spills, though none quite like this. She had scrubbed wine splashed on the furniture after Clint's wife threw a drunken fit over what Clint kept locked behind the basement door. And swept up shards of shattered china when Clint lost his temper over the wine stains. Her life was a constant cleanup after cycles of spills, but the worst of all were her tear stains mixed with Clint's blood on the bathroom tile the day Clint...

A *snap* of a brank yanked her back to now.

While that night was her worst memory, it also gave her the greatest gift: her son. The car keys—that was what she needed right now. And the crimson trail barely visible in the moonlight would lead her to them.

Creeping close to the disturbed mud, she tracked where Fred had dragged himself and scraped across the muck. The gun slipped in her clammy palms. She'd never held a weapon before tonight, but desperation had a way of making the necessary somehow possible. The path led toward a small drop-off where twisted branches snagged at her skin, their gnarled fingers pointing the way forward like ghoulish tour guides.

Silence pressed against her ears. Too much silence. He was out there, waiting. Another twig cracked. She spun toward the sound and took a tentative step. It was too dark to see more than a few feet away.

But there he was, hidden in a bush, chest glistening in the moonlight. His labored breathing carried across the space between them. How was he still moving? The bullet had torn straight through him.

"There's only one bullet left." His voice came out as a wet snarl and he rose to his feet, unsteady but still foreboding. "I hope you're a good shot."

Alice had less than a moment to react as he sprung forward with impossible speed. This was it. Her last chance. Alice squeezed the trigger. But the shot went wide, sparking off a tree trunk behind him.

His cackle echoed through the woods, wild and unhinged. He kept coming, faster now, closing the gap between them. Alice stumbled backward, gun trained on his advancing form. Her finger tightened on the trigger, but the gun was pointless now. It would click empty, but there was that small chance he was wrong… so she aimed and pinched the trigger.

A final shot splintered the night. This time she met her mark as his forehead exploded, and he dropped like a boulder.

"I guess you counted wrong."

She didn't know if anyone had heard the gunshots. Maybe the sound would soon draw the police, and she didn't know the first thing about disposing of a body. None of that mattered right now. She needed help.

She rushed forward, hands searching his pockets until she grasped metal. The car key! She pulled it free, then ran recklessly toward the path she hoped would lead her to the car. Her relief came out in an audible sob when she spotted the Cadillac, then jammed the key into the ignition, missing several times before it slid home. The engine roared to life, headlights cutting twin beams through the murky night.

Tears blurred her vision as she drove aimlessly, searching for something recognizable along winding back roads until she stopped at a street sign. After retrieving the damp square of paper from her panty's elastic waist, she unfolded it and double-checked the address from the phone directory page.

An atlas on the floor of the Eldorado took her the rest of the way to where she was going until the name on the mailbox at the curb told her she had reached the right house. It was tucked at the end of a long path through a cornfield, an old Victorian sitting like a crouching beast among the swaying cornstalks, a fitting end to this nightmare of a night.

Would he be awake at this hour? What would he think when he found out she had killed a *cop*? When she had left the hospital after he delivered her baby, Dr. Kildare had given her his house key and a promise to help her if ever she needed it—but could she trust him?

Acutely aware that she was covered in blood, Alice knocked on the door. She hadn't thought far enough ahead of what to say when the porch light shimmered on, illuminating dancing bugs that matched her jittery nerves. The door swung open.

Dressed in pajamas and fiddling with his black-framed glasses, Dr. Kildare's surprised face appeared in the doorway, his short brown hair disheveled from sleep.

"Alice! Are you okay?" His glasses frames caught the dim porch light as he blinked at her in disbelief.

She glanced down at the blood soaking her nightgown. "I'm hurt. Can you help me? You're the only person I trust right now." *I think*, she didn't add.

He shook his head. "No, you can't trust me, Alice. Not at all. Not after what I've done. I'm the one who destroyed your hospital records."

"I don't care about what you did before, Dr. Kildare. It's what you do now that matters. Will you help me or not?"

Worry—or was it fear?—gave him pause. "What exactly did you do, Alice?"

Shame bent her neck downward, and tears spilled to the porch floor in dime-sized stains. "I killed a police officer, and I need your help getting rid of the body."

Chapter 26

I was staring at a ghost. A ghost who had not only disappeared on June 27, 1969, but had also killed a corrupt cop—and gotten away with it.

"You're Alice Belvedere," I stated.

She nodded.

The three of us—me, Dr. Dreyfuss, and Alice—all perched on the edges of our retro, burnt-orange kitchen chairs in a breakfast nook that belonged to the 1960s. The kitchen was last updated during the Watergate scandal, and the wood-paneled cabinetry and vintage Maytag fridge saluted an era of housewives trapped in their kitchens, popping kids out like there was nothing better to do.

The room was complete with those kitschy, rooster-themed canisters lined up on the counter and a copper Jell-O mold hanging on the wall that could've been twins with the one I had—until Tara informed me that no one made Jell-O molds anymore. The linoleum floor even had that same speckled pattern that made my eyes go crossed if I stared at it too long while eating my morning grits.

"So, now you know what got my husband Greg killed…" Alice's voice was low and measured, like she was choosing each word with care. "Me. Protecting me was what got him killed. He wanted to clear his conscience and Clint Valance killed him for it."

Her eyes held a world of sorrow. When they burrowed into mine, I knew we had ventured into some very dark history.

"That doesn't explain why you never contacted your family," Dr. Dreyfuss said, and the air in the room grew thick as honey. "Surely you missed them."

"I don't have any family," Alice stated.

"Do you not remember me, Alice?"

Alice looked confused, but then her face slowly expanded with recognition and her jaw dropped open. Her smiley-face mug clunk to the table, turning upside-down into a frown as tea stained the tablecloth brown.

"Lea?" Her voice was barely audible.

"Yes, it's me."

Alice jumped from her seat, her face draining of color so quickly I thought she might faint dead away. What remained was a canvas of shock and bewilderment as she gripped the table's edge to steady herself. I knew that kind of reaction. It happened when your ghosts came back to haunt you.

"Lea!" she stammered. "How did you—?"

"Ginger helped find you." Dr. Dreyfuss rose to her feet, and her hands shook so badly her gingersnap crumbled in her palm. "All this time I thought you were... dead."

I'd never seen my therapist look so rattled, and believe me, I'd given her plenty of reasons to lose her cool over the years.

"I'm not yet, at least," Alice said.

The two women hugged, clinging to each other like survivors of a shipwreck finally reaching shore. I shifted awkwardly in my chair, like an intruder witnessing something deeply personal. My tea grew cold as I watched Dr. Dreyfuss and Alice weep into each other's shoulders, decades of separation dissolving in an instant. If I'd known my weekly therapy session would turn into a Hallmark movie reunion scene, I might've worn waterproof mascara.

"I can't believe it's really you…" Alice collapsed into her chair beside Dr. Dreyfuss. "Sitting in my kitchen, still searching for me after all this time. I never thought I'd see you again. Even after all these years you still have that pixie cut that never complimented your face shape."

Dr. Dreyfuss laughed. "And you still have that boring bob I always hated! Why didn't you reach out to me?"

"There's something else, something I could never tell you. It's the reason I stayed away. I couldn't face you." Alice shook her head sadly, the kitchen light sparkling in the white threads of her hair.

"What is it?" Dr. Dreyfuss asked, resting her hand on Alice's. "You can tell me anything."

"Lea." Alice inhaled shakily. "I'm responsible for your parents' death."

Chapter 27

July 20, 1969

For the past twenty days the world was abuzz with chatter about Price Charles being formally invested as the Prince of Whales. But Alice couldn't enjoy such trivial things. Every thought returned back to her recent phone call to the police station.

Greg—he insisted she call him now that they were a proper *couple*—had dropped her off in town at the pay phone near the library. A single dime was all it took to connect with the Bloodson Bay Police Department, who took the anonymous call. She hadn't given herself even a moment to reconsider before she blurted out:

"I'm calling to report child abuse. Clint Valance has been torturing his oldest son by locking him in the basement."

Alice couldn't remember ever hearing the name of the boy. Between his frequent disappearances and her endless housecleaning list, she had never crossed paths with him in the massive mansion during her short tenure as maid. And if she had, Clint's firm instructions were that she never speak to the child.

"Please send an officer to the house to search the basement and you'll find evidence of what Clint is doing to that little boy."

The receptionist promised to pass the message along, but Alice had no idea if anything had come of it. That phone call lingered in her mind days later as she and Greg sat on his sofa watching alongside millions of others a moment that would go down in history.

Neil Armstrong and Buzz Aldrin had just piloted the *Apollo 11* on its first successful moon landing. This was the first time Alice could finally think of something other than Julius, or Officer Fred's body rotting under Greg's barn. For the first time since she arrived here, she felt like maybe there could be a better future ahead. That anything might be possible. We had made it to the moon, after all!

A news break came on after the spaceflight footage. Alice was only halfheartedly listening when a familiar name crashed into the living room through their brand-new Zenith color tube television.

"John and Mary Dreyfuss were both found dead last night," the news reporter stated from in front of a charred Chrysler Newport that Alice recognized as theirs. "A rare engine defect caused an explosion in the vehicle, which left them trapped in the flames. While rescue attempts were made, the couple did not survive."

A terrible fear sunk into Alice. This was no engine defect. This was Clint Valance making a point. He had killed her best friend's parents—and the only family she had—in retaliation for her calling the police on him. There was nothing off-limits to him, no life he wouldn't destroy.

The worst part of it was that Alice knew then and there that she could never face Lea again. How she explain that she was the reason Lea was burying her folks? That her persistence in getting Julius back and taking Clint down resulted in John and Mary's horrifying deaths?

It was the hardest decision she had ever made, but that night Alice laid Julius to rest. Her son would become dead to her, because the cost was suddenly too great.

Chapter 28

Alice spilled the whole sordid story as Dr. Dreyfuss and I listened, transfixed. From the moment Dr. Greg Kildare welcomed Alice inside his home, treated her wounds, then helped her bury the cop's body and hide his Cadillac in the barn, they'd felt a spark. Somehow, being cohorts in crime led to romance, and it started their own version of a macabre happily ever after… until her best friend's parents were murdered, then the love of her life next.

"I couldn't risk putting anyone else in danger. So I stayed hidden. I shut off my heart. I stopped hoping." She wrapped her arms around herself, as if warding off a chill. "It wasn't easy playing dead, being hidden away from the world, but I had to."

A faint smile played across Alice's lips as she recalled her unexpected romance blooming amid such darkness. But when she spoke of Julius—the baby boy her life had revolved around, the son she'd never known—her voice grew distant and hollow, like wind howling through an empty house. Her fingers absently traced patterns on the tablecloth, as if trying to sketch out all the memories she'd missed.

"Why did you stay?" I asked.

"Greg and I had considered starting over in another state, but his career was here, and as long as we kept quiet we were safe… enough." Her words hung heavy with unspoken regret. "But there was another reason too."

"What, Alice?" Dr. Dreyfuss pressed.

"Revenge." Alice's pale eyes turned deep-ocean dark. "And hope that one day I'd be able to see Julius again."

I knew the feeling well. I had stayed in Bloodson Bay for similar reasons when I had given up one son for adoption and my other son was abducted. I was living proof that some tragedies found redemption.

"For years," Alice continued, "I would rock in my chair and imagine holding Julius. I still leave flowers at our home on 1 Crow's End Lane, praying he'll somehow find his way back there. But I don't feel him anymore in those things—the rocking chair, the house, the flowers. Instead, I only feel his absence. But if that's the closest way to touch him, then I'll keep leaning into the empty spaces where he should be, until my dying breath."

That explained the fresh flowers I'd noticed on the porch of the house.

"Oh, honey." Dr. Dreyfuss held her hand, and I was tempted to join them.

All this sentimental crap was starting to thaw my own callous heart.

"By the time I accepted that I would never get Julius back, I had already settled into a life here with Greg. We were happy." Alice's voice softened.

"What have you been doing all these years?" Dr. Dreyfuss asked.

"After Greg was killed, I filled my time planning my revenge. I found the perfect opportunity to come out of hiding. So I filled my hours volunteering at the nursing home where I stayed under the radar. The residents never asked too many questions about my past, and those that did wouldn't remember anything by the next day anyway. It was safer that way, for everyone involved."

"I'm sorry," I said.

"I'm not." Alice turned to me, her gaze chillingly void, her voice grim. "Life has a way of not giving you what you want, but in the end, I took what I needed."

I didn't understand what she meant by that. But the coldness in her expression showed a dark side of Alice Belvedere that made me believe she was capable of taking a life, just like she had taken the police officer's life all those years ago.

"My only regret is that I never tried reaching out to Julius or looking him up. I had chosen not to, partly from fear of what I'd find out about him." Alice's voice trailed off as Dr. Dreyfuss and I shared a glance. "Maybe I should just rip of the Band-Aid and get it over with."

Something frightened me about Alice, warning me to stop digging in her murky depths. I shifted in my seat, the details of what I knew about Ewan Valance pressing against my tongue. The words stuck in my throat until I pushed them through.

"I can tell you anything you want to know," I offered.

"You know what happened to my son?" Alice sat up straighter, and every bit of her body language told me she needed this closure.

"Your son, Julius—though he went by Ewan Valance—is in jail," I blurted out.

Her face crumpled like a discarded paper napkin. Her shoulders curved inward as if protecting her heart from another blow.

"Jail? For what?" Those three small words carried too much

heartbreak.

"Murder, kidnapping, drug trafficking…"

I stopped when I realized this could kill her. I recognized hope running empty. It was the same look I'd seen in my own mirror more times than I cared to count after my husband chose a life of crime over his own family. The empty ache was unfathomable.

"I failed my own son." Alice covered her face with her forearm, and her shoulders shook with sobs. We let her cry it out until her weeping turned to twisted laughter. "Funny how life works out."

I wasn't seeing the humor in any of this, but at least she was no longer sobbing.

"My son ended up a Valance through and through. Maybe that was inevitable. Just like it was inevitable where Clint ended up." I was about to ask where that was when she grabbed my hand and said, "You have no idea how much you both being here means to me."

A single tear traced down her cheek, but she made no move to wipe it away, as if letting it fall was an act of acceptance, of allowing herself to be cared for after so many years of standing alone.

"Any idea why someone would leave an article about your disappearance at a current crime scene of a woman who was killed a few months ago?" I asked, studying Alice for any flash of recognition.

"What was the woman's name?"

"Darla Pearson." I watched as she rolled the name around in her mind like a marble.

Alice shook her head. "No, I don't know anyone by that

name. I'm sorry I'm not of more help." Her hands fidgeted with the tablecloth hem, the same nervous habit I'd noticed from Dr. Dreyfuss. "I had hoped you could help me get justice for Greg. I know Clint was behind his death, but I have no proof. I need a confession."

After all these years, somebody had to stand up for what was right, but I had no idea how to help Alice with that. A little digging had already showed me Clint's current address was unlisted, and I doubted Ewan knew anything about his father's past sins. Not that Ewan would tell even if he did.

"The only way to do that is to find Clint," I said. "But he's unlisted."

"Oh, I already know where he is," Alice stated, like she was holding onto the last thread that would unravel everything. "But he'll never tell you. Trust me, I've tried. And it was a huge mistake."

There was apprehension in her voice that hadn't been there before, and it made me wonder what else she wasn't telling us.

"Then maybe we try a different tactic… together," I suggested.

"What if it doesn't work? What if I lost my son and my husband to that monster and never get justice?"

"Don't give up. I promise you, we'll help you put Clint in jail where he belongs."

Alice closed her eyes, and her sudden calm scared me. "Oh, honey, what I've already done to Clint is far worse than a jail cell."

Chapter 29

The miserable corridors of Happy Homes Assisted Living glinted with harsh fluorescent lights that accentuated every cheekbone and every wrinkle with a sickly pallor. There was nothing happy or homey about this place. It was like walking through a hospital, but instead of the beeping machines and antiseptic smell, we were treated to the faint scent of unwashed hair and stale popcorn from yesterday's bingo night.

My son, Benny, had once tried to force me into this very place, with its pale blue walls and bland tile floors, and the tour was just as depressing now as it was back then. The thought of Benny's misguided attempt to "take care" of me still got my goat. I'd rather eat a plate of rotten eggs than spend my golden years in this soulless institution. I shot Alice a sideways glance, wondering why we were visiting her workplace, but her expression remained a mystery.

Last night's gathering had left me with more uncertainty about Alice after she ushered us out the door, promising answers the next morning. So here we were, at Alice's request, assembling at a nursing home that seemed to have nothing to do with Darla Pearson's murder. I would rather have avoided this facility, given my son's attempt to pawn me off on Happy Homes, but if I hoped to uncover the truth, I had to play along.

And so Dr. Dreyfuss and I stood in the lobby while a wheelchaired patient who must have forgotten the Confederacy lost hummed "I Wish I Was in Dixie" at my hip, and a woman resembling a carcass wandered aimlessly behind me muttering about her roommate stealing her dentures. I was baffled over why we were asked to come and hoped this wasn't some eerie preview of my own destiny. The nurse at the front desk, whose name tag read *Sunshine* in un-sunshiny block letters, perked up when she saw Alice.

"I didn't realize you were on the schedule to volunteer today, Alice."

Her smile widened like the Mississippi, but it faltered for a split second, like she was trying to place Alice in a different context without her scrubs on.

"Not today, I'm afraid," Alice replied, her eyes crinkling at the corners. "I actually brought visitors this time."

Alice gestured to me and Dr. Dreyfuss, and I gave Sunshine a little wave.

"And who are you visiting today?" Sunshine asked, passing over a visitor sign-in sheet for us to fill out.

While scrawling my signature onto the sheet, I glanced over the other visitor entries, discretely looking for any name that might catch my eye. But nothing looked familiar.

"My buddy Clint," Alice chirped, and I nearly choked on my spit right then and there.

Her *buddy* Clint? Since when was her child's abductor her *buddy*?

Sunshine's face registered shock, but not quite the same caliber as mine. "Goodness. I'm not sure that's a good idea. Mr. Valance has been quite agitated this week after his last visitor."

"His last visitor?" Alice asked. "Who was that?"

"Oh, some young blonde who always forgets to sign the

book." Sunshine tapped the visitor log. "Pretty girl, though. Came a couple times to see him. Maybe a granddaughter? It's hard to tell these days when teenage girls look like middle-aged women, and middle-aged women act like teenagers."

Sunshine rolled her eyes at that, and I tended to agree after seeing what Tara let her daughter Nora get away with wearing. Though seeing as Nora was technically an adult, she had the right to dress like a hooker or a hobo—and rarely was there any in-between.

Directing her next words to me, Sunshine clarified, "You see, years ago Mr. Valance's son dropped him off and never once checked in on him afterward. Thank God for kindhearted Alice to keep him company!"

Yes, *kindhearted Alice*… I had a feeling nothing about Alice's visits were kind or from the heart. In fact, I wondered what scheme she was up to.

"Though honestly, it seems pointless to visit him," Sunshine continued, and I could tell she was a talker. "Clint is lost in his own world, convinced he's still in that fancy house where he lived decades ago. The other patients get so worked up when he starts ordering them around like servants, demanding they shine up the cutlery and such." A fond smile spread across her face as she let out a soft laugh. "He's certainly one of our more colorful residents."

"Maybe I can calm him down," Alice said, cutting Sunshine short.

"Are you sure you want to deal with him? You know how he gets…"

"*Absolutely*," Alice said.

But I didn't like the way the word slithered from Alice's

mouth.

"You know where to find him—in his room, as always," Sunshine said.

"Why are we here, Alice?" I demanded to know once we stepped out of Sunshine's earshot. "We already know Julius is Ewan, and Ewan's in jail. What's the point of talking to Clint *now*?"

"You asked how Clint is connected to that Darla woman's death. Well, let's see if he knows anything."

She made it sound pretty simple, but I was about to find out just how impossible a task it would prove to be. Nevertheless, I followed Alice down one hall, then another, all of them exact duplicates and all of them equally depressing until we arrived at Clint's room, which matched every other room in this wing. The walls and single dresser were a sparse, blank canvas, without a single personal keepsake anywhere. I would have felt bad for him if I didn't hate him so much.

In a cushioned chair by the window sat Clint Valance, the cloudy gray daylight highlighting a deep scar etched into the wrinkles of his cheek. His once-imposing frame, which had long ago commanded respect as Valance family patriarch, was stooped and frail like a willow tree battered by a hurricane. Those piercing eyes once rumored to make the ladies weak in the knees—though he wasn't my type—stared vacantly at the glass, a dull, milky film covering them like a thin layer of frost on a winter's night.

This was a far cry from the Clint Valance I'd heard tell of, the one who'd ruled Bloodson Bay with an iron fist and a silver tongue. Now he looked like a rumor of a man lost in the wind.

"Clint never leaves his room," Alice explained, rooting

through her purse. "He paid to upgrade it to a single so he doesn't have a roommate, and he sticks to himself. No one visits him either."

Except for some mysterious *granddaughter* who conveniently forgot to sign in, I thought. I couldn't say it was a cryin' shame that Clint's family had deserted him, because the curmudgeon deserved it.

Only now did Clint acknowledge us with a turn of his head.

"Tell the cook I want my eggs over easy today." His voice was thin and reedy, like an old radio losing its signal. "And I need my suit dry-cleaned right away."

Whatever period his brain was stuck in, he remembered Alice as his housekeeper. He probably thought it was still 1969. I sat uncomfortably on his creaky mattress, feeling like a spectator in this peculiar time-warped exchange.

"It's already taken care of, Mr. Valance, sir," Alice replied, her voice gentle but firm. "I brought a friend to meet you. She wanted to ask you something."

Alice gestured for me to take her place as she slid into the corner of the room, still rummaging in that massive purse of hers. What was she looking for, anyway? Because chances were, I probably had whatever she needed in my own handbag.

"If this concerns one of my court rulings, I'm afraid I have to maintain judicial secrecy," Clint said, glaring at me.

I hopped off the bed and stepped close to Clint, lowering myself to meet him face to face.

"No, this is regarding your son," I said, throwing Alice a sideways look for approval.

"I don't have any sons." And then Clint stubbornly crossed his arms and fell silent.

"This is what I mean." Alice's attempted whisper was loud enough to wake the dead—or the near-dead, I reconsidered, as a bone-thin woman shuffled past the door moaning. "For years, I've been dealing with this. Any time I ask questions, he won't say a word. I don't know what else to do to get him to talk. And believe me, I've tried *everything*."

I didn't dare ask what *everything* entailed.

Maybe Clint had blocked all recall of his sons. As a mother of boys, I could almost understand wanting to erase a few regretful memories. Like the time Benny pranked his fourth-grade teacher by putting a bullfrog in her desk, expecting it to jump out and scare her. The only problem was that she didn't open the drawer until days later, when the stink finally prompted her to discover its remains and Benny gave himself away by screaming, "It's about time!" Benny wasn't the sharpest needle in the knitting bag—he took after me.

Maybe Clint was playing dumb. I'd need to draw him out, outsmart him. And while I wasn't blessed with the gift of cleverness, I had Clint's dementia on my side.

"Ewan needs your help, Judge. You're the only one who can help him." I wondered how creative my story could get while still being believable, even to a senile man.

"Ewan's in trouble? What kind?"

"The woman kind," I stated simply.

Intrigue blossomed on Clint's face. "Who is the woman? I'll take care of her," he bellowed with enough force to make me flinch.

"Darla Pearson," I answered, then watched his reaction carefully.

His rheumy eyes narrowed with the kind of paternal

disapproval I'd seen plenty of times during my own childhood, though this felt different. Heavier somehow, loaded with decades of complicated history.

"Darla. Darla. Darla." He rolled the name around a few times. "You mean Darla Valance? I thought she was dead."

Chapter 30

Clint Valance already knew about Darla Pearson's murder. Except he didn't call her Darla Pearson, he called her Darla *Valance*. That was a plot twist I hadn't seen coming.

"You know about Darla's death?" I asked him.

"Of course," he answered as if we were chatting about the forecast, not murder. "But what's she got to do with Ewan? Darla was Marvin's wife. Or are you telling me that Ewan screwed around with his younger brother's wife?"

Clint was growing more agitated and confused by the second, and I didn't know how to realign his runaway thoughts, which were adding to my own confusion. We were fast becoming two mixed-up peas in a pod.

"No, nothing like that. Ewan is…" I had to think quickly, which wasn't my specialty.

"Ewan is being charged with Darla's murder," Dr. Dreyfuss came to my rescue with a believably fake worst-case scenario.

It was the first time she'd spoken since we arrived. I had almost forgotten she was here. Luckily, her lie worked. Clint was suddenly as talkative as a parrot on speed.

"No, Darla wasn't murdered. She died from an overdose," Clint blustered. "Well, she died and then was revived, and since then she's been dead to the family. Anything that happened to her had nothing to do with Ewan."

"I'm confused. So Darla *wasn't* killed?" I tried to keep up, but the story was circling out of control.

Clint grunted as if I was the one losing my marbles. "When they were married, Darla and Marvin partied too hard, she OD'd, then got revived, and I made Marvin divorce her and give her full custody of the kids if he wanted to stay in the family. So he did. And Darla and the kids have been dead to the family ever since. What's confusing about that?"

This opened up so many more questions, but I didn't know how much more lucidity I would get from Clint before he tapped out.

"Clint," I said slowly, "Darla was recently found dead—again. But this time murdered and left in a cellar. Do you know who might have done it?"

"A cellar, huh?" Clint stared off into space. "My wife hated when I used the cellar for punishment. I got so tired of Ewan crying like a little baby, but it made him a man, didn't it? It's how my father punished me, and look how good I turned out!"

I had no idea what Clint was talking about, but it wasn't about Darla anymore. From the corner of the room Alice darted toward him, her body visibly shaking as she hit the red record button on her phone.

"Clint, did you punish your children by locking them in the basement?"

"Of course I did. It was the only way to keep them in line. Some parents spank, other parents lock 'em in the cellar."

Alice's jaw clenched and her fists pumped, and I almost feared I'd have to hold her back from knocking Clint out.

"You know, I heard the pounding of tiny fists on the door, the cries for help when I worked for you. For so long I thought maybe I was going crazy, but it was true. You really tortured your own son—did you also do it to *my* son?"

"Well, they had it coming, just like Darla did. You wanna know who put Darla in a basement? It was probably Marvin practicing what he learned from me. And good riddance to her!" He jabbed a liver-spotted finger in the air for emphasis. "That woman was poison. None of the family trusted her, especially not me. No good ever came from her and Marvin's relationship—even their kids are money-grubbing trash."

He lingered on the word "trash," and his shoulders tensed beneath his pilled cardigan, as if the mere thought of family— or his warped view of it—was a physical burden pressing down on him. The irony of him rejecting them wasn't lost on me, considering they seemed to disown him back. Misery bred misery, and hatred groomed hatred.

A thread of a detail hung loose, something Sunshine the receptionist had mentioned. If Marvin and Darla had a daughter, maybe she was the girl who had recently visited Clint.

"Do you speak to any of those grandkids?"

Clint closed his eyes, wincing as if mere thinking hurt. It was taking too long for an answer, and I had a sinking sensation I had lost him.

"Clint?" I tapped him on the shoulder, startling him.

"Huh?"

"Do you ever see Marvin's kids?" I tried again.

"I have no use for them," he grumbled. "Darla getting pregnant is the whole reason Marvin is flunking college right now! He keeps saying he's going to start a rock band. The next 'Utopia.'"

"You mean Nirvana?" I guessed.

"I don't care what they're called. They look like bums, and no son of mine will play in some no-name rock band."

Oh, great. Clint's mind had somehow found its way to the early 1990s. It looked like any useful interrogation was over.

"Speaking of Marvin, when you see him, give him this for me." Clint passed me a ceramic mug with MJV painted across it in crooked letters from tremoring hands.

"What's this?" I asked.

"I made it in pottery class. You hear that—pottery! That's what I resort to doing these days. They treat us like kindergarteners here."

"What's the MJV stand for?" Dr. Dreyfuss wondered aloud, looking over my shoulder.

"She should know." Clint pointed to Alice, who returned to the corner, suspiciously hiding something behind her back. "She's his mother, after all. MJV stands for Marvin Julius Valance."

Hell's bells, Clint just confirmed Julius was Marvin—the younger son! And Marvin was… well, I didn't want to tell Alice what I knew about him, as her eyes now lit up with hope as bright as fireflies.

She dropped her purse to the floor and rushed to Clint's side. "Where can I reach Marvin? I'd love to speak with him and tell him about me. I'm sure he's got questions…"

I hesitated, not wanting to speak ill of her son, but the truth was that Marvin had been a crook, drug dealer, and killer. He was the one who kidnapped Emory and chained her in Bloodson Manor's cellar—just like his father had done to him. Marvin was the epitome of evil. But did Alice really deserve to know the truth? I feared it might break her heart… or worse.

"Alice, Marvin is… dead," I began, uncertain how to explain the long, sordid story of how Ewan had plotted his murder. It was very Cain-and-Abel—if Abel was also evil, like his brother.

"He's… gone? So I'll never get to know my son?" Alice mumbled as Dr. Dreyfuss glided to her side and tucked Alice under her arm. "What happened to Julius… I mean Marvin?"

I decided to go with short and simple. "He got caught up in the, uh, family business."

"How so?" Alice pressed, and I hated what I had to do next, but she needed closure, and the truth would at least give her that.

"He was a drug dealer and a murderer, I'm sorry to say. You're better off not knowing who he turned out to be."

Alice didn't know this about me, but I had personal experience missing out on my child's entire life—two sons, in fact, though one I had surrendered for adoption and one was taken from me. I intimately knew the ache of years spent wondering who my boys had grown up to be until our recent reunion. But finding out your son was an evil good-for-nothin' who ended up murdered by his brother was a whole new level of pain I couldn't imagine and didn't want to cause for someone who had already suffered plenty.

"I wish I could tell you something better about your son," I added.

"Well, it makes me feel okay about what I did, I guess," Alice said cryptically.

"What do you mean?" Dr. Dreyfuss asked. "What did you do?"

"Nothing. Don't worry about it. Are we done here?"

I couldn't reunite Alice with her son, but I could still help

Tara. If I could figure out why Darla's body ended up in Bloodson Manor, I had a feeling it would lead me to the person who poisoned Tara.

Piecing together what I knew, a history began to form. Marvin and Darla were married with kids—probably sometime in the early 1990s, if my Nirvana math was correct. Marvin would have been in his mid-twenties back then, according to when Clint's mind was trapped. Which would put the grandkids in the thirty-something ballpark right now. And Sunshine had mentioned a *"blonde"* visiting him. So my suspect list was narrowed down to a thirty-something blonde female. Easy peasy.

"Where's my eggs?" Clint barked.

We'd clearly exhausted whatever strength remained in him when he snapped at us to get him food or get out. Alice and Dr. Dreyfuss offered to chase down a phantom nurse, since it seemed like no one paid any heed to any of the residents. At least this gave me a chance to take a peek in Alice's purse.

While lurking in the corner, she had been hiding something, and I could sniff out a secret like a bloodhound. I knelt and opened her purse. Sitting on top was a bottle labeled sodium pentothal, prescribed by Dr. Gregory Kildare himself ironically right around the time he died. I wasn't sure how a dead man could write a prescription, but I was about to find out.

A quick internet search listed it as truth serum. Alice had been dosing Clint to get him to confess his crimes. That must have been why she recorded it. While it wasn't exactly scandalous, it was certainly illegal for her to forge a script in order to manipulate his confession.

When a prickle ran up my neck, I turned around to find a

pair of legs blocking my view. My eyes trailed upward to find Clint standing over me. I couldn't tell what he was thinking behind that gauzy gaze.

"What's that you've found?"

I quickly dropped the truth serum back inside and snapped the purse shut. "Makeup," I lied.

He stared at me and his lips slowly lifted to something resembling a smile. The scar gnarled the patch of skin on his cheek. I grinned back innocently.

I seemed to convince him, because he turned slowly and shuffled back to his chair against the window. What did men know about makeup anyway? I decided then and there to keep Alice's secret for her. It was the least I could do after everything this monster had done to her.

By the time Alice and Dr. Dreyfuss returned empty-handed, a terrible stench permeated the room. Alice looked at Dr. Dreyfuss, who looked at me, and I shrugged since I sure as heck didn't cause the smell. Then leaning forward ever so slightly, Clint stared directly at Alice and smirked. The old man had crapped in his adult diaper, and it sure seemed like he'd done it on purpose.

"Cleanup in Aisle 6," I muttered. "I'll get the nurse."

"No!" Spit clung to Clint's quivering bottom lip as he spoke at Alice. "I want *you* to clean me up." As Alice stood shell-shocked, I overheard his whisper intended for her ears only: "I've known about your plan, trying to get me to confess to Greg's *tragic death*. Don't be a fool, Alice. I'm untouchable."

Alice gasped. Clint knew about the truth serum. And he was taking great pleasure in this disgusting form of punishment.

"We'll send a nurse in anyway!" Dr. Dreyfuss said,

grabbing my arm and leading me out of the room.

I left with a sick feeling that Clint was more aware—and more malicious—than I thought. Everything he had told us was now cast in doubt—because Clint had fooled us all.

Chapter 31

I strutted into Tara's hospital room carrying my latest creation: a bedazzled baby mobile featuring miniature disco balls and lights that played "Stayin' Alive." A fitting song for a woman who had survived poisoning, in my opinion.

"Sugar, your little one needs to come into this world with style!" I held up my masterpiece.

Tara's eyes widened, but I couldn't tell if she was impressed or horrified. When it came to me, Tara's expressions often meant both at the same time.

"Ging, that's… something else."

I was about to launch into details about my visit with Clint Valance when the doctor breezed in, flipping through Tara's chart.

"Well, Mrs. Christie, your bloodwork shows the antifreeze has cleared from your system. You and the baby are free to go home, but please be vigilant about what you consume. This could have been devastating. Luckily your friend here," he gestured to me, "got you to the hospital so quickly."

"That *Dukes of Hazard* driving was a one-time thing," I said. "No more emergencies better happen again!"

After the doctor left, Tara sank back into bed, protectively holding her newborn. With her disheveled hair sticking to her pale face, the poor girl needed a shower something bad, smelling as fresh as week-old potato salad left out in the North

Carolina sun. Though, giving birth was enough to make anyone look like they've been dragged backward through a hedge. I never trusted post-birth pictures on social media where the mother looked as made-up as a beauty pageant queen at an acceptance speech.

"I'm terrified whoever is after me will make another attempt on my life—or the baby's. How can I trust anything I eat or drink anymore?" Tara's gaze never left the bundle in her arms, but I could read her worry like a roadmap.

I reached out and took her hand, giving it a reassuring squeeze. "I'll figure this out. I promise I'll get to the bottom of it."

"Ging, you've done enough. Chris and Detective Hughes are working on it. I have filed a police report already and Chris is down at the station right now. They're looking into a connection between Mikhail's lawsuit and Darla's murder and my poisoning." Tara grinned weakly at me. "You can let go."

"You're my daughter-in-law, Tara. You should know better."

It wasn't in my nature to let go. When I got hold of something, my grip was relentless. It applied to almost every area of my life: when my home was under threat of being taken; when my husband tried to leave me; when I lost my boys… no matter how strong the pull against me, I never let go. And now clues to a murder investigation involving my best friend were dropping in my lap left and right. No way was I giving up on solving this.

Grabbing Tara's overnight bag, I ambled around her hospital room collecting her things. While folding the half-finished, asymmetrical, crabapple red baby blanket I had attempted to knit, I was reminded of Mayor Rose Crabtree.

The town council's agenda was adamant about forcing Tara and Chris out, and the timing sure seemed awfully convenient. I'd lived in Bloodson Bay long enough to know these small-town politicians were like greased pigs at a county fair: slippery and messy. Those councilmembers, sitting up there on their high horses, had some developer whispering sweet nothings into their ears about turning our town into another money-making, soulless tourist trap. I couldn't sit by and watch it happen.

It was dark by the time the hospital discharged Tara. I dropped her off at home with orders to rest and eat the innovative spaghetti casserole I threw together after I realized lasagna required sheet pasta and cheese, which I didn't have. I had one more place to go before calling it a night. But when I arrived there, the driveway was empty and the Christmas lights were off. Since no one looked home, there was only one other place I knew to look.

The Bloodson Bay Town Hall parking lot was empty except for Rose Crabtree's custom canary-yellow Bentley SUV that I wondered how she afforded on a humble mayor's salary. With no one else here, I'd have Rose all to myself without having to fight off her girl gang, too.

I stomped into Rose's office with righteous indignation and found her preening behind her glossy mahogany desk like she owned the whole dang town. Her salt-and-pepper hair was hairsprayed into a perfectly round helmet that only politicians and 1960's housewives could achieve.

"Ginger Mallowan," Rose seethed as she slammed her pen down on the desk and drummed her fingernails.

Tap-tap-tap-tap. Tap-tap-tap-tap.

"Rose Crabtree," I retorted, though I desperately wanted to quote Pee-wee Herman and say, *"That's my name, don't wear it out,"* because I knew it would leave her flabbergasted.

"What brings you to my door, Ginger?"

Tap-tap-tap-tap.

"Tara Christie is why I'm here. I want you to leave her family alone." Planting my hands on the desk, the stack of papers beneath my palms slipped off the waxy surface and scattered all over the floor. "Oops."

I hadn't intended to do that, but it felt good.

Rose's face twisted like she'd just bitten into a green persimmon. "Absolutely not. The Christie family is a danger to our town. They should relocate to where it's acceptable to impale kids and let drug dealers take over their houses."

"Tara didn't know that was happening."

"Exactly," Rose agreed. *Tap-tap-tap-tap.* "Darla and her son Brock were selling drugs to kids right under Tara's nose. Those 'Curse Day Parties' the kids hosted every year were drug orgies hosted in Bloodson Manor!"

Orgies? I hadn't heard anything about that! I wondered if Rose even knew what one was. But I had a more pressing question.

"And how exactly do you know Darla was dealing drugs?"

Rose's manicured *tap-tap-tap-tapping* suddenly stopped.

"Because my daughter almost died from what that woman sold her!" The words exploded from Rose's mouth, her face flushing an angry red that clashed with her Christmas-green blazer.

"Well butter my biscuit, it sounds like you had a reason to want Darla dead. I think they call that *motive*," I drawled, watching her reaction carefully.

Sometimes you have to poke real hard to see what falls out of the tree.

"How dare you accuse me of murder!" Rose leapt up and lunged at me, her chair screeching against the floor and falling sideways.

Now, I may be getting on in years, but I still remember how to throw a punch from my roller derby days. Back when I was a Dixie Devil, they called me the Ginger Menace. I left more than a few ladies crying in the rink.

I'd never forget when the renowned Blonde Bomber Joan Weston knocked me on my rear in the 1968 Roller Games. I had never been prouder. That woman had an arm like a freight train and the determination of a bull seeing red.

I spent three days nursing that bruise, showing it off to anyone who'd look. It was prettier than a sunset, all purple and yellow. Those were the days when we didn't wear all that fancy protective gear, just our skates and our gumption. And believe me, I had gumption by the bucket load.

I put that gumption on full display with Rose Crabtree as we tussled, knocking over her filing cabinet and sending papers flying everywhere like confetti. I got a shiner that would have my bridge club gossiping for weeks, but Rose's nose would never be the same after meeting my right hook.

One last shove sent Rose flying as she slip-slided across the papers on the floor, her arms windmilling as she went down. Served her right. Nobody came at the Ginger Menace without getting a taste of Southern hospitality, roller derby style.

"You'll be hearing from my lawyer!" Rose shouted as she pointed me to the door, her nose already swelling up like a summer peach gone bad. But that woman must have had hairspray harder than granite, because not a hair was out of place.

I sat in my car parked out of sight for over an hour, nursing my throbbing hand until Rose left, but I noticed she didn't turn out of the parking lot toward her house. Instead, she headed in the direction of town. My Spidey-sense told me to follow. Then the oddest thing happened. It didn't make sense. Rose Crabtree pulled up to Sloane's empty office.

She was anything but subtle in her bright yellow SUV and matching fur coat. The building was dark as molasses, but Rose let herself right in. A moment later, a flashlight beam danced inside, bouncing off the windows like fireflies in July. Then another flashlight joined the first. Two flashlights meant two people, but I hadn't seen another person enter with Rose… which meant the other person had snuck in before I arrived.

I ducked low in the seat of my car when two figures slipped out. When one turned to the other, I caught a glimpse of their faces in the streetlight. The first was Rose Crabtree as expected, but her companion made me scrabble further down in my seat. When my elbow bumped the horn, both of them swung around toward the noise.

I held my breath, begging my arthritis to have mercy on my scrunched legs that had done more kneeling today than a prostitute at confession. Finally, they turned away from me, giving me time to grab my phone. My fingers jabbed at letters across the screen, warning Sloane before it was too late:

You're in danger!

But then a little red exclamation point flagged the message: *Unable to send*. This required a face-to-face conversation, so I headed straight to Sloane's house.

Part 3
Sloane Apara

Chapter 32

Winter became a bully this year. Harsh. Cruel. And relentless. Nothing like its kinder, cooler predecessor Autumn, who draped the world in colorful foliage and invited us outside with sweater weather and campfires. Even Summer had the courtesy of making amends for its brutal heat by offering beach days and firefly nights. But not Winter. Oh no, he was a brute.

The roads were already precarious enough with the slush, until I passed a car that looked a lot like Ginger's swerving all over the road. A weather advisory had ordered residents to stay home, except in cases of emergency. I wasn't sure this would qualify, but it was too late now.

A black pool of ice formed outside the Feel the Noize Party Planning office, creating a slick patch. This was the second time something had tripped the alarm in the past week, and I was determined to get to the bottom of it.

I stepped carefully from the warmth of my car into the crisp winter air. The darkness outside mirrored the growing unease within me, that familiar tension creeping up my spine like a spider.

My stilettos lost traction for a worrisome moment against the frozen pavement as I navigated to the door. Here in the South, we didn't get much practice maneuvering "weather." My mother, who'd grown up in Nigeria, could barely tolerate a chilly breeze.

I caught my balance with a practiced grace that came from years of walking in heels designed for looks, not comfort, at luxury events. I couldn't help but roll my eyes at my own stubbornness. Any sensible person would have worn boots, but image was everything in my line of work—even at this ungodly hour when the only witness to my fashion choice was a woman in a flashy yellow fur coat turning the corner, and a homeless man pacing the sidewalk.

I fished out a $20 bill from my purse and handed it to him, and he thanked me with what I guessed was "have a blessed day," but I couldn't clearly read his lips behind his unruly beard.

After entering my office building, I reset the alarm, my hands already numb despite my designer leather gloves. As I stepped into the deserted corridor, I caught my reflection in the darkened windows—a tall, elegant figure wrapped in a wool coat that had seemed like overkill when I bought it last month but now felt completely justified.

A buzz vibrated against my thigh. My phone glowed with a new email alert, illuminating the main office and casting angular shapes on the walls. I slid my finger across the screen, surprised at the sight of Mayor Rose Crabtree's name in my inbox. That woman had been blowing up my notifications lately, and nothing good ever came from her midnight messages.

I clicked on the email, my jaw tightening as I spotted the snobbish tone not very well-hidden in each perfectly punctuated sentence:

Dear Sloane:

Your contract for the town's Christmas holiday celebration has been terminated. Your association with Tara Christie is to blame for this recent development. Furthermore, I will be taking steps to ensure you are not hired to plan any future gatherings in our community. No hard feelings!
Sincerely,
Mayor Rose Crabtree

No hard feelings? Sterling had already spent countless hours planning and purchasing for the winter-wonderland-themed Christmas party that was mere days away. Now Rose Crabtree had the audacity to cancel it and threaten to blacklist me due to my choice of friends?

No, I think not.

In Nigeria, we had a saying: "It's not fishing if you don't have a net; it's simply bathing." Rose Crabtree *thought* she had power, but she was just a bobblehead who nodded at the townspeople's whims—but the townspeople loved me.

We also had another Nigerian proverb: "A disobedient fowl learns obedience in a cooking pot." Rose was a rebellious bird that was about to get a life lesson in humility.

After years of building my reputation as the go-to event planner for the elite, Rose Crabtree thought she could destroy my business with a few pointed words and veiled threats. She was mistaken. I had battled spinal meningitis that had left me Deaf as a child. I'd faced my father's killer, and in Nigeria I once used my attacker as a human shield from his detonated bomb.

Certainly Rose Crabtree, with her discount department store

suits and desperate grasp at small-town power, was no threat to me. She was about to learn what happened when you crossed someone who had survived far worse than petty council politics.

The floor trembled. The rhythmic vibration of footsteps alerted me to a presence. Someone was here. Most likely whoever had tripped the alarm.

I felt it again, the light tread of movement. Deafness had made me extra attuned to my other senses, and they rarely let me down. I whipped around at the sensation of someone behind me. No one was there, that I could see.

Searching my desk for something I could use as a weapon, I grabbed the closest object that could do some damage: a stapler. Holding it over my head, I crept toward the entrance and hid behind the wall, every nerve in my body pulsing. When the figure passed over the threshold, I swung the stapler down—

And stopped right before impact.

My assistant Sterling Jones's platinum blonde head merrily bobbed inside. Apparently she hadn't seen me behind the partition as she bustled to her desk, removing her coat and tossing it on her chair. I approached her from behind. When I rested my hand on her shoulder, she jumped and screamed, whipping around in circles until she saw me and keeled over, hands cupping her face.

"Oh my gosh, Sloane, you scared me to death!" By the exaggeration of her mouth movements I could tell she was yelling while signing at the same time.

"Sorry," I signed. "But you scared me first. What are you doing here so late?"

Sterling stood awkwardly silent as she conjured words that wouldn't come. I wondered what she was hiding. Her skittishness made me uneasy. Finally she seemed to come up with an answer.

"The mayor emailed me cancelling the town Christmas party, so I wanted to check the copy of the contract to see if we had any recourse," she signed with an exaggerated frown.

This was not part of Sterling's job description, so I wasn't sure what made her think she should get involved.

"Yes, I'm aware. I'll deal with it. You can go home."

"Is there anything I can do to help?" she offered a little forcefully.

"No, I'll take care of it." I returned the stapler to my desk, but something nagged at the edge of my awareness. Something was missing. From my desk? I couldn't quite place what it was.

Just as Sterling shrugged on her coat, a teenage version of her suddenly appeared and plopped onto the sofa next to an expresso bar I relied on during late-night work sessions. Her hair matched her mother's platinum blond identically. Even their facial features were remarkably similar.

"You have a daughter?" I signed point-blank.

But Sterling wasn't looking at me. "I told you to wait in the car," I read on her lips, each word exaggerated with rising irritation.

"I was tired of waiting," the girl replied. "And I got cold."

"Who is this?" I instantly knew my question added to the rising tension, but I couldn't shake the feeling that I was missing something crucial about this odd mother-daughter standoff.

"This is Charity," Sterling explained, her neck splotched with pink.

"I didn't know you had children."

We'd talked about kids only once. Sterling had asked me

why I wasn't married and if I ever wanted children. I told her in confidence about my deceased ex-husband Benny and how we had tried for years to get pregnant. Infertility was the first hurdle, and then miscarriage after miscarriage. Eventually, I gave up.

My business became the baby I put my everything into. Sometimes I still thought about motherhood, but I saw how tough solo parenting had been for my mother. I didn't think I was strong enough for that.

"My *mother* apparently forgets she has a child, too." Charity mouthed the word *mother* like it burned her, then crossed her arms. "She only remembers me when she needs me. Like when she had me keep tabs on your friend in Wilmington—"

What was Charity talking about? I had only asked Sterling to pick Tara up in Wilmington for me, not to *keep tabs on her*. Maybe something had gotten lost in translation.

"Enough!" Sterling's glare silenced the girl. "Charity now lives at Loving Arms Children's Home. I should have been upfront with you, Sloane, but I worried you'd judge me for not being able to raise her myself. That's the reason I'm here in Bloodson Bay—to try to get custody."

"There is nothing shameful about fighting for rights to your child, Sterling," I signed.

Then I grabbed my dry erase board that I used for new clients and sat down next to her. I wrote on it, *I'm Sloane, and I'm Deaf. What is your name?*

The girl finger-spelled in response: "C-h-a-r-i-t-y."

I grinned, finding myself pleasantly surprised by her knowledge of the ASL alphabet. I signed back, slowly so she could keep up, while speaking each word: "Wonderful to meet you, Charity. How did you learn to sign?"

"They teach a class at the children's home. I only know the basics, but I want to learn more," she enunciated.

"I can teach you if you'd like," I offered before thinking it through. "If your mother is okay with it."

I glanced at Sterling, who shrugged.

"Yes," Charity agreed with a simple nod of her fist. "I'd like that."

"I'll give you a sign name. Only Deaf people can bestow those." Examining her, I wanted the perfect sign to capture who this girl was… or maybe who she wanted to be. I formed a C that transformed into a giving motion. "This represents you being a gift to those around you."

It was either the exact wrong thing to say, or the right thing to say, because a tear slid down her cheek a moment later.

"Thank you," was all Charity signed before Sterling dragged her up off the couch and out the door.

When I returned to my desk feeling encouraged by the first teenager I actually liked, the high quickly faded. I realized what was missing. My breath caught as I searched for my laptop containing all my files, including confidential client information and upcoming event details. That computer held everything, from the intricate plans for next month's celebrity beach wedding to the detailed proposals for three Fortune 500 company galas.

And it was gone.

There was only one other person who had a key to my office, with access to my laptop. And she appeared in the doorway, pulling something out of her pocket and staring at me with a look that could kill.

Chapter 33

Sterling appeared in the doorway just as my phone blushed to life on my desk, then vibrated its way to the edge. I warily caught it before it fell and saw part of a text from Ginger on the home screen:

You're in danger!

Another text popped up immediately after, and I swiped to open my phone, keeping Sterling in view while reading:

Your assistant is working with Mayor Crabtree. I caught them sneaking around your office. Don't trust her. Watch your back!

Then one more text, from Ginger again:

I'm at your house. Where are you?

Sterling watched me watching her, both of us unmoving except for the twitch of her arm. She was holding something, but I couldn't see what. If she was trying to intimidate me, it wouldn't work. Bristling with pissed-off-ness, I stalked toward her, my hands talking for me with controlled fury.

"You took my computer, didn't you?" I had trusted her, given her a second chance when no one else would, and this was how she repaid me? "And I know you're working with Rose Crabtree. What are you both up to?"

"I... I can explain."

Caught off-guard, Sterling stumbled backward, her spine hitting the wall behind her with a dull thud that quaked the floor. Sterling's face had paled to corpse white, making her hair seem almost yellow in comparison, and a faint sheen of sweat beaded on her upper lip.

She glanced at the exit like a cornered animal searching for escape, her perpetually nervous energy now cranked up to eleven. Then her chin dropped to her chest. Her gaze fixated on the floor. No, not the floor. Her *hand*. She gripped something, but her sleeve covered it.

Her body shook, perspiration streaking down her temples, and a moment too late I saw why. A knife whizzed across my chest, grazing and snagging my top. I was lucky; it was just a small pocket knife. Easy to jab at someone within arm's reach, and easy to dodge if you're quick enough.

I was, but barely.

I put my hands up in surrender and created some distance between us. The irony was unsettling. My timid assistant had somehow found the courage to steal from me and now was trying to attack me.

"Sterling, I've been nothing but good to you. I gave you a job, despite your background. I've kept your secret all this time. What's this about?"

My arms weakened with the force of my emotions. When I'd hired her, I had vowed to keep her past private. Now, we both knew that the moment I got away—*if* I got away—I would go straight to the police, and I would not be as forgiving as her previous employer. Sterling's face remained blank, her shoulders rigid. The stillness stretched between us like a rubber band ready to snap.

"I appreciate all you've done for me," Sterling spoke while jabbing the knife out in front of her. Each movement was jerky and uncertain like a puppet on tangled strings. "But history has a way of repeating itself. I'm sorry, Sloane."

Her chin lifted, a sad smile playing at the corners of her mouth—the kind of smirk that spoke of inevitable doom. Then both of her hands cupped the knife's handle, her arms swaying back and forth like she was conducting a funeral march.

Her eyes met mine, cold and unfamiliar. "You never should have trusted me."

Then she lunged at me.

Chapter 34

Did I mention that I once dodged a bomb by using the bomber as a human shield? Well, my knack for survival didn't happen by chance. It happened because of a lifetime of careful observation and heightened awareness. And right now I was aware of a deadly threat that took the form of a skinny, platinum blonde swinging a pocket knife at me.

Pivoting to the right, I spun out of Sterling's reach, ending up on the other side of her arm. She was too frenzied to react. Jabbing the knife in my direction, she missed again as I side-stepped her aim.

She might be fire, but I was smoke drifting around her.

I positioned myself behind her. Yanking on her arm, I held it behind her back and twisted, until she dropped the knife. But she was stronger than I expected and rammed her full weight backward, smashing me against the wall. I released my hold on her, clenching empty air as she bolted out the exit. I charged after her, my thin heels wobbling in the cracks of concrete as I burst onto the sidewalk.

Sterling sprinted ahead, her hair whipping in the wind. The beat-up car she had arrived in idled at the curb, puffs of exhaust pouring from where a muffler should have been. Sterling yanked open the driver's side door and dove inside. The lock clicked down as I reached the passenger door and tried the handle, then slammed my palm against the window, the impact stinging my skin with each hit.

Through the glass, Sterling's face was a pale oval. I expected to find Charity inside, but the other seats were empty. Then the car peeled away from the curb, leaving me in a cloud of exhaust fumes.

When I returned to my office, my heart was a frantic, trapped bird. Charity's previous spot on the waiting room couch cushion still held the indent of her small form. I had no idea if the children's home knew she had been with Sterling, or where Charity would have gone now. The thought of that troubled child alone with my mentally unstable assistant made my stomach churn.

I didn't know who to contact, or how. Being Deaf made communication like jumping through flaming hoops if the personnel you were trying to reach didn't accept sign-interpreter calls or texts, which was common in this backward little town. It would have been easier to get a Nigerian prince to show up than to get an interpreter for the town hall meetings. And yes, in case you were wondering, there were, in fact, real-life Nigerian princes.

I figured the police would be the easiest way to locate Charity, but the Bloodson Bay Police Department didn't have a video relay service that gave emergency access to Deaf callers. After a lawsuit threat from yours truly (and believe me, I can be quite persuasive when needed), they had finally updated their service to accept emergency texts. Small victories in a hearing world, I suppose, though right now that triumph felt hollow with a child's safety at stake and the night growing colder.

Then Deputy Joe Speers came to mind. He had signed to me

when he and Detective Hughes had first come to Bloodson Manor. But I didn't have his personal contact information, and I didn't even know if he was on duty tonight.

I opened a text to 9-1-1, hoping I could convey the problem easily, though explaining emergencies through text felt like trying to suck a Debbie's Diner extra-thick malt shake through a straw. As any milkshake aficionado knew, Debbie's shakes required a spoon.

As I typed my message, I fought the urge to add multiple exclamation points, which would only make the cops assume I was hysterical. I ended up with a simple, urgent explanation:

I am Deaf and I came across a child named Charity Jones from the children's home that ran away. She could be in a dangerous situation. I need help finding her. If Deputy Speers is on duty, please send him to this address, or any other officer who knows sign language.

I was about to send my office location, then thought better of it. Would Charity return to the children's home? Probably not. Where else could she go, now that Sterling seemed to have left her behind? And more importantly, how would Charity survive the cold tonight? Foster kids tended to be street smart, so Charity likely would have returned to someplace familiar. One location came to mind.

I found Sterling's home address in my phone contacts and had to double-check to be sure it was the right place. It was a gamble, but it was all I had. So I texted the exact location to the BBPD, grateful that at least GPS coordinates couldn't get lost in translation like so many other things in my daily interactions with the hearing world.

The text screen remained stubbornly blank, no reassuring dots to indicate an incoming message. My leg bounced with nervous energy as I stared at the phone, willing it to light up with a response. When none came, I remembered that this part of town was an internet dead zone.

Deep down I already knew I was too late. My gut instinct, which had guided me through countless business deals and social catastrophes, screamed with the same certainty that told me when a client was about to make an unreasonable demand: Charity was long gone.

A moment later, a text bubble popped up on my phone, the screen's vibration making my hand tingle. A deputy would be dispatched to the address listed to take a statement—another tedious interaction where I'd need my tablet to communicate. In the meantime, I needed to find out what Sterling had been up to. I had about five minutes before I should head out.

That woman had been acting strange from day one, with her perpetual deer-in-headlights expression and those vague, noncommittal responses to even the simplest questions. My ability to read people's mannerisms had sent up red flags about her. After my marriage imploded due to my scheming ex-husband, I learned to always trust my instincts.

That was why I had a backup laptop hidden in a false bottom of my filing cabinet, a precaution no one but me knew about. My ex-husband had made me paranoid. Sometimes, like now, my paranoia paid off.

After opening the computer up and powering it on, I navigated straight to the contract I had put Sterling in charge of:

the town Christmas festival contract with Rose Crabtree. Unrecognizable charges filled my monitor. Numbers jumped out at me, each one more damning than the last.

The catering budget was inflated by thousands. The decorations, the entertainment—all of it marked up beyond reason. The total discrepancy: $867,539. More than $800,000 was unbudgeted for.

My hands trembled as I logged into my bank account. The absolute worst possible scenario flashed on-screen before me. The business account had been drained. Only a couple hundred dollars remained in my balance. Almost every penny gone, along with my laptop containing my entire client database, contracts, everything I'd built over years. A decade of meticulous planning, of transforming lavish dreams into Instagram-worthy realities, wiped away like footprints in the sand.

I'd made my fortune helping others create perfect moments, and now my own world was crumbling in the most imperfect way possible. Sterling's threat echoed in my head: *History has a way of repeating itself.*

The secret I had kept for her—a stint in jail for felony theft when she'd stolen from a law firm she had worked at—had cost Sterling her career, her daughter, and her freedom. She had gotten released due to a legal technicality when the firm dropped the charges, but now she'd committed fraud again—and this time, I was the victim. She'd hurt the only person willing to cut her a break.

I leaned back in my chair, an elusive thought taking shape. Sterling had no idea who she was dealing with. I had clawed my way up from nothing, built a social media empire, and survived countless attempts to tear my success apart. I wasn't used to backing down when things got complicated.

She thought she had me cornered? Please. I'd orchestrated events for billionaires and royalty, managing crisis after crisis with a smile on my face. One woman with sticky fingers wasn't about to be my undoing. It was time to show Sterling Jones how wrong she was.

I considered my next move. In my world, revenge was best served with a filter and the right lighting. But life had taught me that sometimes, it meant getting a little blood on my hands.

Chapter 35

No one with any dignity or hygienic requirements stayed at the So-So Southern Motel, a pay-per-month rundown excuse for shelter. Not unless they were okay with live-in bed bugs and the fragrance of black mold. But when I plugged in the street address Sterling had listed on her job application, that's where GPS took me. The motel screamed "on the run" rather than "sticking around for my daughter." So much for fighting to get her parental rights back.

The glow from the parking lot security light was like a lighthouse standing guard, casting its steady beam to guide late-night wanderers through the sea of darkness. A rusty HVAC unit droned next to the front office, the vibration across the broken pavement ominous, like a mechanical predator humming a discordant tune.

A $50 bill convinced the unfortunate motel owner, Mr. Soren Sosa—hence the motel's ironic name—to tell me "the pretty blonde girl's" room number, because he had never gotten her name when she first checked in. But he refused to hand over her room key.

"I can't just hand you her key. It's motel policy—for customer confidentiality reasons," he justified. "But she's usually there."

His clientele tended to pay with cash and preferred the

anonymity that only lodging like the So-So Southern Motel could offer. God forbid he tarnish that reputation.

He shuffled along the narrow veranda leading me to Room 13, his frame stooped with age. We arrived at her door and knocked. While we waited, I scribbled my questions:

"How long has she been living here?" I wrote.

"Been here since September, which surprised me. Most of our guests don't stay that long," he answered.

"Did you see her tonight?"

"Nope."

"What about anything suspicious?"

"Nah." His one-word answers reminded me of a gnome guarding his small domain. "Wait a minute." He held up a gnarled finger. "A woman I've never seen before came by just a bit ago and then left in a hurry."

I flipped my notebook page over and scrawled: "Did you get a look at her?"

He gave a jerky bob of his head and took my pen, his fingers surprisingly strong despite a tremor. He drew what looked like a child's stick figure, all spindly limbs and a circular head. I had to press my lips together to keep from laughing. Unfortunately, this was going nowhere fast.

"Any specifics?" I added a pointed underline for emphasis. "Hair color? Eyes? Height?"

"I'd say medium height and normal eyes. I don't know if she had hair."

"I don't understand. Was she bald?" I pressed, frustrated that our language barrier was making this Q&A session nearly impossible.

"She wore a sweatshirt hood over her head, but her face

kinda looked like the Room 13 gal," he said.

A sweatshirt. Something a teenager would wear. It sounded like Charity had been here.

"Did you see where she went after she left?"

He nodded confidently. "A car—nice one, too."

I figured I'd gotten as much as I was going to get. Getting details was like trying to grasp fog. Mr. Sosa wandered back to his office and I turned to leave when something caught my eye—Sterling's car sat nestled between a beat-up pickup truck and a minivan with a bumper sticker that proclaimed *I <3 My Grandkids.* At this late hour, unless she'd taken an Uber or sprouted wings, she had to still be here.

My knuckles were raw from pounding on the door of Room 13, its rusty door number matching the overall despair of the complex. Maybe Sterling had taken her stolen $867,539 and upgraded to someplace nicer, but I hoped she had left something behind in the room that could lead me to her. Or at least to her daughter Charity.

A broken tricycle lay abandoned in the long porch, its bent frame intermittently reflecting the red lightbulbs winking at every door. This motel gave *The Shining* a run for its money when it came to creepy vibes. The small portico in front of Room 13 reeked of stale cigarettes and dumpster garbage. I knocked one final time, trying to ignore the judgmental stare from the elderly neighbor peeking at me through a crack in the doorway.

"She never answers," the old woman growled, only her lips and one eye visible. "A bit of a recluse. But I guarantee she's in there."

"You saw her go in?" I typed on my phone and showed her

the screen.

The woman pointed to a hearing aid in her ear, showing me she understood my communication dilemma. "Yep, she was just here not long ago. And she never left. Kinda like 'Hotel California.'"

Which meant Sterling was either hiding out inside, or she had snuck out another way. My phone buzzed, the screen lighting up with Deputy Joe Speers' name and a FaceTime request. Finally, *someone* in emergency services who knew how to handle a Deaf caller! I stepped away from the curious neighbor, attempting privacy.

"I saw your emergency text," the deputy one-handedly signed with a confident flow and natural rhythm that showed he'd been practicing. He pointed over his shoulder at his police cruiser. "I'm on my way."

"Thanks," I signed with one gesture, then added, "You might be the only other person in Bloodson Bay I can talk to, other than Ginger and Tara."

Two dimples tucked into his cheeks. He was actually kind of cute, if you liked the cleanshaven, bald-headed type, which I was still undecided about.

"I figured it was time someone in law enforcement stepped up. We can't have our most famous—and beautiful—resident feeling left out."

I couldn't help but chuckle, genuinely impressed despite my usual skepticism of law enforcement. His dimples deepened as he grinned back, creating little valleys in his face that made him look boyish and charming. Was he flirting with me?

The thought was both amusing and slightly unsettling. I'd spent so many years being the "Deaf woman" in town that having someone actually see me as a romantic interest felt foreign.

"About Charity Jones," he continued. "I found a match… sort of."

"What do you mean by *sort of?*"

His dimples disappeared. "I'll tell you when I get there."

Chapter 36

Deputy Speers met me in front of Room 13 of the So-So Southern Motel with a key dangling from one hand and a timid wave from the other. At least he had better luck with Mr. Sosa than I had.

"Miss Apara, it's nice to see you again," he signed.

I hadn't remembered thinking he was *hot* before now, but as he shyly greeted me, a stir flittered in my stomach. No, it was more likely the flu than feelings I was catching.

"You can call me Sloane, Deputy Speers." I figured since he went out of his way to learn sign language for me, we were officially on a first-name basis now.

"And you can call me Joe."

"Okay, Deputy Joe."

"Just Joe," he corrected me.

"I like Deputy Joe better."

His mouth opened in a hearty, wide-mouthed laugh, and I wished I could hear the sound of it. "Alright, only because I like you."

My cheeks heated with a flush I hoped the darkness hid. I absolutely was not on the market for a boyfriend, and I didn't want to give him the wrong idea.

"So, Deputy Joe, tell me what you found out about Charity Jones."

"For starters, Loving Arms Children's Home has record of a Charity *Valance*, not Charity Jones. And she's been missing for about a week. The Amber Alert's already out."

Valance? My tummy flutters coiled into a tight ball heavy in my gut.

"I'm guessing her mother—my assistant—who went by Sterling Jones is actually Sterling *Valance*?" I clarified.

"Yep. Your assistant and her daughter share a last name with the town's most notorious crime family, but there's more. You know the body found in Bloodson Manor—Darla Pearson? She's also a former Valance. I pulled up her records and found out she was married to Marvin Valance."

Now *that* put an interesting spin on the investigation. "That's an awful lot of connections to the Valance family."

"You'd better be careful getting involved in this, Sloane."

It was too late for that. I bit my lip, considering my options. If Sterling needed money so desperately that she would steal from me, filing a police report about her theft would only divert resources from finding Charity and solving Darla's murder. My theft charges would have to wait. We had a kid to find and a killer to catch.

It was clear Sterling wasn't going to answer the door after several knocks. But now that a child was missing, Deputy Joe felt justified letting himself in. He fidgeted with the key, then inserted it into the lock and clicked it open. He pushed the door slightly, then hesitated.

"I don't know what we're going to find inside. But just in case Sterling is connected to Darla's murder, don't touch anything. We don't want to add your fingerprints to the mix or disturb possible evidence."

The undercurrent of what he was suggesting felt ominous—that my assistant might have tortured Darla and killed her. The thought terrified me. But then again, Sterling had neglected her own child, lied to me, and stole almost a million dollars. Plus, she was a Valance. I had no idea what she was capable of anymore.

My heart pounded a frantic rhythm as Deputy Joe shoved the door fully open, dragging along a towel that had been tossed in front of it on the floor. Whoever was inside could not have easily placed it there on the way out. That meant they were still here.

A shiver of unease snaked down my spine.

Inside, a packed suitcase gaped open in the middle of the living area floor. I recognized a sweater from Sterling's wardrobe, its sleeve reaching toward the door like a desperate plea for help.

The air smelled musty with the lingering scent of her vanilla perfume, mixed with something else—rot. After years of planning luxury events, I'd developed a sixth sense for atmosphere. Right now, every instinct alerted me that something was terribly wrong.

Deputy Joe made his way around the edges of the living area, then cleared the bathroom, glancing back every now and then to see if I was still there... or to make sure I was okay. It would have been thoughtful if not so unnerving. I couldn't ignore the eerie stillness, how it amplified the sense of wrongness that permeated Room 13. Something bad had happened here. I felt it in my bones.

"No Sterling, and no Charity," I signed to Deputy Joe. "What now?"

"We look around," he replied.

On a long dresser beneath a television old enough to still use a bunny-eared antenna, a stack of papers caught my attention. A legal document with Sterling Valance's name printed across it sat on top.

Sterling's job application had listed a law firm she had worked at, and when I asked about her experience there, she cagily confessed to embezzling from the company. They had initially pressed charges, which had landed Sterling in jail, but eventually the charges were dropped. Thinking she was a reformed person after her release, I stupidly hired her anyway.

I didn't dare touch the paper, but I didn't need to. The cover page contained plenty of information about a Record of Appeal. More shocking was finding Sterling Valance's name as counsel for the appellant Ewan Valance in his upcoming appeal. Sterling was Ewan's attorney.

The date scheduled for the appeal held especially interesting timing. Sterling's theft and disappearance weren't coincidence. They were meticulously planned. She was spearheading the appeal for Ewan Valance, and the court date was set for *tomorrow*.

"Look at this." I tugged Deputy Joe's sleeve to get his attention and pointed out the document. "Sterling was listed as counsel in Judge Ewan Valance's murder conviction appeal. She was trying to get him released from prison."

"Ex-judge," Deputy Joe corrected me. "Any idea why she'd want to help free a convicted drug trafficker and murderer?"

It was good to know that Deputy Joe didn't side with the corrupt judge, because that would have been a deal-breaker for me. In Bloodson Bay, you never knew who to trust.

"Somehow they're related and she actually liked him," I guessed. "I'm betting not a lot of lawyers would want to touch his case. This appeal must have been filed before she was disbarred."

From what Sterling told me, after her charges were dropped she was able to reinstate her law license. I took a picture of the appeal document in case I needed it later, then kept looking around. Something else of importance was here.

Hidden behind an empty, open pizza box was a framed picture. It appeared to be a family photo from ages ago. I recognized Sterling and a toddler-aged Charity, but no one else looked familiar. I reached to pick it up to get a closer look when a hand grabbed mine.

"No touching." Deputy Joe looked at me intensely as he spoke this, cupping his palm around my closed fist.

Then he gently flipped my hand over and intertwined his fingers with mine. His gaze was soft, and his touch was reaffirming. The sweet connection lured me in so tenderly that I couldn't resist him. I held my breath, waiting for something to happen, but I didn't know what. We held this moment in unmoving, unbreathing silence for so long my vision started to darken around the corners.

Then Deputy Joe leaned in. I met him halfway. The kiss was brief but devastating. How did I let this happen? We were two pairs of lips touching in a no-touching zone. It felt forbiddingly delicious. But this was not the time or the place.

I was the first to pull away, keenly aware of the location and situation we were in. A dingy motel room that reeked of decay was not where I wanted to be making out with a cop, of all people.

"Look, you're very sweet—" I began to sign with my free hand, vaguely aware that my other was still trapped in his.

"You're beautiful," he signed back. "And intelligent, creative, and did I mention beautiful already?"

I rolled my eyes, but I had to admit, he was smooth—especially when he signed one-handedly. "Yes, you mentioned it."

"I've liked you for a long time, you know," he admitted aloud.

"I figured," I spoke back to him. I didn't usually like using my voice to talk because it made me self-conscious, but for some reason I trusted Joe with my insecurities. "No one learns a whole new language for someone they detest."

Then Deputy Joe dropped to one knee. Okaaay, what the heck was he doing?

"Please do me the honor of letting me take you out to dinner and a movie on a proper date."

Thank God that was all he wanted to ask. For a minute there…

"What—this isn't a date?" I teased. "I figured you kissing me made it formal."

"Hm, a date investigating a missing person? Wow, a woman after my own heart." He patted his chest as his expression feigned awe.

As much as I wanted it, I needed to put a stop to this. With the demands of both of our jobs, the timing was less than ideal.

"Look, I like you a lot, Joe, but dinner and a movie are out of the question."

"Why?" He moved nervously to his feet.

"Because unless the movie has closed captioning, I'll have

no idea what's going on."

"Oh." His expression brightened. "Then how about just dinner?"

I sighed. Boy, was Deputy Joe persistent. "I'm not really in the mental space to start dating someone," I tried to explain.

"When is anyone ever? That doesn't mean we can't be friends and see where it goes."

"So this isn't a date then? Because I usually don't kiss *friends*."

A grin spread across his lips. "Sloane, you drive me crazy. But in the best possible way. Lucky for you, I'm a patient man. So yes to dinner then? As friends?" His eyebrows lifted hopefully.

"Fine," I agreed. "But right now we need to focus on finding Sterling and Charity and put a hold on the kissing and hand-holding."

I glanced down at his hand that refused to release, then removed his warmth from mine. Although I resented the cold emptiness that replaced it, we had to get back to work. The night was getting later and colder, and finding Charity urgently needed my focus.

The kitchenette yielded nothing but a half-eaten box of stale crackers and a lingering smell that I still couldn't identify. A faint, sickly-sweet smell, like overripe fruit and something vaguely chemical.

"Do you smell that?" I signed to Deputy Joe, who had slipped on a pair of latex gloves and was opening drawers and checking under the bed.

"I think you need to use the bathroom," he signed.

"Excuse me?" I wasn't the one who made the odor, if that's

what he was implying.

"I meant *check* the bathroom," he corrected himself with a laugh, shaking his hands as if to erase the mistake. "The garbage can in there might have a clue."

I would have laughed if I didn't feel so anxious. My chest tightened as I held my breath and pushed on the crooked bathroom door that didn't want to stay open. The door hinges resisted in protest as I eased it forward, inch by inch, the smell invading my senses. My hands trembled against its cheap, hollow core. The door flung closed as soon as I released it. Everything in me wanted to turn back.

What I walked into made me gag. The window was open behind cheap metal blinds, and pouring into the bathroom was freezing air and a horrible stench. I yanked the blinds up and streetlight poured in. Grabbing the outside of window sill, my hands landed in something sticky… and when I turned my palms over, they were covered in blood.

I peered out the window to the dumpster below, and a scream trapped in my throat, unable to escape. My feet reflexively backed away, while my eyes refused to avert from the horror before me.

"Joe!" A single syllable of name tumbled up from my chest.

My legs felt like lead as I stumbled backward out of the bathroom, my heels catching on the carpet threads and sending me sprawling. Deputy Joe rushed to my side as I collapsed to the floor. His arms holding me upright couldn't ward off the image seared into my mind.

I would never forget seeing her body drained of life, and I could never forgive myself for letting it happen. Then a terrifying reality hit me like a punch to the gut: I should have never started digging.

Chapter 37

As the last known person to see Sterling Valance alive, I officially became a suspect in her murder. To make matters worse, the one guy I had entertained the possibility of dating was the one to drag me in for questioning. Deputy Joe Speers had been a gentleman during Detective Hughes's interrogation, but it was mortifying dodging her insinuation that I had both motive and means to kill my assistant once they found out about the theft.

There would be no chance of a second date with Deputy Joe. Not that our first unofficial "date" was one to brag about or anything. Eventually, they released me to go home. But my freedom wouldn't last long.

After a long night that led into a short morning, I didn't go home to bed like I should have. Instead, my first stop was the one place I shouldn't have gone.

Ginger's front door swung open before I reached her porch. She blinded me with her tie-dyed muumuu paired with cowboy boots—an outfit that would look ridiculous on anyone else, but somehow worked perfectly for her. Her flame-red hair was a nest of curls piled haphazardly on top of her head, catching the morning sun like a burning halo.

"You'll catch your death out there!" she scolded.

She waved me inside, guiding me around stacks of clutter

and boxes of junk scattered across the entryway. Ginger could never throw anything away, no matter how many times Tara and I had tried to host a hoarding intervention.

"That's an ironic choice of words, considering the night I've had," I signed.

"Good heavens, sweetie, you look like you've seen a ghost!"

"You could say that," I spoke because my hands were shaking too furiously to sign anymore.

I struggled to push away the gory scene I'd witnessed outside the bathroom window of Room 13. Sterling's limp body slumped in the dumpster, her neck bent at an unnatural angle. Crimson streaks splattered across the garbage bags propping her up, while the odor of death mingled with the stench of discarded fast food. The horrifying snapshot was stuck in my brain. Sterling, my thieving assistant, murdered. And her daughter, Charity, still in the wind.

Deep in my gut, I worried that Sterling's fate was somehow my fault. I couldn't process it enough to form the signs to describe it. My throat tightened, the phantom feeling of a cry trapped within. Somehow, my life became a true-crime documentary like the ones Ginger was obsessed with—only this was real, raw, and terrifyingly close to home. I shuddered, realizing how exhausted I suddenly felt.

"What happened?" Ginger pulled a tissue out of her sleeve like a magician and began dabbing at my cheek with motherly concern. "You've got a little something on your face. I think you're bleeding."

Except it wasn't my blood. My stomach churned at the memory of how it got there, and Sterling's vacant stare as I rushed outside and climbed into the dumpster toward her dead body, then attempting futile CPR. I lifted my hands, displaying the crimson stains that had begun to dry and crack in the creases of my palms.

"Got enough tissues in your sleeve for this?" I asked.

"Good God! Are you hurt?" Ginger began searching my torso for signs of injury.

"No, I'm fine." Well, not really *fine*. I wished I could wash away more than just the physical evidence of the gruesome scene I wanted to forget. "It's Sterling's blood. She's dead."

"Lord have mercy," I read on Ginger's lips. "Let's get you cleaned up then have some tea and cookies."

Tea and cookies were Ginger's solution to everything.

We wove around clutter that threatened to climb the walls. I stepped over a vintage *Tiger Beat* magazine so old that the cover article touted an exclusive interview with The Monkees. When we reached the kitchen, I headed to the sink to wash up while Ginger went for the pantry.

"I've been at the police station all night explaining why I showed up at Sterling's motel room in the first place. She stole over $800,000 from me." I rubbed my temples.

The fluorescent lights of the interrogation room had sparked one of the worst headaches of my life. I accepted a Christmas-decorated sugar cookie, figuring some calories might help with the headache.

"Didn't you get my message? I told you I saw Sterling and Rose Crabtree breaking into your office. Why on earth would you confront her after that?" Ginger shook her head, her permed bun toppling over to the side.

"I didn't get your message until it was too late. And by then, I had met Sterling's daughter Charity, and I felt like I needed to help that poor kid… I thought Sterling was only trying to fix her bad situation."

"You think it takes $800,000 to fix a bad situation?" Ginger's lips pursed in a disapproving pout. "Now you're looking at motive for murder, honey."

"Thanks, Ginger. I feel so much better now." I made sure to coat my signs with a sarcastic glare, matching the acid churning in my stomach. Leave it to Ginger to state the obvious in the least helpful way possible.

"Do you want my help or not?" Ginger asked, propping her hands on her hips.

"I guess." I wasn't sure taking Ginger's advice was the best idea, but it was the only one offered at the moment.

"Then we need to follow the money, honey."

"How do we do that?"

"By following *me*!" Ginger declared, grabbing her purse and puffy jacket, then leading me outside.

I didn't know where we were going as Ginger's car bounced through town to somewhere she wouldn't divulge. Only when we were knocking on a stranger's door, and that stranger answered, did I realize how terribly stupid this idea was.

"What on God's green earth are you doing here?"

Although it was barely past eight in the morning, Mayor Rose Crabtree answered the door wearing a taxpayer-funded silk pantsuit that probably cost more than most people's monthly mortgage. Her professionally coiffed hair remained unmoved in the morning breeze.

"We just wanted to chat," Ginger answered.

"Chat to my lawyer." Rose grabbed the edge of the front door, ready to slam it shut in our faces, when Ginger thrust both arms out and blocked it.

"I don't think you want your lawyer knowing what you're up to."

The diamond tennis bracelet on Rose's wrist sparkled, reminding me that this woman had enough alimony money and gossipy friends to make our lives difficult if she chose. Her eyes, cold and calculating, passed over me and Ginger with barely concealed disdain.

"I know you and Sterling were in cahoots," Ginger began.

"I don't know anyone named Sterling." Rose leaned against the door casually.

Rose knew how to play the game. Deny everything with the practiced ease of a career politician, while keeping her face a mask of polite confusion. Until Ginger raised her bruised fist, the purple-yellow marks a testament to their recent scuffle.

"Sterling is dead, Rose. So you better start talking."

Rose didn't flinch. Did she already know?

"Unless you want to talk to my fist instead?" Ginger drawled. "Although a little battered, these knuckles still work just fine, honey."

Even in her tie-dyed dress that looked like it had been sewn from a hippie's bedroom curtains, Ginger managed to be intimidating.

"Are you threatening me?" Rose scoffed, but I noticed her fingers drumming nervously against the doorframe.

"How about we discuss what I saw you doing at Sloane's office? I'm sure the police would love to hear more about your breaking and entering... especially since I caught you and Sterling together on video right before her murder."

Now *that* got a reaction from Rose. Ginger was lying

because there was no recording, but it was believable enough to make Rose stiffen. Nobody in their right mind messed with Ginger when she got that look in her eye. I'd seen grown men twice her size back down when she fixed them with that steely gaze.

"A child's life is at stake!" The words burst from my throat.

The thought of Charity in danger provoked an unfamiliar protectiveness within me.

"What do you mean?" Rose asked.

"Sterling's daughter is missing. She could be hurt… or worse. Please help us…" I begged while Ginger translated for me.

Rose wasn't a monster. She had kids and didn't want a child to get caught in the crossfire. That stoic demeanor crumbled as she explained how Sterling had first approached her months ago at a town hall meeting, offering to help fund Rose's plans to push Tara Christie's family out.

"Why did Sterling care about Tara?" I asked.

"That sounds like Ewan Valance's bidding," Ginger said. "Sterling was Ewan's little puppet all along."

I read Rose's lips as she confessed, her iron-clad composure dissolving. The revelation didn't surprise me—Sterling had been playing everyone like a chess master, and Rose was just another pawn in her game.

What *did* surprise me was the genuine remorse etched across Rose's face as she detailed their clandestine meetings in my office, searching for my laptop and bank access, while Sterling guaranteed Rose's grand vision for transforming our sleepy town into an overcrowded vacation spot.

"Look, I didn't do anything illegal other than trespassing.

Sterling did the rest," Rose insisted. "But I can get you every dollar back! After she emptied your bank account, she left the full amount of cash for me in a safety deposit box. So please don't press charges—I'll pay back every cent… with interest! I can take you there to get it as soon my meetings are over today."

I frowned. It didn't make sense. "Sterling didn't want anything in return for handing over all that money?"

Rose glanced away shiftily.

"Rose, tell us what you agreed to do or else I'm sending the cops the footage I have of you and Sterling breaking into Sloane's office!" Ginger raised her fist and aimed it at Rose's chin.

"Okay, okay," Rose grumbled. "She said I could keep all of the money in exchange for a favor in case she ever needed it. All I could think of was what kind of person steals money and doesn't want any of it?"

That was a good question. Rose had no reason to kill Sterling if she'd already gotten the money. So who killed Sterling—and why?

"We need to figure out what Sterling's angle was. Once we know that, we can trace our way to the killer," Ginger concluded as we walked back to her car.

My mind wandered through the potential culprits. I doubted that Mayor Crabtree used Sterling to get access to me, then killed her in a money grab. The plot sounded too far-fetched, even for Rose. She might be unhinged by ambition, but she wasn't a murderer.

Or maybe Sterling's death was connected to Ewan Valance's appeal. Killing his counsel would put a pause on his court date, maybe even derail it completely. Out of all the theories, this one rang truest because no one wanted Ewan Valance released. But who would kill Sterling to keep Ewan behind bars?

I had taken a picture of the appeal paperwork before Deputy Joe took the paper as evidence, so I pulled out my phone and found the photo. A car whizzed by, nearly hitting me as I stood at Ginger's passenger-side door re-reading it.

There it was: my answer in black and white.

"I might know why Sterling was targeted," I signed, a chilling realization creeping in. "I just found something interesting about her… something that could *definitely* get her killed."

Chapter 38

Ginger's *computer room*, as she called it, housed everything but a decent computer. It was more of a craft room with clear bins full of scrapbook papers, collector edition Beanie Babies that no one else wanted to collect, and a mismatch of every type of craft supply you could imagine. In the corner crowded by fabric scraps and a sewing machine sat a desk housing a desktop monitor and tower old enough to still use floppy discs.

We sat scrunched together surrounded by junk, and I thrust my phone at Ginger. I tapped on the screen, enlarging the image of Ewan Valance's court appeal document. She squinted to read it, her mouth forming a perfect O of surprise as she absorbed what I was showing her.

"Look at when this appeal was filed." I pointed to the date signed at the bottom of the page.

It was filed shortly before I hired Sterling. It was also when Mr. Sosa said she had first checked in at the So-So Southern Motel. And right around when Darla was murdered.

But that wasn't all.

"And check out the law firm listed under Sterling."

The court document had Sterling Valance listed as counsel at the top. But below her name was a name I hadn't given much thought to before now:

Slick & Quick Law Firm

I was pretty sure Tara's attorney also worked for Slick & Quick Law Firm, and she was previously the ADA who had initially put Ewan behind bars. Why would the firm represent his appeal when it was clearly a conflict of interest?

I googled the law firm's name, and a college alumni magazine web page popped up giving the history of two graduates, sisters Sterling and Silver Valance. Apparently they had started the firm together years ago and worked as partners ever since. I wondered if I'd be able to get in contact with Sterling's sister Silver.

"S-i-l-v-e-r V-a-l-a-n-c-e?" Ginger fingerspelled. "Is that a joke?"

Sterling and Silver Valance. Twins, perhaps?

"From what I found out, I think they're Marvin Valance's estranged kids." Ginger spun in her computer chair with giddiness at her new lead.

I hadn't heard about the family tree yet, but there sure were a lot of branches.

"We need to figure out all of the familial connections. Maybe we can find out how they're all related in an internet search." My hands moved faster as we created a disjointed image. A Picasso, if anything.

"Who would want to stop Ewan Valance's appeal enough to kill Sterling, though?"

"Every law-abiding citizen in Bloodson Bay?" I guessed.

Ginger nodded. "Yeah, that man's got more enemies than a mosquito at a garden party."

There was something else we were missing from the bigger picture. While Ginger spent five minutes opening the search engine on her ancient, outdated computer, I searched *Sterling*

Valance Bloodson Bay on my phone.

A recent Instagram post came up for one of my events that included her first name. I tried *Sterling Valance, Court Appeal.* This search resulted in a bajillion articles about Ewan Valance's appeal scheduled for today, far too many results to sort through. The internet, usually my faithful ally, was being stubbornly unhelpful.

"Let me show you how it's done."

Ginger pounded on her keyboard with surprising one-fingered dexterity, found the Instagram post, and screen-captured it. Her tongue poked out in concentration as she added *Sterling Valance* to the image search. A photo and corresponding article from the *Bloodson Bay Bulletin* popped up.

"Since when did you become a tech whiz—on this old desktop, no less?" I was genuinely impressed by her newfound digital prowess.

"Since I started hanging out with you young'uns. Look at this article. It explains a lot." Ginger zoomed in on the image.

The entertainment news piece was an archive from 1995 and celebrated Judge Clint Valance's imminent retirement from the bench, noting how his son Ewan had followed in his father's remarkable footsteps, creating his own legacy.

The snapshot listed over two dozen Valances over three generations, and showed all the hallmarks of mid-nineties style, making me cringe at the fashion disasters on display. I spotted at least two sets of jelly shoes, several slap bracelets, combat boots, and at least three Jennifer Aniston haircuts.

My focus drifted down to scan the caption identifying each relative in the picture in order of their appearance, starting with my person of interest, Clint Valance:

Clint Valance (father), Ewan Valance (son), Sterling Valance (granddaughter), Marvin Valance (son), Silver Valance (granddaughter), Darla Valance (daughter-in-law), Leonard Valance (grandson)...

And the list went on and on.

I noted Darla's name, except she was *Darla Valance* back then.

"I forgot to tell you I found out that Darla is a former Valance," Ginger said as she started drawing a family tree on a scrap of paper.

Ginger wrote *Clint Valance* at the top with an accompanying stick figure, and his two sons Marvin (aka Julius) and Ewan were connected to a line below him. Next to Marvin was his wife Darla's stick figure.

It took me a moment to pick out Sterling from the crowd in the photo, her tiny frame hugging the leg of Ewan Valance. She looked around kindergarten age, wearing a frilly dress and butterfly clips in her hair that seemed at odds with her somber expression. But she still had that recognizable white-blonde hair. It was long and styled in tight ringlets, but that same haunting lingered in her eyes. Even as a child, she seemed to shrink away from the camera, half-hiding behind Ewan's pressed suit pants.

"Sterling and Silver were Marvin and Darla's kids," Ginger speculated aloud, creating more branches of names on her family tree.

Marvin's stick figure held Darla's hand, and under their names were Sterling and Silver. Three generations of Valances in total, starting with Clint and ending with Sterling and Silver.

I took a closer look at the sisters, who looked completely different. Silver had black hair, in stark contrast to Sterling's platinum blond. And Sterling was quite a bit taller, which presumably meant she was older. That crushed my twin theory.

"Those girls look terrified," Ginger commented.

"I'd be scared too, if I was Marvin's kid." I suppressed a shudder, knowing what I knew now. Marvin had murdered a teenage girl two years after this picture was taken, a fact that made the innocent family portrait feel sinister in retrospect. No wonder Sterling wore that troubled expression. Even though she couldn't have known what her father would do, children often sensed darkness. My fingers traced the edge of the photograph, wondering what other secrets this "perfect" family portrait was hiding.

I refreshed my internet browser, this time typing *Sterling Valance murder*. Breaking news detailed Ewan's postponed appeal and how his lawyer Sterling Valance was found dead in her motel room at the So-So Southern Motel late last night. The article went on to describe how her death had put a hold on the appeal that was speculated to set former Judge Ewan Valance free.

The medical examiner had already determined Sterling's death was homicide, but that much had been obvious even to me. My vision blurred as I looked away from the details that I had witnessed firsthand mere hours ago, the reported facts of which were sparse but chilling.

Thankfully, Deputy Joe had managed to keep my name away from the press as the person who had found her, but my anonymity was short-lived. The words "murder suspect" made my stomach clench as the article asked for any witnesses to come forward.

My cell phone lit up with a text from a private number. I hesitated to open it, but ignoring the looming dread, I swiped to read it:

Sterling's favor request just came in.

It was Rose Crabtree. I replied with the following text:

How? Sterling is dead. She can't ask for favors beyond the grave.

Well, she can and she did.

And?

And I wasn't totally honest with you. Her favor was that I give her an alibi if she ever needed one. She suspected someone was going to kill her and wanted to get ahead of it. Obviously she doesn't need the favor anymore, but someone else does.

Fine, I'll bite. What's the favor now?

I'm stepping forward as a witness who saw you at Sterling's motel room right before she was found dead. Sorry to send you to jail, but I have no choice. It's either you or me.

What do you mean? You do have a choice! A dead woman can't hurt you…

But her family can.

After my text exchange with Rose ended, Ginger read it over my shoulder, mouth opening in what I assumed was a gasp or a shriek or any other natural sound of shock that I couldn't hear.

"Who do you think is ordering Rose to implicate you?" Ginger signed.

"Rose said it's Sterling's *family*. So I'm guessing it's the same man Sterling's been protecting—Ewan Valance. He must have found out someone killed his star lawyer grand-niece—is that a word?—and he must think it was me."

"That's no surprise. He's been paying off cops in the BBPD for years. One of them must have leaked word to him that you were a potential suspect."

Rose had no idea of the danger she was putting herself in. Whoever had killed Sterling could go after Rose next if they thought she was working for Ewan.

A killer was out there roaming the streets of Bloodson Bay, and we knew their plan. They had already killed Darla to frame Tara and get control of her land. Then they silenced Sterling permanently in order to keep Ewan Valance in jail. And now they might set their sights on our insufferable town mayor next. The Valance family's web of corruption seemed to ensnare everyone it touched.

"Should we warn Rose?" The danger of the situation felt deadlier with each decision.

As much as I despised Rose Crabtree for her constant harassment of Tara, she didn't deserve to die. Even Rose's relentless crusade to turn our homey coastal town into some tacky tourist trap didn't warrant a death sentence. Yes, I was contemplating saving someone who'd made my friend's life miserable for months. Still… I couldn't let something horrific happen to her.

"You want me to help the woman trying to kick my best friend out of town?" Ginger grabbed her phone anyway and shook her head in disbelief. After scrolling through her contacts, she hit the call button, then mouthed to me, "Voicemail."

Ginger spoke into the receiver, "Hey, Rose. You need to go to the police right now. The person who murdered your partner-in-crime Sterling is probably coming for you." She paused, then added, "Oh, and don't forget you owe Sloane a trip to the safety deposit box!"

She hung up, muttering something about karma that I couldn't quite read on her lips.

"You have no tact, do you?" I signed.

"You don't need tact when you're my age, dear."

Thirty minutes later I arrived home. By this point my body needed a nap after the longest night of my life. But I couldn't rest without checking something first. It had been badgering me for the past several hours.

After I settled into my comfy but tastefully modern home office chair with a plate of my favorite Nigerian snack of deep-fried *chin chin*, I pulled out my laptop to double-check my upcoming event schedule. I took inventory of the clients whose parties Sterling had sabotaged, hoping I could get everything straightened out. I didn't know if I would ever trust another person again after what my assistant had done to me.

Next I went through Sterling's to-do list. Each event she had been assigned was color-coded according the type of event—red for weddings, yellow for baby showers, and purple for birthday bashes. But Sterling had an item color-coded black, which was one I had only used once before for a funeral.

I clicked on the task set for tomorrow and found a cryptic notation with it: *Delete CC*.

What did that mean? Delete a carbon copy, or a credit card number? Or did *delete* have a more ominous meaning—as in the color-code black for death? Sterling had put a funeral on the event schedule. If I wasn't mistaken, this seemed awfully like a cryptic murder hit-list.

My head felt like it exploded, along with the ceramic plate of bite-sized chin chin balls I dropped on the floor. Who was going to be killed next?

Part 4
Ginger

Chapter 39

Nothing on earth smelled sweeter than a newborn baby's head. Sitting in Tara's living room, I fussed over the cutest bundle of joy I'd ever laid eyes on, my heart instantly melting into a pool of goo. And as a Baby Boomer myself, I'd been around long enough to see my fair share of babies, so I knew my grandson was particularly good-lookin'. Just like his *mamó*—me!

"Would you look at those precious little fingers," I cooed.

Tara placed him in my arms, his rosebud mouth working in his sleep as he gripped my finger with surprising ferocity for a hand so tiny. But I was equally wrapped around this sugar dumpling's itty-bitty finger faster than you could say "sweet tea."

The way his eyelashes fluttered against those plump cheeks got my baby fever risin,' even though I was well past my prime and more likely to wear a diaper than to change a baby's.

"We finally came up with a name," Tara said.

"It's about time. I was starting to think we'd have to call him *Hey You* for the rest of his life."

"We decided to name him after your daddy—his great-grandpa." Tara's eyes were bloodshot from lack of sleep, but her smile could've powered all of Bloodson Bay. "Flynn Christie has a nice ring to it, don't you think?"

I dabbed at my eyes with the hem of my sleeve, not caring

one whit that I was getting mascara all over my favorite floral-print blouse.

"Honey, you're gonna make this old lady cry. My *athair* would've been over the moon." My voice caught as I remembered how much my father always wanted a son to carry on our family name, but he got me instead.

The name *Flynn* traced back to our Irish roots, meaning "descendant of the ginger-haired one"—a perfect fit for my carrot-topped grandson. The way sunlight hit those copper strands of his reminded me so much of how *Athair's* hair used to shine.

I touched Flynn's downy fluff, remembering how my *athair* used to joke that our family had been kissed by fire. Lord, what I wouldn't give for him to be here now. He'd probably be strutting around Bloodson Bay like a rooster in a henhouse, bragging about his great-grandson to anyone who'd listen. He'd have been at the hospital every day, probably driving poor Tara crazy with his endless stories about the Irish War of Independence and that booming laugh of his that used to make the rafters quiver.

"I'm glad you like it, Mom." Chris appeared equally exhausted but ecstatic. He rose from the sofa across from where I sat and grabbed his car keys. "I'm going to run over to Debbie's Diner and pick up something to eat."

"Not on your life!" I handed Tara the baby and headed into the kitchen. "Your family needs proper sustenance. My famous fried chicken will put some color back in those cheeks."

Chris chuckled. "Because your grease is so much healthier than Debbie's?"

"Hush your mouth." I started pulling ingredients from

Tara's cabinets, realizing I didn't have nearly enough breading. "Now go make yourself useful and run to the store and grab me bread crumbs so I can fix up some real Southern home cookin'."

Chris gave me, then Tara, pecks on the cheek before heading out, while Tara carefully transferred Flynn to his basinet and slumped at the kitchen table as I prepped.

"Talk to me, Ging." Her eyelids fluttered closed. "I need something to keep me awake. Catch me up on what's been going on."

Pans clattered while I coated chicken breasts in my secret blend of spices and crumbs—the secret being a dash of every spice I could find.

"Well, first off, Darla was married to Alice's son Julius— also known as Marvin. And they had two girls—Sterling and Silver. While she was working as an assistant and robbing Sloane blind, Sterling was also the attorney who was supposed to appeal Judge Valance's conviction, but she got murdered. And we still don't know who her sister Silver is."

Tara's gaze glassed over. I admit it was a convoluted mess, but there was no simpler way to explain it. Eventually, her brain must have caught up when she asked, "Do you think the same person who killed Darla also murdered Sterling?"

"It's the most logical conclusion since they were mother and daughter. Whoever killed them really didn't want anyone to spring Judge Valance from the slammer."

"Why do you think Sterling stole the money from Sloane?" Tara asked.

"That's the weird part of all of this—she gave the money to Rose Crabtree to use for her town revitalization project," I said. "And it wasn't even the first time she'd done it. She also stole from her own dang law firm!"

"There has to be a reason why she'd risk everything to embezzle—*twice*."

"It turns out she stole from Sloane in order to pay for a favor from Rose Crabtree."

"What was the favor?"

I shrugged. "Sterling paid off Rose to give her an alibi because she thought she might need to kill someone who was after her. But now Sterling's too dead to tell us who it was."

Then Tara was quiet for so long, I thought she had fallen asleep. Then she said, "Is the Record on Appeal document for Ewan Valance public?"

I had tried to search for it online but had no luck accessing the actual record. "You'd either have to be pretty law-savvy to find it, or it was exclusive to those in the court system."

"So the question is, who would have access to the list of lawyers on that document?"

She was on to something, even as she slouched against the counter, clearly running on empty. Bless her heart, but that investigative brain of hers was as brilliant as always. Our perpetrator was someone who knew the legal system and despised Ewan Valance enough to murder not one but two women connected to him—first Darla, and then Sterling.

I'm coming for you next, the threat on the cellar door had warned. The killer also wanted Tara gone.

Only one person who knew the law, financially benefitted from Sterling's death, and wanted Tara out came to mind: Rose Crabtree.

Chapter 40

I wouldn't have been surprised if Chris had planted and grown the wheat from scratch to make the bread crumbs I was still waiting on, because hours later, Tara was asleep on the sofa and Chris still hadn't returned from the grocery store. I vaguely remembered what new parenthood was like, and I figured Chris thought any chance to get out of the house was a welcome one—even if it was only to wander aimlessly around grocery aisles.

Luckily, I was good at detours, so instead of fried chicken, I made chicken cordon bleu. Still home-cooked, and still edible. Though Lord knows my *máthair* would've had a conniption fit seeing me serve fancy, French cuisine instead of a robust, Irish meal.

The phone ringing with a video call alert woke Tara up, and I glanced over as the call connected. Tara's attorney, Ms. Deere, materialized on a laptop in the kitchen as I finished washing the last pan. Since when did video calls become the new norm? Gone were the days when you could answer the phone in a brassiere and curlers. Now you had to dress up and put on your face just for a phone call. I missed the simpler times.

"Hi, Ms. Deere." Tara pushed a breast pump and bottles aside out of the screen's view. "Excuse the mess. I'm taking the call on my laptop since my phone battery is almost dead."

"I understand. So, your husband contacted me earlier today

mentioning something about evidence surfacing regarding Darla Pearson's death." Ms. Deere cut to the chase. "Did the police name a suspect? Chris was supposed to meet me in person but never showed up."

I could tell Ms. Deere was sitting in her car because I could see the headrest directly behind her. Although the background was blurred, seagulls squawked somewhere off-camera. Wearing a pressed suit jacket and silk blouse, she was professionally dressed, even for a day at the beach.

I self-consciously patted my hair, wishing I had brought some hairspray and lipstick with me. And maybe worn something black, which I heard was slimming. Didn't the camera add ten pounds? God only knew what terror I resembled on the lawyer's side of the video.

"Um, I see you have company," Ms. Deere wavered. "Do you want me to call you another time?"

"No, this is fine. It's just my mother-in-law."

"Oh, you must be Ginger. I'm Bella Deere, attorney-at-law," Ms. Deere introduced herself with a tight lift of the lip that didn't qualify as a grin. "I've heard good things about you."

"And I've heard you're a lawyer," I joked, but she didn't crack a smile. Maybe I needed to try again. "Ms. Deere, how does an attorney sleep?"

"I'm sorry?" She looked anguished. Maybe she'd heard this one before.

"First she lies on one side, then she lies on the other." I chuckled, but apparently my lawyer joke didn't land because Ms. Deere frowned.

So much for lightening the mood. With her slicked hair and rigid expression, she looked like the kind of woman whose handshake was firm enough to break phalanges—which are hand bones, for those who don't know hand anatomy like I do, no thanks to my carpal tunnel.

"Chris must have called to give you the latest updates on Darla and Sterling being mother and daughter," Tara interjected, to my relief.

Ms. Deere smoothed her barely ruffled hair, despite the fierce winter winds the beach was notorious for this time of year. "Interesting…"

As Tara filled her in on Sterling's theft and murder, plus Darla's connection to Sterling as her mother, I couldn't help but notice how the attorney's manicured nails drummed against the steering wheel with increasing intensity. The rhythmic tapping reminded me of something…

"You worked with Sterling at Slick & Quick Law Firm, right?" I asked Ms. Deere.

"Yes, until she embezzled money from my firm. I had to fire her over it. She's a Valance through and through—she got greedy and backstabbed her own partner to get rich. I dropped the charges because she paid me back, but I never trusted her after that."

That seemed to be par for the Valance course.

"Just curious," Tara's forehead wrinkled, "but who would have access to a court appeal's attorney list ahead of time?"

"Why do you ask?"

"We think whoever killed Sterling is trying to keep Ewan Valance in jail. Sterling was listed as the counsel for the appeal, and now she's dead. I think the same person killed Darla, too. Once we know who, I'll be exonerated."

Ms. Deere's lips tightened until they nearly disappeared.

"Anyone could go to the court and request the list. But let's hope the appeal falls through. Ewan was a corrupt judge, and his criminal activity has tainted the purity of the justice system."

Ms. Deere checked her watch with the kind of urgency I usually reserved for two-for-one sales at the Piggly Wiggly.

"Well, Tara, I'm sure you don't want to pay for a full hour," she announced. "I'll touch base with the BBPD and Mikhail Pearson to see how this might impact the lawsuit. If we can prove you had nothing to do with Darla's death and that Sterling was the culprit, it might convince Mikhail to lower his compensation demands. In the meantime, take a break and stop playing detective."

I thought of my own tentative legal situation with Rose Crabtree. My arthritic joints were still tingling with satisfaction from our earlier scuffle.

"Do you offer senior citizen discounts?" I held up my bruised knuckles, admiring the purple splotches like badges of honor. "I might need to lawyer up if Mayor Rose Crabtree presses charges for that knuckle sandwich I served her. Worth every broken nail."

I wiggled my fingers with a wince, though I couldn't wipe the smile off my face. That woman had it coming, trying to strong-arm Tara out of her property like some fancy-suited vulture. Sometimes a lady my age had to remind folks that Southern charm is layered with steel underneath.

"Not really, Ginger, but Tara can give you my contact info if Rose decides to pursue it." Then the laptop screen went black.

In the living room where Flynn stirred from his nap, the television murmured in the background. Tara scooped the baby up, cradling him against her as she swayed while standing. I watched her, pained to see her wrestling with all this worry over Darla's murder when she ought to be savoring these precious early days with her baby.

Another glance at the clock revealed that Chris was beyond the normal *Twilight Zone* getting-lost-in-housewares-aisle. But I only had a moment to dwell on that before the television news station updated with an urgent report. The local anchor's grave expression filled the screen as she announced someone had just discovered Mayor Rose Crabtree's body at her residence this evening.

"Today our town's beloved mayor was found dead at the bottom of her staircase. The cause of death was blunt force trauma to her head during the fall. Police have ruled it accidental, and a memorial will be held to honor this town hero we all loved," the reporter said.

An *accident,* my ass! I wasn't sure how falling down stairs qualified her with hero status, but that wasn't my concern. A third death in our little town? This was officially a serial killer!

The reporter interviewed a visibly shaken friend of Rose's. I never knew Rose had a real friend. The woman had found her after Rose missed their power-walking date and wouldn't answer repeated phone calls. Tara stopped swaying and instinctively pulled Flynn closer to her chest.

"Well, I guess you don't have to worry about Mayor Crabtree suing you for assault," Tara remarked with grisly humor, dabbing at the spit-up on her shoulder with a burp cloth.

"Except my DNA is all over that woman's face," I commented. The news was sparse with additional details, showing only police tape and somber-faced officers milling around Rose's home. "I still might need Bella Deere, attorney-at-law's, info after all."

Then I laughed. It was too terribly comical not to.

"What's got you giggling?" Tara asked.

"Marvin Valance's biological mother is named Alice Belvedere. And your attorney is Bella Deere. *Belvedere, Bella Deere.* Get it? The resemblance is ironic to me, that's all." I shrugged, because saying it really wasn't as laugh-out-loud as it was in my head.

Tara bolted up, and I knew I must have stumbled onto something big. There was no such thing as irony in a murder investigation. The wheels in my head started turning. The way Ms. Deere tapped on the steering wheel in our video chat was just how Rose tapped on her desk. Something was connecting, but it lingered just out of reach.

"Wait a second… Bella would have had access to the appeal petitioner's list!" I realized aloud.

"And when we ran into Sterling at Debbie's Diner, Bella acted like she didn't know who she was. Meanwhile they were co-workers at Slick & Quick Law Firm," Tara added.

"Do you think your attorney is somehow related to Alice Belvedere?"

"Alice only had one son, which was Marvin. And Marvin only had two daughters: Sterling and Silver. So if Bella is related to Alice, wouldn't that make her—?" Tara didn't finish her question, but I already knew what she was thinking.

"Sterling's sister!" we both screamed simultaneously.

That 1995 Valance family photo flashed in my mind. Two little girls had been listed: Sterling standing next to her grand-uncle Ewan Valance, and Silver beside her mother Darla. I hadn't connected it at the time because I was only looking for

Sterling's name. But only someone high as a kite like Darla could come up with something as quirky as *Sterling* and *Silver* to name her two non-twin daughters.

I'd come across my fair share of unusual names in Bloodson Bay, for we weren't exactly known for our conventional ways, but this one took the cake and the whole dang bakery.

"But why would Silver Valance change her name to Bella Deere in order to escape her matched-set identity?" I wondered aloud, the logic of it eluding me.

"She hates Ewan Valance and seems to hate the whole dang family," Tara concluded. "She probably didn't want any connection to the Valances."

"But *why*? It still doesn't explain her motive for murder. Ewan was family—her uncle. There's got to be a reason she hated Ewan enough to kill her own sister and mother and possibly Rose in order to keep him behind bars. Something doesn't add up…"

"I don't know why, but when does a murderer ever use sound logic?"

Tara had a point.

"What do we do now?" I asked. The revelation about Bella Deere's true identity as Silver Valance, and what that meant, had my mind spinning like a tilt-a-whirl at the county fair.

"I need to call Detective Hughes. She'll know what to do." Tara's hand was already reaching for her phone while the other held tightly to Flynn.

But before Tara could dial, both of our cells started ringing with that distinct chime that meant trouble was brewing. It was Sloane requesting a group video chat. I nearly dropped my phone when I saw Sloane's face. Her dark eyes were wide with fear, and her hands were moving so fast I could barely keep up.

My stomach clenched with leaden gravity as I interpreted Sloane's message:

You need to warn Chris that he is the killer's next target!

Chapter 41

Chris? A *target*? I squinted at Sloane signing on my phone screen, wishing I'd remembered to bring my readers instead of leaving them Lord-knows-where in that disaster zone I called a house.

Both Tara and I were still trying to make sense of what she was telling us between frustrating freezes in the video stream and misunderstood signs I hadn't learned yet. She was saying something about a hit that Sterling had scheduled, and CC—Chris Christie—was going to be "deleted."

"What do you mean *deleted*?" I let the words hang in the air like wet laundry. "Chris isn't dead!"

And then it hit me. Chris still hadn't come home. We had no idea where he was, and it had been hours since we'd seen him. Were we too late?

"It sounds like Sterling was fixin' to kill Chris, but she clearly can't do it, since she's at the morgue." I tried to sound hopeful, but it didn't quell my fear.

"So we don't need to worry about it, right?" Sloane's signed words were punctuated by frantic glances at something off-screen.

"Uh, well, we think Sterling's even-more-psycho sister Silver is the killer."

"And you'll never guess who Silver's alias is," Tara

interjected. "It's going to sound crazy."

"In this town?" Sloane's eyebrows arched dramatically. "The crazier it sounds, the more believable it is."

I took it from here, relaying our suspicions about Bella Deere, aka Silver Valance, being the missing sister and vengeful niece of Ewan Valance.

"We think she's been pullin' the strings all along. With her being Tara's attorney, she knew the ins and outs of everything going on."

"But why would she frame Tara for Darla's murder? And why threaten Chris? I don't know that the cops will buy that a renowned attorney is also a killer," Sloane signed back doubtfully.

"Sugar, that's exactly why she's perfect for it. Who's better at committing a crime than someone who knows all the legal loopholes? Besides," I tapped my temple with one bejeweled finger, "sometimes the ones with the fancy degrees are the most dangerous of all."

Sloane still looked skeptical. "But what is her motive?"

I was thinking so hard that my brain nearly split in half. Was the whole thing about the $800,000 Sterling had stolen from Sloane? Was this Bella/Silver's way of getting her hands on it? And then it hit me as my memory grabbed on to that moment when we first found Darla's body.

"Ewan Valance was responsible for his brother Marvin's death this past year, right? Meaning Ewan killed Silver's daddy."

In the 1995 Valance family picture, Sterling had clearly favored her Uncle Ewan, while Silver clung to her daddy, Marvin.

"Maybe this is revenge against her Uncle Ewan," I continued. "Silver is the one who put him behind bars right after her father's murder, and then here comes Sterling trying to set Uncle Ewan free. Maybe she wants to keep him in prison, even if it means… well, you know, taking out her own sister."

A sister killing her own blood wouldn't be a new low for the Valance family. But why would she have killed her mama, too? Darla's death still had me stumped.

"That could be motive… except, what does any of that have to do with *my* family? Why am I being dragged into this?" Tara asked. "Speaking of which, I'm going to try calling Chris again."

Tara had started all the signs of early panic. Pacing the living room. Looking out the window. Call after text after call.

I kept Sloane updated through video chat while Tara punched in Chris's number for the umpteenth time. Silence. Then we both heard that dreaded automated voicemail telling us to leave yet another message. Chris *never* turned off his phone, and *always* answered it, ever since they managed to land on the radar of every psychopath in Bloodson Bay.

Dread clawed at me. This was getting worse by the minute.

"Maybe Nora's seen him?" I suggested.

Tara nodded doubtfully and called Nora, her voice strained and tight. "Is your daddy with you?" A pause, filled with static fear.

I could just make out Nora's concerned reply through the line: "No, Mom. Why? What's wrong?"

Tara rattled off a quick "nothing, honey, but whatever you do, don't answer the door" to Nora and quickly hung up. "We have to find Bella—or Silver, whatever the hell her name is."

"But where do we start looking?" I asked.

Tara froze, a strange thoughtfulness in her eyes, like a lightbulb of an idea had just flashed on. "The memo!"

Was that some kind of code? "What are you rambling on about?"

She muttered something about Silver and a rapist, and then about a $500 monthly payment to a rape crisis center.

"*A Silver Lining*. That's what the memo said on the checks Chris was sending to the rape crisis center!" Her eyes widened. "Silver was the name of the girl he witnessed getting attacked at Lover's End," Tara breathed, her voice barely above a whisper.

"Huh?" I blinked, confused.

Tara sighed, steadying herself. "A long time ago, Chris saw a girl get attacked on the beach, and he didn't do anything to help. After he witnessed it, she ran away, but Chris never forgot. And that girl—she knew Chris! She even said his name that night on the beach. I bet she never forgot either."

Tara gently placed Flynn into his car seat, then grabbed the diaper bag and car keys. She rushed into the kitchen and came back holding a huge knife. My educated guess was we were going to stop a murderer—or end up being more victims.

"He's been making payments to a rape crisis center for years, and the memo he's been using is *A Silver Lining*. I think the girl he witnessed getting attacked was Silver Valance."

My conversation with Clint at the nursing home came to mind. "It makes sense that she'd run away, since the Valances basically disowned her whole side of the family... which is typical for them anytime a scandal pops up involving the family."

Tara clipped Flynn. "What if Bella… Silver… is still pissed, all these years later?"

The ultimate grudge. That tracked, when it came to the Valances.

"Let's say that's true," I speculated. "Where would she take him?"

Tara's eyes narrowed with the same look she got when she was about to march into a horse kill pen determined to rescue the whole lot of them. Her fortitude settled it as she hauled the car seat out the door, made even more fierce by her familial instincts kicking into overdrive.

"You're not actually going to confront Silver, are you? Let the police handle it," I pleaded.

"I am not letting her destroy my family. If this is about a grudge, I know exactly where to find them and how to stop her…"

Chapter 42

The wheels of Tara's truck crunched over gravel as she pulled up to the desolate beach parking lot two hours later. The dashboard clock glowed in the dark cab, and the dusk pressed in around us like a thick velvet curtain. Flynn, strapped in his car seat, slept soundly despite the apprehension crackling through the air.

By the time I spotted a sleek sedan parked crookedly across two spaces, Tara was already out of the truck and ordering Sloane to stay put to watch the baby. She moved faster than any woman who had just given birth had a right to.

"I sure as heck ain't letting you deal with her alone!" I called out, hustling after her down the wooden steps to the beach.

The tide was coming in, and the sand shifted treacherously under my feet as we made our way under a salmon sky toward a lone figure walking the shoreline. I didn't see Chris anywhere.

A woman's silhouette shrank in the pink distance as she headed for the dark mouth of the seaside caves farther down the beach. Waves crashed against the rocks around Lover's End, drowning out our approach until we were right behind her standing above the mouth of the massive pipeline.

"Bella!" Tara shouted over the wind and surf. "Or should I call you Silver?"

Silver whirled around, surprise flickering briefly across her face before settling into something calculating. There was no mistaking what she held. A deadly black barrel shimmered in the lingering twilight that was surrendering to night. Silver tossed it from one hand to the other, almost playfully, before straightening her arm and aiming the gun at Tara.

"You found me," Silver stated. "I'm guessing that means you figured me out."

"Where's my husband?" Tara's voice barely carried over the raging waters.

"I think you know, Tara." Silver's lips curved into a predatory smile.

"What do you want in exchange for my son's life?" I begged. "Money? Our silence? We'll give you whatever you want if you let us save Chris."

"Oh, I've already lost everything that was important to me. The only person I loved—my sister—chose Ewan Valance over me. I have no one else, and what's the point of money if you can't spend it enjoying time with the person you loved?"

I couldn't understand why Silver had done all of this just because Sterling appealed Ewan's conviction, but maybe if I could get Silver talking, I'd buy some time to figure a way out of this mess alive.

"Are you going to kill us too?" I asked.

"Yes," Silver's shoulders lifted slightly, "unfortunately I was raised to always tie up loose ends. That'd be you."

"Can you tell us why? I'm sure you want your monologue moment before you kill us off. Plus I think closure would be good for all of us."

Silver considered my request, then said, "Fair enough. Give me both of your phones and I'll tell you."

Her eyes glittered with malice, reminding me of a cottonmouth snake right before it strikes. Against all sense of survival, we handed the phones over, watching helplessly as she launched them into the churning water. The devices disappeared with barely a splash, swallowed by the ocean that seemed hungrier than usual tonight.

"I forgot the knife in the car," Tara signed to me sneakily. We had zero weapons and no way to call for help.

"What did you just say to her?" Silver demanded.

"I was speculating how you managed to overpower my husband." Tara was a much quicker thinking than I was.

"Oh, that was easy. I *happened* to bump into him at the grocery store and asked him to meet me for a quick drink to discuss the lawsuit. It only took a couple roofies to make him pliable enough to get into my car, and from there it was easy tying him up."

"So all of this was about what happened on the beach all those years ago?" Tara's eyes gravitated toward the cave entrance below where Silver stood. The water was quickly rising with the tide. "Even killing your own sister and mother?"

Tara's voice splintered on *mother*, and I couldn't blame her—the horror of a child murdering the woman who brought her into the world was almost too cruel to process.

"Wow, you should be detectives. That's good sleuthing, ladies." Silver's snicker was joined by a yell from inside the cave beneath us, the walls scattering the sound. Chris was still alive... for now. "But you're missing the best part of the story."

"So tell us..." I prodded, then I realized we were down to mere minutes before the cave entrance was completely submerged. "But quickly. I've got bunions the size of Texas."

What followed was a confession so horrific I felt dreadful even hearing it. And it all started with a mother who turned two sisters against each other.

"Deadbeat Darla," Silver referred to her, "was no mother to me. She cared more about getting her hands on Valance money than her own children. She always pitted me and Sterling against each other, forcing us to compete for our grandfather Clint's love. It was the only way he would give Darla money—if we made him proud. You can imagine what that does to a child, feeling like a circus animal performing for attention in your own family."

"But sibling rivalry doesn't justify murder," I tried to reason.

"It does when your own grandfather locks you in a basement for not being good enough. Then deprives you of food and sleep for days…all because your older sister is better than you."

Apparently they didn't reserve the basement punishment just for the boys. They all fell victim to it. Then Silver told us something completely unexpected.

"My father was the only one who cared about me." It was hard for me to imagine Marvin Valance having a heart, but maybe he hadn't been as damaged back then.

"I was too independent for Uncle Ewan's taste," Silver continued, "but he adored my sister. Sterling worshipped him, and he fed on adoration. Even after Sterling found out Uncle Ewan killed our dad, she forgave him without hesitation!"

Sure enough, as Tara and I had deduced, Sterling—a sister only by name, not by love—had planned Ewan Valance's murder conviction appeal. She was clever about it, too.

"My sister and I used to support each other. Slick & Quick Law Firm was our legacy—we partnered in it together with plans to represent the downtrodden, the town's victims. People like me who had been raped and cast aside with no justice!" Silver's passion was evident, and I could see how she would have been a damn fine lawyer… if she wasn't a killer.

"But when my Uncle Ewan convicted my father in 1997, I decided one day I'd pay him back for taking my dad from me. I knew Uncle Ewan was heavily involved in trafficking, so I became an ADA with the sole goal of taking him down. And it paid off! But then everything went wrong. My sister not only stole money from our firm, but she wanted to free the man I just put behind bars! At that point I knew my sister was too far gone to save. We were no longer sisters after that. But I couldn't find the strength to banish her from my life. She needed to die."

"Is that why you dropped the charges?" I asked. "You wanted her free from prison so you could kill her?"

"Wow, that's dark," Silver stated, "but yes. Now you know everything and can die in peace. I'm actually quite the humanitarian, you know."

"How so?" Tara asked, and I noticed that as Silver talked, the gun slowly lowered.

"Well, Darla was drinking and drugging herself to death in her new loveless marriage to Mikhail, so me killing her was a mercy murder. And my half-brother Brock needed a little *nudge* to get off the same track." Silver smirked at her play on words.

"What do you mean?" I was afraid to ask, but I had to keep her talking.

The gun was almost completely pointed at the sand, and she didn't seem to notice as I shuffled inch by inch toward the cave.

"It was too easy convincing Darla to party with my jackass half-brother at Bloodson Manor. I hooked them up with the drugs, and they did better than I'd hoped! Brock hurt himself—which he did all on his own—and Darla disappeared with a trucker I introduced her to. When the trucker was done with her a few months later, at least she gave me the one thing I needed from a mother in the end," she added wistfully.

"What did she give you?" I suspected Silver's love language wasn't gifts or quality time.

"She became the perfect casualty, a body that I could deliberately plant to frame the Christies. Which brings us full circle to you and Chris, Tara. You're probably wondering why you got dragged into this, aren't you?"

"You're upset that Chris didn't save you the night you were raped," Tara stated.

Silver laughed, and her cackle grew louder and louder until suddenly she stopped. It was a strangely disturbing reaction, highlighting just how Jekyll-and-Hyde this woman was. I continued my tiny shuffles, waiting for the perfect moment to run, which seemed like it would never happen.

"Oh, you were serious, Tara? Well, yeah, I'm pissed at Chris for that. But that's not why I want *you* to suffer. After Uncle Ewan was sentenced to prison earlier this year, I went to visit him in jail. Do you know what he told me? It was the craziest thing, and it stuck with me."

I couldn't imagine where this was going. There were more twists to this tale than my last perm. But as long as we could keep her talking, I was only a few feet from the icy churning water that was about a foot from the top of the cave. If Chris was bound up, I didn't know how long he'd be able to keep his head above water like that.

"Uncle Ewan told me that back in 1997, you testified against my dad, accusing him of murdering that girl Emory McAlister." Silver was so focused on waving her gun at Tara that she didn't seem to notice me slinking away in the darkness. "You ruined any chance of reconciliation for my family. That's why he couldn't raise me—because you put him in jail. I became fatherless because of you!"

I remembered reading the newspaper when the story went national. Tara's witness statement at Marvin's trial in 1997 had condemned him to life in prison. That one event started a chain reaction more than two decades later.

"I must applaud you, Tara."

Silver steadied the gun and pressed it to Tara's temple. She was winding down. I watched her arm stiffen, her trigger finger tighten. I needed more time.

"What for?" Tara's voice shook. That gun was awfully close to her head.

"You are one tough cookie to crumble. When the police removed you as a suspect in Darla's death, I couldn't even kill you."

"You tried to kill me?"

Tara's gaze darted at me then back at Silver, and we both knew she had to keep the focus on her if I was going to make it inside the cave. Now whether I made it back out was another matter.

"Who do you think poisoned you? I put it in your tea when we were at lunch. And I snuck more poison into Tiny Tots Tote water. I was so worried you'd figure it out."

"You could have killed my baby!" Tara shouted.

Her hands flew out like she was going to strangle Silver, until Silver fired off a warning shot at Tara's feet.

"Stay back! Because I promise, this time I'll make your baby an orphan."

"Wow, you are just like your father. Your dad murdered an innocent kid, and you almost killed my baby. Prison was exactly what he deserved," Tara spat back. "And it's exactly what you deserve."

"I guess the apple doesn't fall far from the tree." Silver's smile looked deranged—fake and wide and toothy. "If I could change history I would. But since I can't, I have to embrace how beautifully poetic this all is."

She cocked her head at Tara, closing one eye as she took aim. Her index finger wrapped around the trigger, tensed, and—

"Wait!" I screamed.

The ripple effects of each choice had a terrifying impact on time. Except it didn't start with Marvin going to jail for murder, or Chris witnessing Silver's rape, did it? It started with a baby named Julius and a woman named Alice whose son was taken from her. Had Julius been raised by Alice, none of this would have happened.

A thought occurred to me… something that might save us all. I could barely keep my voice steady when I finally broke through the alarming silence with a sledgehammer of a question:

"What if I can change history for you?"

Chapter 43

Silver gawked at me like I had spinach stuck in my teeth. "Do you have a time machine I don't know about?"

It was probably too late to admit that I could not, in fact, go back in time and change history. But in a way, I could. I studied Silver's face in the dying, peach-hued light, searching for any trace of the innocent young girl I had seen in that Valance family photo. I saw nothing but bitterness.

The darkness sharpened her features, transforming her appearance into something more sinister than sympathetic. But she had once been a traumatized girl, and that was who I needed to reach.

"Hear me out," I began.

"I'm listening."

"You originally became an assistant district attorney to help other victims, right?" No matter how Silver answered this, I would never understand how someone could betray her passion to seek justice and twist it into wreaking vengeance.

"Yes, that's true. But it's funny how life works out—or doesn't work out, in my case." Silver's chuckle was hollow.

She kicked at the sand with her shoe, the heel and toe both ominously pointy. And terribly uncomfortable-looking. I imagined I'd break my foot trying to slide into one.

The waves crashed harder against the shore, spraying us

with salty mist and skimming the mouth of the cave. The entrance was nearly submerged now, so high that the surf curled with icy, foamy pools around my shoes and ankles. If Chris was incapacitated in the cave, it wouldn't be long before he drowned. Or froze to death.

The sea spray plastered her short, dark hair to her face, making her look like a madwoman escaped from the loony bin. The way her finger arched around that trigger told me she wasn't bluffing—she had gone full-on psychopath. The wailing wind provided a sinister soundtrack to this nightmare.

"Please let me save Chris!" Tara pleaded.

"No—eye for an eye, Tara. I lost my father, and you're going to lose your husband. We'll call it square."

But Tara kept inching toward Silver, and I worried she was going to get herself shot.

"I told you I can change the past for you. But not if Chris dies," I warned.

"You can't bring my father back, so there's nothing you can offer that I want."

"I'm betting I do." Silver didn't know just how savvy a gambler I was. In fact, my winning spree made headlines in every Atlantic City casino, which was also around the time I got banned. "Before you do something you can't take back, there's something you need to know about your grandmother, Alice Belvedere."

"What makes you think I give a crap about a dead grandmother I've never met?" she asked.

"You picked her last name as your alias, *Bella Deere*." I steadied my voice, channeling every therapy session I'd spent with Dr. Dreyfuss. "I have a feeling she was important to you, and I know something about her that might make you reconsider all of this."

I gestured to the gun in her trembling hand, then at the cave.

"What's the point? She died before I was born."

"No, Alice Belvedere is very much alive, honey. And she's nothing like the rest of your family. You know that goodness in Marvin that you loved? That came straight from her."

I watched Silver's face carefully, noticing the first crack in her resolve, like ice breaking on a winter pond. The gun lowered an inch.

"You're lying!"

She wanted to believe me but wouldn't let herself. I needed to convince her to trust me.

"I've never been more truthful in my life. I can take you to her right now—but only if we get Chris out of that cave alive."

Silver's face contorted, tears I hadn't noticed before now gleaming like tiny diamonds.

"How do I know this isn't a trick? That you won't turn me in the second Chris is safe?" A war was waging behind her eyes, hope wrestling with suspicion.

"Because you're a woman of the law, aren't you? Deep down, you believe in justice. And I do, too." I took a careful step into the surf, wet silt shifting under me as the water rose to my hips. "You killed three innocent women—Darla, Sterling, and Mayor Crabtree. We both know you will need to answer for that. But meeting your grandmother before you turn yourself in? That's a gift I can give you."

I stepped further into the bitter water, my joints clenching in pain. The tide was chest height now, but my son was worth every blistering moment. If Chris was still alive, he wouldn't be for long.

Silver's arm lowered, the gun thudded silently to the sand, and Silver collapsed to her knees, sobs wracking her body like a storm-tossed ship.

"If you let me meet Alice first, I'll turn myself in." She looked up at me, mascara streaking down her cheeks like black rain.

As soon as the gun hit the sand, I swam into the cave to save my son.

Chapter 44

I might as well have been swimming in the artic with penguins, it was so cold. I wondered what kind of crazy people did this for fun.

As I treaded water deeper into the cave, there was about a six-inch gap between the surface and the pipe, enough that if Chris kept his mouth facing upward, he could catch breaths between each wave. But if he was bound or knocked out... I shuddered at the thought. And the cold. Damn, was it cold!

I was about ten feet into the makeshift cave when I saw him. His body was limp, and his arms were secured with a bungee cord. I bounced my way across the concrete pipe toward him, snatching quick breaths with every leap since the water was higher than me now.

When I grabbed him by the arms, he drifted easily toward me. Almost as if he were... dead. I couldn't think like that. Clinging to desperate hope and surging with adrenaline I didn't even know I still had, I dipped my head under his bound arms and through the hole they created, hauling him up as far as I could position him so that his head remained above the water.

Bouncing my way back out of the cave, I dragged him up to the shore, across the sand, and laid him gently down. When I turned him over, his skin was blue. Cold blue or dead blue, I couldn't tell the difference.

Everything Sloane had taught me during our CPR class came back to me in an instant, and I sat on his chest and began the compressions and mouth breaths without hesitation. I continued pumping and exhaling until my arms were sore and breaths were ragged, praying that for once I could be more than just an old, useless lady.

And then Chris sputtered.

Chapter 45

Six months later we still hadn't figured out who killed Mayor Rose Crabtree or why, but it wasn't Silver who did it. She had confessed to killing Darla and Sterling, but Rose's death was a mystery. Maybe it was murder, or maybe it was an accident. But by the following June, I didn't even care. Today wasn't a day of investigating murder or solving crime. Today was a day of happy endings and new beginnings.

Bloodson Manor was officially gone, bulldozed down to nothing but a hayfield. Tara and Chris could finally focus on parenthood. I even watched Flynn so they could take a belated babymoon, which lasted all of four hours as their outing consisted of dinner and a movie before Tara was overcome with mom guilt and rushed home. I figured we could try again once Flynn started high school.

Even Silver got her happy ending when Alice hugged her before escorting her to the police station. Her grandmother had been visiting her in jail every week since. But the justice system got the raw end of the deal. Every case Silver had worked on ended up under scrutiny, which gave every locked-up criminal a field day as they demanded appeals.

Chris's fake funeral service, hosted by Feel the Noize Party Planning, ended up being put to good use as well. Sloane offered to donate a memorial to Mikhail Pearson as a tribute to Darla's tastefully curated memory, and as a thank-you, Mikhail ended up dropping all charges against Tara for Brock's injuries.

Silver probably helped nudge him in this decision when she threatened to expose Brock's drug dealings to the police. It was clear why she'd excelled in law; her powers of persuasion were remarkable.

What thrilled me most was seeing Sloane become the legal guardian of Sterling's teenage daughter, Charity Valance—who quickly took on Sloane's last name. *Charity Apara* had a nice ring to it.

She was the only youngster I'd ever seen Sloane take a liking to. Probably because they shared the same stubbornness that I knew would one day cause them to butt heads like two bulls. But if I knew one thing about bulls, it was that when their horns locked, they were inseparable. Sloane and Charity also became inseparable.

As for me, I was still waiting on my happy ending—in every sense of the word. I was still a hotblooded woman, after all. After officially breaking things off with Gunther Jones in person a couple months ago, I missed our weekly jail visits and letters that bordered on pornographic. Only Gunther could make talk about dentures and bunions hot.

Sure, dating a convict with a ten-year sentence had been destined for failure from the start, but our connection had been real. Hadn't it? Or maybe I had never been anything more to him than a redheaded sex toy—minus the sex, since his request for conjugal visits had never gotten approved. And so I ended up back in the eligible bachelorette pool, and that was okay. I had survived worse.

I settled into my favorite rocking chair on Tara's back porch, watching six-month-old Flynn crawl across the grass while Sloane and Charity played chess on the patio table. The June heat pressed down like an electric blanket set on high, but the breeze carried the sweet scent of honeysuckle from the garden.

"Look at you, handling those mom duties like a pro." I shot Tara a playful wink as she expertly managed Flynn's squirmy attempts to explore a pile of horse poo their mini-pony Havoc must have left behind during one of his escapades.

"I couldn't do it without your endless supply of babysitting," she said as she kissed the top of Flynn's red head.

Sloane's hands flew in animated signs as Charity captured her queen. Those two were thick as thieves these days. Who'd have thought the woman who once declared she'd rather eat glass than babysit would end up adopting a kid?

A piercing scream crushed the peace as a figure rushed into the backyard. When I saw Havoc the mini-pony chasing a man in uniform, I almost thought the summer heat had fried my brain.

"I'm just trying to deliver a package!" the delivery guy yelled, jumping up on the porch while I shooed the playful pony away. The poor man was still catching his breath as he read aloud the name on the box. "It's for Sloane Apara. Is she here?"

I waved to Sloane, signing to her that she had a special delivery—and I made sure to mouth *special delivery* followed by a suggestive air-smooch.

She opened the box and looked utterly baffled. Then she pulled out a hideous pair of glasses, placed them on her face, and looked utterly ridiculous. A note was included with the spectacles, a style so clunky that even I wouldn't be caught dead in them—and I gave a whole new meaning to the word *eccentric.*

"What's it say?" I asked.

Sloane passed me the card, expressing shock and confusion and curiosity all at once:

How about that movie date now?

And at that moment, another man in uniform showed up—only this one realized Havoc was no threat at all and didn't scream like a little girl.

"Deputy Joe?" Sloane signed. She glowed, and I knew I was witnessing a major crush. "Are these from you?"

"They're captioning glasses," he explained. "I had to walk through fire to get these, but they will give you real-time captions that work for movies, social settings, anytime you need to follow a verbal conversation. As people talk, a transcription captions each speaker, making conversations easier to follow."

I never would have known how romantic a pair of ugly glasses could be.

"Yes," Sloane replied, making no sense whatsoever.

"Yes?" Deputy Joe wondered.

"Yes, I'll go to the movies with you! And I'll even let you call it a date."

Wearing her new gift, Sloane challenged Deputy Joe to play a game of chess, while Charity took that moment to approach my rocking chair.

"Miss Ginger?" Charity stood at my shoulder, fidgeting with the hem of her shirt. "Can I talk to you for a minute?

Privately?"

"Sure." I got up with a grunt and followed her to the far end of the porch, where passionfruit vines provided a curtain of purple-flowered privacy.

The girl pulled an envelope from her back pocket and held it out to me. "I have something I want to tell you. A secret."

"What is it, honey?" I took the envelope, curiously opening it.

"I, uh, want to donate some money I've saved to Tara's horse rescue… anonymously."

Inside the envelope was a bank statement with a number that made my eyebrows shoot straight up to my hairline: $867,539.

"I couldn't write a check that big, so I figured I'd just give the whole bank account to Tara and Chris."

"Wow, that's a lot of money, Charity. Where'd you get this kind of cash?"

"Uh, well, my bio mom left me some cash when she died and I was able to move it into a bank account. But when Sloane wanted to adopt me, I realized I didn't need it anymore. I have a real mom who'll take care of me now. So I want it to go toward something good—and Tara's horse rescue could really use it."

The dollar amount niggled at something in my brain, that oddly specific number tugging at a memory. Something about it felt off, like wearing someone else's shoes—and I was speaking as someone who'd accidentally worn enough mismatched pairs at church socials to know.

Looking at Charity's face now, with those big, worried eyes and trembling hands, pieces clicked into place like a Rubik's cube completing itself. Like when you suddenly realize you've been forcing the wrong pieces together all along and a prodigy kid comes along and in two minutes solves the dang thing.

It was the exact amount Sterling had stolen from Sloane's business, which had been reimbursed to Sloane through her insurance company when the police couldn't find the missing safety deposit box key to retrieve her cash. But Rose Crabtree confirmed that Sterling had given her the full amount. If Sterling didn't end up with the money, how did Charity get it? Somehow Charity got her hands on the safety deposit box key before Rose took a tumble down the stairs that killed her.

A long moment passed before I connected the blaring red dots. Rose Crabtree's murder wasn't Silver's crime, just like she said. Was it actually an accident, or was it was Charity's handiwork, killing her for the money? It probably wouldn't have taken much effort for her to break into the house, find the key, and catch Rose off-guard at the top of the stairs. One little push and she was financially set for life.

I knew from the moment I met Charity that a darkness lurked beneath the surface. I had hoped Sloane's love could heal that.

The police had ruled Rose's tumble down the stairs as accidental, but now I wasn't so sure... I wrestled with the idea of telling Sloane what I suspected, but my thoughts scattered when Charity wrapped her arms around me.

"Thank you, Miss Ginger. For everything. For the first time, I truly feel safe, like I belong somewhere."

Her happiness radiated through me, pure and sweet as summer sunshine. Staying with Sloane offered Charity her last hope of ending the darkness that had claimed everyone else in the Valance family—her mother Sterling, her grandmother

Darla, her grandfather Marvin, her Aunt Silver, and Grandpa Ewan, as far back as her great-grandpa Clint. The bloodline had endured enough tragedy across the decades. I couldn't let anyone discover what I knew.

The apple doesn't fall far from the tree…

Silver had said this that night at the beach cave. She was right. Even sweet Charity ended up infected with that dang murder gene, while she smiled at me as genuine a smile as I could tell.

Yes, I would keep her secret, but I would also keep a close eye on her…

Epilogue

I noticed the front door before I even pulled all the way into the driveway. Just hanging there, slightly ajar, like it was waiting for me. A sliver of darkness slid out from between the jamb and the doorframe, maybe an inch wide.

I knew I'd locked it. I always locked it. Living alone in Bloodson Bay, I'd be stupid not to. I kept the porch light on a timer. I double-checked windows. I had a deadbolt and a chain. And yet, here it was, open.

I sat in the car for a few seconds too long, gripping the steering wheel so hard my palms began to sweat. Maybe it was the wind. Maybe I left in a rush this morning and forgot to pull it shut. But that voice in the back of my head? The one that sounded like my *máthair* and smelled like cigarette smoke and Irish cream coffee?

You know better than that, Ginger.

I stepped out of the car. The air was still—too still. No breeze. No rustle of leaves. Just the creak of the door drifting wider as I walked up the porch steps. When I pushed it open the rest of the way, I knew instantly—this wasn't my forgetfulness. This was a break-in.

The living room was just how I left it, a hazardous mess. No robber would want to come within fifty feet of my house. Where would he even begin? Boxes stacked up against every wall, knickknacks covering every surface… this was no theft attempt. And if it was, I would probably send them a thank-you note.

"Tara?" I called out doubtfully.

Tara wouldn't have left the door open. She was a mom of a crawling baby and made a habit of closing doors and picking up choke-able objects. My house was her worst nightmare.

"Who's here?"

Nothing but silence answered my question.

I needed a weapon. My gaze landed on the fireplace poker standing in its brass holder by the hearth. It was heavy, solid metal, with a pointed hook on the end. Perfect for a clean impaling. I crept over, my footsteps muffled by the rug, and I grabbed it. The cold weight felt strangely comforting in my hand. Gripping it like a battle axe, I moved slowly, clearing the living room.

The kitchen was empty. Even the fruit bowl buzzing with fruit flies remained untouched. No signs of anything missing— not that I would know until I did a thorough inventory of my stuff. I backed out slowly, the poker slipping in my sweaty grip.

"Hello?" I said.

That's when I heard it. Water running. From the bathroom. My prowler was still in the house. I listened intently. It was the sound of the shower, a low and steady thrum of water hitting ceramic. It seemed highly unlikely that an intruder would pause his intruding to grab a quick shower. But then the water stopped.

The door to the bathroom was closed, steam swirling out from underneath. Holding my breath, I reached for the handle, the metal cool and slick beneath my fingers, and I slowly turned it.

As it creaked open, I dropped the fireplace poker.

There he was. Standing in front of the sink, a towel slung low around his hips and droplets dripping down his shoulders. He turned, just as shocked as I was.

"Gunther?"

"Ginger!" he said, like it was nothing. Like he hadn't just broken into my home and taken a shower as if this was the pay-per-hour So-So Southern Motel.

Prison had aged Gunther Jones only slightly, but his skin looked brighter and healthier than when I had last seen him months ago across the metal table in the correctional center's visitor's room. His wet white hair was plastered to his forehead, and there was a hardness in his gaze.

A thin scar stretched across his collarbone that hadn't been there before his incarceration, and I briefly worried over what inmate had put it there. But it was him. The quasi-ex-boyfriend I had sworn off was now back in my home. In my life.

"What are you doing here?"

He glanced at the fireplace poker at my feet and smiled. Like he wanted me to be afraid.

"Gunther," I repeated, bending down to pick up the poker without taking my eyes off him. "How are you out of jail? I thought your next parole hearing wasn't until next June 27th."

He ran a hand through his wet hair, water dripping onto the tile. "I needed to talk to you. You haven't answered my letters."

"You mean the ones from prison?" I snapped. "I burned them."

His face twitched. I should've turned and walked away. I should've run and called the cops—but something stopped me. Maybe it was curiosity. Or maybe it was that look in his eyes. The one that didn't say *I'm dangerous* but instead whispered

You don't know everything.

"Oh," he said. "You shouldn't have done that."

THE END… FOR NOW

There's more murder, mayhem, and mystery brewing in Bloodson Bay that only Tara's Angels can solve in *The Last Thing She Knew*, the next book in the IF ONLY SHE KNEW MYSTERY SERIES.

Did you know that reading provides health benefits including better brain connectivity, lowering blood pressure, reducing stress, fighting depression, and increasing longevity? While the victims in my stories clearly did not read enough Pamela Crane books, you don't have to be one of the statistics. Enjoy a long, healthy life by grabbing your next read at www.pamelacrane.com.

Do you want to find out when I'm hosting a giveaway or releasing a new book? Follow me on Facebook, Instagram, or join my mailing list HERE for chances to win free prizes and pre-release offers.

About the Author

To know PAMELA CRANE, you first need to know her husband. He sleeps with one eye open. He checks the knife block to make sure none are missing. It could be because they have four kids and a farm full of mischievous animals. Or it could be because she writes murder mysteries, or about characters who have lost their marbles (not based on her real-life psyche, she swears!). Don't worry—her husband is safe...for now. Her books range from witty whodunnits to psychological suspense and even humorous women's fiction thrown in for good measure. She's a USA TODAY bestselling author of over a dozen novels (who's counting?), but her biggest accomplishment is keeping her zoo of animals alive...and her husband in check. Grab a free book at www.pamelacrane.com.